SINS OF THE LINES

SHARHONDA EXANTUS

ISBN for paperback: 979-8-218-07751-8

ISBN for E-book: 979-8-218-12785-5

For my husband, Christian

PROLOGUE

BEFORE

THE WOMAN WATCHED THE CLOCK, COUNTING EACH TICK AS the second hand traveled round and round. The ticking was deafening —reverberating off the hollow, white walls of the hospital room. She glanced nervously at the door and then back at the clock, a feeling of dread building in the pit of her stomach.

7:45 a.m.

The procedure would be starting soon. She could feel her heartbeat quicken. The small room was eerily quiet except for the sound of the clock and the beeping of the monitors that she was hooked up to. She glanced down at her arms and gently touched the clear syringes that pierced her skin. They pulsed fluids through her body from the IV bag hanging on the silver pole next to her bed. The light pink hospital gown that the staff had given her to wear was flimsy, barely covering her naked body.

She felt exposed. Vulnerable.

The thought of what was ahead terrified her. Dr. Southerland had explained the procedure a hundred times, yet she still felt uneasy. A hysteroscopic operation was what he'd called it—a procedure that would allow him to remove the uterine adhesions that had plagued her life for years. It was their last attempt to repair some of the damage that had been done—to give her a chance at a life free from pain.

The procedure was by no means a cure; Dr. Southerland had been clear on that. "Don't expect a miracle," he'd warned her. Even with this intervention, the odds of restoring her fertility were slim to none. It had been a devastating blow, a hard reality to face. After years of treatments and seeing countless doctors, she was hit with the harsh truth that she would probably never bear a child of her own.

Dr. Southerland had described her case as severe—unlike any other that he had ever seen in all his years of practice. He'd once been optimistic, indulging her requests to try new treatments as they became available. But as the months turned to years, even she could see his optimism fading. With her complex medical history and advancing age, her odds of conceiving again were slim.

At her last visit to his office, he'd sat her down and delivered the news she'd been dreading. She could still remember the look on his face —his worn, pale skin with those sad, blue eyes looking at her with pity from behind his large-framed glasses. "Performing a hysteroscopic operation is your best option at this point," he'd explained. "Asherman's syndrome can be severe for some women, and I'm afraid that is what we're seeing in your case. Unfortunately, I don't think the procedure is going to do much good as far as your fertility. At this point, the removal of the uterine adhesions is solely to improve your quality of life."

She'd sat there motionless as the shock of the news sank in. "There are always other options," he'd said, hoping to lighten the mood of the conversation and provide her with a glimmer of hope. "There's always surrogacy or even adoption. You can still have children."

She stared back at him but didn't speak. A surrogate was out of the question. Women paid tens of thousands of dollars for those services, and that was something that she and her husband just could not afford. They had already spent thousands on fertility treatments, draining their savings account until they had next to nothing left. And the idea of adoption had never crossed her mind. She didn't want someone else's baby. She wanted her own.

There was a soft knock at the hospital room door. She sat up in the bed and wiped away the tears that streaked her face. "Come in."

The door opened slowly. An older nurse appeared in the doorway. She was a small, wiry woman with scrubs that seemed too big for her small frame. She took small, shuffling steps over to the bed and smiled down at her. Her oversized veneers were the same color as the blanched hospital room walls. They seemed to take up her entire face as she smiled. "We are all set to start your procedure, hun."

She stared back at the nurse, her eyes blank and emotionless. She couldn't speak. Tears were stinging the backs of her eyes again. She turned away as she tried hard to force them back.

"We're going to wheel you down the hall to where Dr. Southerland is going to do your procedure," explained the nurse. "Before we start, we're going to give you something to help you sleep since this procedure will be a little more involved."

She nodded her head but remained silent. Her mouth had gone completely dry. She fought the urge to jump out of the bed and run as fast as she could out of the room and away from this place.

A transporter walked into the room and released the brake at the bottom of the bed. The woman felt herself moving as he wheeled the bed slowly out of the room and down the brightly lit corridor. The overhead lights in the hall whizzed by above her head as he picked up speed. They made a sharp turn at the end of the hall and went through a large set of steel double doors.

She found herself in the middle of a large operating room. The staff wore starched blue scrubs and surgical caps. A long steel table stood a few feet away, an assortment of medical tools placed strategically across the middle. Everything was so sterile, so cold. The staff even moved around like robots, mumbling medical terms that she didn't understand.

She propped herself up on her elbows, the urge to run overtaking her.

The older nurse walked up to her and gave her a reassuring smile. "It's ok, dear. Just lie back."

Just lie back. The words hit a nerve, paralyzing her. They were the same words that had been spoken to her that fateful day—the day when her baby had been ripped from her body. The events of that day suddenly came rushing back, flooding her mind with memories that she'd tried so hard to forget.

She could still envision the clinic with its outdated furniture and peeling blue walls. The smell of antiseptic and metal hung in the air. The thought of it made her want to gag. She could see the doctor's face who had performed the procedure—could still picture her between her legs that had been propped up on stirrups. She was an unsmiling woman with hands as cold as ice. There was no talking—no words between them. She could still feel the metal of the speculum stretching her insides, the hollowness that was left behind. It was over almost as quickly as it had begun.

"Are you ok, hun?" The nurse's voice broke through her thoughts, bringing her back to reality. Her mouth was like cotton. She tried to spread her lips to speak, but her tongue was stuck to the roof of her mouth. She managed a simple head nod.

"Just relax," said the nurse. "We're going to give you the anesthesia now to help put you to sleep. Just breathe normally."

The nurse squeezed her hand and slipped an oversized breathing mask over her face. Her heart felt like it was going to break through her chest wall as she struggled to calm her breathing. The large light above her head shone brightly, causing little black spots to flood her field of vision. She shut her eyes and turned her head to escape its overwhelming glare.

She tried to focus on other things, to push away any reminder of that day. She couldn't change what had been done, for the decision had not been hers. She couldn't have known that there was something bigger at play. She never saw any of it coming …

Chapter 1

Evie

I'm standing on the front lawn of the sorority house, my eyes fixed on the front door. It is just as I remember it—the potted plants hanging from the eaves, the neatly trimmed shrubbery, the garish lavender paint covering its exterior walls. It's been years since I last stepped foot on the property, and it's the last place that I want to be—except I have no choice.

I take a deep breath and adjust my sunglasses before walking up to the door. My purse is heavy on my shoulder, and beads of sweat erupt from my hairline and make their way down my face. My shirt sticks to my chest. There are cars parked in the driveway, and I can hear the low sound of voices coming from inside. I knock on the front door, my heart pounding in my chest as I brace myself for what happens next.

The lock turns, and Ms. Maggie appears in the doorway, her large brown eyes peering at me through her thick-framed glasses.

"Yes?" She looks me up and down, her forehead wrinkling as she frowns against the glare of the sun. She must be in her late sixties now, and time seems to have taken a toll on her. She is gripping a cane tightly in her hand. Bony nodules protrude from her fingers where arthritis has set in. The cocoa-brown skin on her face is covered in wrinkles, giving her face a leathery appearance. She pushes a silver strand of hair back from her face as she studies me closely.

I remove my sunglasses and give her my best smile. "Ms. Maggie! It's me, Evie."

Her mouth drops open as she finally recognizes my face. "Oh, my word! Evie, is that you?" She takes me into her arms and gives me a long hug. "Yes ma'am! It's me," I say. "It's so good to see you!"

She squeezes me tight. I can smell the familiar scent of White Diamonds coming from her. It's always been her favorite scent. "I—I can't believe it!" she says, looking me up and down. "It's been so long, child. How've you been?"

"I've been good! How are you?"

"Oh, I'm good now that you're here. Come in, come in! It's scorching out there." She hobbles out of the way, and I step inside. The layout of the house is the same. Everything is just as it had been, even down to the furniture. Ms. Maggie hasn't changed much of anything, but then again, I'm not surprised. She has always been a stickler for tradition.

She leads me over to the couch in the sitting area and sits down next to me, taking my hands in hers. "Oh, you don't know how happy it makes me to see you. One of my girls has come back to see me."

I blush, lowering my eyes to the floor. "I'm happy to see you too. It's been so long."

"How've you been, baby? How's life treating you?"

"Things are good! I moved back in town about a year ago. I just started a new job."

"A year ago? And you're just now coming by to see me?" Her face sags with disappointment, and I can tell that she is slightly hurt that I hadn't visited sooner.

"I've been meaning to come by," I lie. "But things have been so hectic with the move and with work. I just haven't had the time."

"Oh, I understand," she says. "Everyone is so busy nowadays. All that matters is that you're here now."

I look away from her, avoiding her curious gaze. What I'd told her wasn't a complete lie. It had taken some time to get adjusted to moving back here after all these years, but that isn't what stopped me from visiting sooner.

"Actually, I'm glad you picked today to come by," she says, tapping my hand. "The new pledge line is having their probate show on campus this afternoon. I would love for you to meet the girls."

"Oh really?" I try my best to sound surprised. I know the probate is today—it is the real reason for my surprise visit.

"Uh-huh, in a couple of hours. The girls are in the back now getting ready!" She stands to her feet and hobbles on her cane toward the door. "Don't you remember your probate show? How many years ago was that, Evie?"

"Oh, too many years," I say casually.

She leads me down the long hall. My eyes scan the large array of photographs of past sorority members lining the walls. Now that I'm back here, everything comes rushing back. The smells and the sounds hit me all at once. My stomach lurches.

Ms. Maggie turns and looks back at me. "You girls looked so beautiful! I remember it like it was yesterday."

I force a smile.

She turns and walks into the den at the back of the house. There are about fifteen girls crammed into the small space. Pallets of makeup cover the floor, and clothes are strewn across the furniture. A large mirror has been propped up along the back wall. Several girls are crowded in front of it as they meticulously apply makeup to their young faces.

Diana is sitting on a small loveseat in the corner of the room. She looks up from her phone and notices us standing in the doorway. Our eyes lock for several seconds before she turns her attention back to her phone. To her, I'm a stranger.

Ms. Maggie clears her throat and leans against her cane. "Girls!"

The noise in the room dies down, and suddenly all eyes are on us. "This is Evie," she says, motioning in my direction. "She is one of our former chapter members."

"Hey, ladies! Nice to meet you all."

The young girls smile and say hello before turning back to their preparations. I glance over at Diana again. She's distracted, still preoccupied with her phone.

"They're getting ready," Ms. Maggie whispers to me. "You know how that is."

I place my hand on her shoulder. "I remember all too well."

"Ms. Maggie?" Diana walks over to us. Her face is pale underneath the layer of makeup she's applied. "Nia hasn't shown up yet, and she's not answering her phone."

"What do you mean she's not answering?" asks Ms. Maggie.

"I can't reach her," says Diana. "I've called her at least a dozen times, and she hasn't returned any of my text messages."

"Well, she has to be here soon. The probate starts in a couple of hours."

"I'll keep trying her," Diana says. I can see the worry on her face, but I pretend not to notice.

Ms. Maggie points at several boxes stacked next to the door. "You girls need to start wrapping up and getting some of these boxes loaded into the cars. Is all of this stuff going?"

"Yes ma'am," says Diana. "Those are the masks and some other things the girls want to take."

Ms. Maggie taps her cane lightly on the tiled floor. "Alright, let's get this stuff loaded up."

I bend over and pick up the first box. "Let me help. It's the least I can do."

"Oh, you don't have to do that," says Ms. Maggie.

"It's fine." The box is heavier than it looks, and I have to shift it in my arms to get a better grip. "Let the girls finish getting ready. I can help load everything into the cars."

Ms. Maggie rubs my back softly and smiles. "You're such a sweetheart, Evie. Always taking care of everyone else."

"It's no problem at all." I turn to Diana and give her my best smile. "Where should I put them?"

CHAPTER 2

TORI

THE CROWD OUTSIDE OF UNIVERSITY HALL IS MASSIVE ... past the point of containment. It stretches out in every direction, covering every inch of central campus and spilling over into the adjacent quadrangle that borders the library. People perch on the balconies of the neighboring dorms and lounge in folding chairs as they wait restlessly for the show to start. I take a few steps forward and crane my neck as I try to get a better view of the stage. Dozens of balloons float high above the crowd. Spectators flood the overcrowded courtyard, toting bouquets of flowers and gifts for the new pledges.

I have a spot beneath one of the few trees on the outskirts of the courtyard. The heat is unbearable today. The cellophane wrap from the bouquet of flowers I'm holding sticks to my arms. If it were any other day, I wouldn't have come. But today is different. I feel a surge of excitement as I wait for the probate to start—for the moment when Nia is finally revealed as a new member of Kappa Theta Theta sorority.

"Who are you here to see?"

A voice comes from behind me, and I turn to see a girl smiling in my direction. She's wearing a Magnolia State University tank top with a pair of denim shorts, but I've never seen her on campus before. I return the smile. "I'm here to see my best friend, Nia."

Her eyes widen. "Nia? Nia Bryant?"

I nod, but I instantly regret saying anything. Nia had sworn me to secrecy about her pledging process. Even though she's just minutes away from crossing the stage, I wonder if I've spoken too soon.

"Um, what about you? Do you know someone being revealed today?" I ask the question to be polite, but the girl doesn't hear. She's already deep in another conversation with someone else, and I suddenly feel awkward standing by myself. Even though I've gotten through my first semester at MSU, it's no secret that I don't fit in very well. If I'm honest, Nia is my only friend here. Now that she's preparing for her probate, I'm forced to be alone. I watch as everyone around me socializes, laughing and talking amongst themselves.

I stand on my tiptoes to get a better view of the stage. It's already fifteen minutes past the show's noon start time. The humidity is slowly creeping up, and I can feel myself beginning to sweat. As I look around at the horde of people gathered in the courtyard, I realize that I'm not the only one growing impatient. Several people are beginning to grumble about the heat.

A flash of movement catches my eye. Diana McNamee, the MSU chapter president of Kappa Theta Theta sorority, has just walked out of University Hall. She looks upset about something, and I have a feeling that things aren't going as planned with the preparations. She scans the courtyard and walks quickly toward a group of guys standing near the front of the crowd. They're members of Lambda Nu Phi fraternity, one of the more well-known fraternities on campus. Nia's boyfriend, Byron, is a member. He's standing with several of his line brothers, waiting for the show to start.

Diana pulls Byron to the side. They seem to be having a heated conversation, and I watch as his facial expression changes. Something is wrong, but I can't tell what's going on from where I'm standing. I take out my phone to text Nia when I notice Diana staring in my direction. A chill runs up my spine as she turns and begins walking toward me. I hold my breath as she comes closer, unsure of what's going on.

She finally reaches the tree where I'm standing and takes several deep breaths as she tries to slow her breathing. Her pressed hair has gone stringy in the heat, and her mascara has started to clump in the corners of her eyes. She looks wilted in the spring heat.

"Hey! Have you heard from Nia?"

"No," I say, shaking my head. "I haven't seen her. She's not here?"

"No! No one has heard from her or seen her since last night." Diana is not her usual composed self. I can hear the panic in her voice. To hear that Nia isn't with her line sisters worries me.

"I haven't seen her since yesterday," I say.

"Alright, thanks." She turns on her heels and walks back towards University Hall.

A feeling of dread comes over me. The bouquet of flowers feels like it weighs a thousand pounds, and I shift it in my arms. The probate show is all Nia has talked about for the past few weeks. I find it hard to believe that she would miss it on purpose.

A call to Nia goes straight to voicemail. I wait another minute and try calling her again, but she still doesn't answer. Has she gotten cold feet? Overslept? Dozens of possibilities run through my head, but I know that they are all unlikely. Nia isn't the type to oversleep or miss an event like today.

Someone taps me on the shoulder. The girl with the tank top asks me what's going on. Before I can answer, a burst of applause and loud cheering erupts from the large crowd. The show has finally started. I take a few steps forward as I try to get a better view of what's happening. The crowd is thick, but I'm able to see the new pledge line of Kappa Theta Theta sorority emerging from the side door of University Hall. They're dressed in identical lavender-colored dresses and matching heels. Black masks conceal their faces. They walk slowly in a single-file line. Diana and a few of the other Kappa Theta Theta girls are walking alongside them, making sure each girl is in coordination with the group.

I feel a rush of relief now that the show has started, but the feeling is short-lived. The pledges have climbed the steps to the stage and are standing in a straight line in front of the crowd. I shield my eyes with my hand and begin counting the number of people on stage. There are supposed to be a total of ten pledges, but there are only nine girls on stage.

They are one girl short.

I watch closely as the probate show begins, wondering if maybe, by chance, one of the girls behind one of the masks is Nia. The tree seemed like a good place to stand to escape the heat, but now that the show has started, I can barely hear anything that's going on. I decide to move.

As I make my way through the mass of people, the noonday sun beats down on my head. I find an open spot next to a group of girls and stand where I have a better view of the stage. The pledges are chanting loudly in unison, eliciting loud applause from the audience. I study each of the girls, looking for anything familiar in their movements that will allow me to recognize Nia.

"I thought there were ten girls being revealed today?" One of the girls standing in front of me is whispering in a hushed voice to her friend standing next to her.

"That's what I heard too. Maybe one of them didn't make the cut."

I fight the urge to set the record straight—to defend Nia in her absence. I know it won't solve anything, though, and I turn my attention back to the stage. A loud roar erupts from the crowd as the pledges begin taking off their masks one after the other, revealing their faces. I hold my breath as each girl is revealed, hoping that by some stroke of luck that Nia's face will be behind one of the masks. One by one, the masks fall to the ground, and I wait—but deep down, I know. Finally, the last girl is revealed. An uneasiness comes over me.

Nia isn't on stage.

Chapter 3

Tori

I stay until the end of the show. A part of me hopes that Nia will show up, running out of University Hall and taking her place on stage with her line sisters. But by the end of the probate, there is still no sign of her. The new pledges run off the stage and fall into the arms of loved ones who have traveled from all over to support them. I stand there and watch as family members and friends snap pictures of the newly inducted members. Nia should be here celebrating with everyone else. Instead, the flowers I've purchased for her have now withered in the heat.

Nia hasn't returned my calls or responded to any of the texts that I sent during the show. Byron and two of his line brothers, Drew Bradley and Tre Thomas, are still standing on the other side of the courtyard. I make my way over to them, weaving in and out of the dense crowd.

Byron looks up when he sees me. "Hey! Have you seen Nia?"

"I was just about to ask you the same question," I say.

"I haven't been able to reach her. I've been calling and texting her. I can't believe she didn't show up!"

"I've tried calling her, too. She didn't answer for me either."

He shrugs his shoulders and looks around at the crowd. "I don't know what's going on. This isn't like her."

An awkward silence grows between us. I don't care much for Byron, and I think he knows it. Things have been rocky between him and Nia for the last few months, and I've seen firsthand how much of a toll it's taken on her. When he'd been discovered cheating, I was the first person Nia called. Their relationship woes quickly became the talk of the campus, and Nia was devastated. I was relieved when she'd broken up with him. She seemed to be on the mend, but he had somehow wiggled his way back into her life. They've been back together for a few weeks now, and things have been awkward between him and me ever since.

I take out my cellphone again and log into my Facebook, but there's no recent activity on Nia's page. Her Instagram and Snapchat are also surprisingly quiet.

"She hasn't posted on social media since yesterday."

"I know," he says. "I saw that too."

"I just talked to Diana," says Drew. "The girls still haven't heard from her since they last called her before the show."

Byron puts his head in his hands. "I'm really worried! She doesn't do stuff like this. She always answers her phone."

"You think she got scared?" Tre asks. "Maybe she decided not to go through with the probate?"

"Nah. She was so excited about today. She's been talking about it all week. In fact, she wouldn't shut up about it!"

"So, what do you want to do?" asks Drew.

"I don't know! I guess we should look around for her. I can drive by her house and check to see if she's there."

"Do you think we should call the police?" Everyone turns and looks at me, and I immediately regret making the suggestion. The last thing I want to do is overreact and send everyone into a frenzy if there is a simple explanation for Nia's absence.

"Maybe we can look for her first," Drew says, turning back to Byron. "Make sure we exhaust all options. If she doesn't turn up by tonight, then I think going to the police would be the next best step."

Byron considers the suggestion. "Yeah, let's do that."

"Take my number," I say. "Call me as soon as you hear anything."

I say goodbye to them and make my way through the dwindling crowd toward the courtyard exit. My phone begins vibrating, and I yank it out of my pocket, praying that it's Nia finally calling back. I look at the call screen and brace myself before finally answering the phone. "Hey, Ma."

"Hey, baby! How was Nia's probate?"

I contemplate what to say, especially since the last thing I want is to cause my mom to worry. She knows how close Nia and I are; we rarely go anywhere without each other. Hearing that Nia has disappeared will only cause her to overreact. She's been on edge since I started at MSU and still isn't too thrilled that I'm attending an out-of-state school for college. My decision to live with my aunt off-campus was what eventually shifted things in my favor. She was content with me moving away as long as I was living with family.

"Um, Nia didn't show up to the probate," I say finally.

"Didn't show up? Where is she?"

"I don't know. No one has been able to reach her. But I'm sure she's fine."

She's silent on the other end of the line. I hold my breath as I wait for her to respond. "When was the last time you talked to her?"

"Yesterday afternoon. She came over to the house before her probate practice."

"You don't think something bad—"

"No, Ma!" I say, cutting her off. "It's probably nothing."

"Where are you?" I can hear the worry creeping into her voice, the anxiety building. She's already thinking the worst, going to the extreme like she always does.

"I'm leaving campus now, headed back to Aunt Lyn's."

"Good. I feel better with you at home. If something is wrong—"

"Ma, look I gotta go," I say, rushing her off the phone. "I'll call you once I hear from Nia." I don't give her a chance to answer, hanging up before she can get another word in.

Nia is fine. I say the words over and over again in my head. I want to believe my own thoughts, to believe that there is a simple explanation for Nia's absence at the probate. I have to believe that she's ok. I don't want to think the worst, to succumb to my fears. I force myself to think positively, even though deep down I have this nagging feeling that something isn't right.

CHAPTER 4

CHRIS

THE BRIEFING ROOM IS MOSTLY EMPTY WHEN I ARRIVE. I take a seat in the front row near the podium. Lieutenant Stokes is standing at the door, wringing his hands nervously as he stares at the clock. The briefing is scheduled to start promptly at 3 p.m., but most of the officers still haven't arrived yet. Emergency squad briefings aren't usually called so late in the day, especially on a Friday.

Officers continue to straggle in, and Lieutenant Stokes takes his place behind the podium. His eyes are fixed on the door as he waits impatiently for the entire group to arrive. I check the clock again. There's still no sign of Cramer. Even though we've been partners for a little over two years, I still haven't gotten used to his habit of running late. I hope for his sake that he's on time today because the lieutenant looks more tense than usual.

The door opens, and Cramer waltzes into the squad room. He sits down in the seat next to mine and whispers as he leans in close to me. "What's going on?"

I turn my head to escape the smell of cigarette smoke on his breath. "Don't know. But it must be pretty serious for us to get called in so late in the day."

Lieutenant Stokes clears his throat and checks the clock as he begins the meeting. "Well, I think we have everyone, so let's get started," he says. "I apologize for the late notice with this meeting, but this was a request straight from the chief." A request from the chief is rare. The fact that the briefing is at his request has already piqued my interest.

"A young woman who attends MSU was reported missing this afternoon," says Stokes. "We were alerted to her disappearance not too long ago by her parents, who were contacted by her boyfriend. The young lady, Nia Bryant, was last seen sometime after midnight last night and apparently did not show up for a show that she was supposed to participate in at the campus this afternoon. Her vehicle was just uncovered by her boyfriend at her residence with the keys still inside, but no one has seen or heard from her."

Cramer raises his hand. "So, it hasn't been twenty-four hours yet?"

"Correct," says Stokes. "According to her parents, friends last report seeing her approximately fourteen to fifteen hours ago."

Cramer looks perplexed. Normally, we don't start investigating missing persons cases until the person has been missing for at least twenty-four hours.

Lieutenant Stokes seems to sense the confusion in the room. "I know we wouldn't normally start working this case so soon, but the chief has asked that we make finding this young lady a top priority. I know we are all strapped right now, but this case takes precedence for the time being. We need all hands on deck."

The other officers begin to grumble amongst themselves. Our caseload has been higher than average over the past few weeks, and I can't help but think about the pile of cases already clogging my desk that need attention. Adding another case to the mix is not something that anyone wants, especially one that doesn't technically meet the criteria for a true missing person's case.

I raise my hand and ask the question that is on everyone's mind. "Excuse me, Lieutenant? May I ask why this case is so different? You said yourself it hasn't even been twenty-four hours. Why are we being asked to look into it now?"

Lieutenant Stokes walks from around the podium and comes to

stand directly in front of me. "Because Nia Bryant is Congressman Dwight Bryant's daughter."

Cramer and I exchange worried glances. Congressman Bryant is part of a long list of famous graduates from MSU, and is one of their major donors. It's no secret that he and the chief have had a longstanding relationship for years.

"The congressman's daughter?" I ask.

"That's right. Hence the urgency for this meeting. Congressman Bryant called the chief personally with concerns for his daughter's safety."

I can feel my body deflating as I sit back in my chair. The fact that Nia Bryant is a congressman's daughter changes the whole trajectory of how the case will be handled. Lieutenant Stokes directs his attention to the front row at my partner and me. "Evans and Cramer, I want you both to take the lead on this case. Stay afterwards and we can discuss what steps we need to take. I imagine we will need a few teams to cover all of our bases."

The assignment surprises me, but I don't show it on my face. Lieutenant Stokes looks around the room at the rest of the officers. "As for everyone else, we have very little to go on, and we need to gather as much information as we can to establish a timeline. An alert has been issued to all surrounding agencies. We need everyone to get out and start canvassing the area. Anything you find, make sure to bring it to myself or Evans and Cramer. Any questions?"

He scans the room with his eyes. "Ok, let's get to work."

The other officers begin shuffling out of the room. Lieutenant Stokes grabs a small folder from the podium and places it down on the table in front of us. Once the room is clear, he closes the door and takes a seat.

"I know I don't have to tell you two how important this is," he says. "The chief wants the best of the best heading this case, and I chose you two for a reason. If either of you sees any reason why you wouldn't be able to have your head in this case, I need to know now."

He turns his attention to me, but I look away. It's no secret that things have been rough for me lately. Even though it's been several months since my involvement with the Zakari Stanton case, it's taken me a while to get a handle on things. My work performance has suffered, even catching the attention of several of my supervisors.

"Evans?" Lieutenant Stokes gives me a stern look. "Can I count on you to have your head in the game?"

"Yes, sir." I try my best to sound as convincing as possible. "I'm all in. Tell us what you have."

Stokes opens the thin manila folder in the middle of the table. "That's the problem. We don't have much of anything yet."

Inside the folder is a photograph of a young woman. She's an attractive girl with medium brown skin, shoulder-length dark hair, and large brown eyes. The date on the photo is from less than a week ago.

"I had IT pull up her social media, and we were able to get this photo of her," he says. "It's the most recent one. We need to start circulating it around to see if anyone has seen her. It's also important that we start interviews ASAP with everyone connected to her." He closes the folder and slides it across the table to me. "The chief wants this case handled quickly and efficiently. The fact that she's the daughter of a politician makes things complicated. The last thing we need is outside agencies coming in to take over our investigation, but that's exactly what will happen if we don't get ahead of this."

I open the folder and glance at the girl's picture again. Over the years, I've seen more than my fair share of missing persons cases. Many times, the person declared missing would show up a few days later, telling stories of wanting to get away or needing a break. Those are the cases that end well, but that isn't always the case. Every now and then, we get cases where foul play is involved. As I stare at Nia Bryant's photo, I can only pray for her sake that it isn't the latter.

"I'll let you two decide how you want to work this," says Stokes. "I'm giving you full discretion to use whatever resources you need to track this girl down. You know my door is always open if you need anything."

"Thanks, Lieutenant," says Cramer. "We will get to work on this."

Lieutenant Stokes looks back and forth between us before walking out of the room. Cramer picks up the photo and studies the young woman's face. "I don't like this at all."

"Me neither," I say. "Her father's political status alone makes things tricky. Cases like this get messy quick."

"Well, let's hope we can find her."

"I'm sure we'll find her .... Let's just hope we find her alive."

CHAPTER 5

CHRIS

We work well into the night. Going home is not an option, even if we want to. The squad room, which is normally quiet at this hour, is alive with activity. Several detectives are huddled around a large conference room table in the middle of the room. They've made a temporary workstation of computers and phones as they work on information requests, including Nia's phone and bank records. Getting access to records can be a challenge and may take several days, but they are our best hope in helping to develop a timeline to track Nia's last movements.

I sit hunched over my laptop at my desk. Nia's Facebook page is pulled up on my screen as I browse her profile. "Jesus! Is there anything these kids don't put on social media?"

Cramer looks up at me from his desk. "You know how it is! We are in the age of sharing. If it's not online, it never happened."

"Yeah, but this is a little much. There are hundreds of photos here. And this is just the first site. I'm sure she's on multiple platforms."

"I'm sure she is. And guess who's going to have to comb through all those pictures? We are. It's gonna be a long night."

I continue scrolling. At first glance, nothing looks out of the ordinary. Her most recent post is from yesterday morning, but there's been no activity since.

"No posts since yesterday morning," I say.

"Does she post regularly?"

"She does. Usually more than once a day."

"That's not a good sign. If she wasn't a regular on social media, I wouldn't be too worried. But if she's gone dark suddenly, then that's a red flag."

I move further down the page and click on a photo of her with another male student. A photo tag redirects me to his profile, where I notice that Nia is tagged as his girlfriend.

"I found her boyfriend," I say. "Name is Byron Clarke."

"He was the one who found the car, right?"

"Yeah, that's him."

"Anything interesting stand out to you?"

"Nothing out of the ordinary. Just typical stuff kids post on social media."

"Well, the patrol officers have already done an initial interview with him," he says. "But we need to sit down with him as soon as possible. You know the boyfriend is always suspect number one."

I return to Nia's page and take one last look at the photo of the smiling couple. They appear to be happy and in love, but I've worked this job long enough to know that things aren't always what they seem, especially on social media.

I spend the next several minutes searching the internet for anything else I can find on the missing girl. Several articles populate from my search, including one from her local hometown. I click on the article and read the caption below her photo: *Seventeen-year-old Nia Bryant, pictured above, makes history as the first student in her high school to be accepted into three Ivy League schools.*

"It sounds like this girl was a star student," I say. "This article I found says she was accepted to over ten colleges, including three Ivy leagues."

Cramer raises his eyebrows. "Sounds like a smart kid."

"Yeah, she sounds responsible. Which makes it hard to believe she would just take off like this."

I close my laptop and stand slowly to my feet. My body is tight, and my eyes are heavy with sleep. Scouring Nia's social media has taken me hours, and my legs are numb from sitting for so long. It's been a long day, and we still haven't scratched the surface of everything we need to dig through. "I'll be right back," I say to Cramer. "I'm going to grab another coffee."

The second-floor lounge is empty, and I close the door to give myself some privacy. The standard troffer lights in the room have recently been replaced with recessed lights, and I'm still trying to get used to them. The room seems too bright now, and it takes a few seconds for my eyes to adjust. Hours of staring at the computer screen haven't helped.

I take one of the flimsy Styrofoam cups from the cabinet and pour myself enough coffee to get me through the next few hours. It's not the best coffee, but it'll have to do. After a few sips, I can already feel myself perking up.

I check the door to make sure it's still closed before calling Rosalind. Even though we've only been on a few dates, I don't want people around the department to know about our relationship just yet, even if it's just casual right now.

She answers on the second ring. "Hey you!"

"Hey, how's it going?"

"Pretty good," she says. "I had a long day at work. Case after case."

"Yeah, same here. That's kind of why I'm calling." We are due to meet downtown in a few hours at a local restaurant for dinner, but those plans will have to wait.

She sighs. "No need to explain. I already heard about the missing girl when I was leaving work today."

"I'm sorry. You know how these things can be." I'm grateful that I don't have to explain myself to Rosalind. As the county Medical Examiner, she's accustomed to the unpredictable nature of our work.

"It's fine," she says. "We can reschedule for another day once all of this calms down."

"Yeah, that sounds good. After the week I've had, though, I sure could've used some drinks tonight."

"Have you guys made any progress with finding her?"

"No, not much. But we have every available officer working this one. If she's out there, we'll find her."

"Ok, well, try to get some rest when you can. Call me tomorrow." I say that I will, even though I know I'm going to be tied up with this case for a while.

Back in the squad room, things are even more chaotic. Night shift officers have just come on duty and are being briefed on the search efforts. A large whiteboard has been set up at the far end of the room. Nia's picture has been taped to the front, along with the details of her last known movements.

Cramer is still parked at his desk, his eyes glued to his computer screen.

"What are you looking at?"

"Some of the initial reports submitted by the responding officers," he says. "According to what they have here, Nia was supposed to take part in a probate show today."

"Yeah, that's right. It's basically when the new inductees into a Greek organization are revealed. She must've just joined a sorority."

He shakes his head. "I can't imagine how worried this girl's parents must be. You send your kid off to school to get an education—you don't expect them to just disappear into thin air."

"I know. It's every parent's worst nightmare."

"I hope we find her soon, alive and well. After what happened with Zakari Stanton, I don't think this community can handle the death of another young person."

My stomach sinks at the mention of Zakari's name. It's been six months since the sixteen-year-old was shot while walking home from a friend's house, and his case still haunts me. Shootings are rare in Magnolia, especially shootings involving juveniles. Zakari was just two blocks from home when he was shot during a shoot-out between rival gangs. He was a good kid from a good family—the last person you'd expect to be gunned down in the middle of a residential street. Being in the wrong place at the wrong time had cost him his life.

I was the first officer on scene after the call came through. He was alive when I got to him, bleeding out in the middle of the street. I'll never forget the look of fear in his eyes during his last moments. I pleaded with him to hang on for the ambulance that was just a few miles down the road, but he was too far gone. He died in my arms just as the ambulance arrived, and it's something that has tormented me ever since.

I take a seat at my desk and open my laptop again. I push aside thoughts of Zakari Stanton for now. I couldn't save him, but it's not too late for Nia. We can still bring her home.

I pull up Nia's Facebook again but stop when I notice Detective Jacobs enter the squad room. He's working closely with us on the case and has been out in the field heading the search efforts. I wonder if he's found something, and I brace myself for bad news as he makes a beeline for my desk.

"What's going on?" I ask.

"I just got a call from the guys stationed at Nia's apartment where her car was found," he says.

Cramer closes his laptop and walks over to my desk. The room has gone quiet as everyone turns their attention toward us. A pit has formed in my stomach. I don't want to ask the question, but I have to. "Did they find something?"

He nods. "The crime scene techs have just started processing the car. There's blood inside—a lot of it."

Chapter 6

Evie

"Excuse me ma'am, have you seen this girl?"

A young officer steps out in front of me, blocking my path. I watch as another group of young women is stopped by another officer as they try to walk into a nearby restaurant. I look the officer standing in front of me up and down. He has the face of a teenager and looks like he's barely out of the academy. The loose-fitting uniform that he's wearing is two sizes too big for his small frame.

In his hand is a freshly printed flier with Nia's face plastered on the front. I freeze. I can feel his eyes on me, and I try my best to appear composed.

"I'm sorry, I haven't seen her," I say, shaking my head.

He glances down the busy sidewalk. Friday nights on the downtown strip are usually busy, and tonight is no exception. Music blares from clubs and bars as people flood the streets, looking to unwind from the work week.

"Are you sure?" he asks. "She attends the university here and frequents this area often. We are hoping someone may recognize her."

"She doesn't look familiar," I say. "I work a few blocks down and am just getting off for the night, but I've never seen her around here before. Is she in trouble?"

"We are just trying to locate her. No one has seen or heard from her since early this morning, and her family is worried."

I feign concern. "Oh, how awful. I'm sorry to hear that."

"Well, if you see her or hear anything that may be helpful, please give a call to the tip line." He hands me a flier from the top of his stack.

"I certainly will, Officer. Thank you."

He flags down a couple walking arm-in-arm in our direction. I turn quickly down a side street where I'm less likely to run into anyone. The sound of the music and loud voices fades as I walk away from the strip toward the parking garage.

It isn't until I'm finally out of sight that I stop holding my breath. I push the button for the elevator and wait impatiently as it slowly makes its way down from the top level. The cops are already out in full force, and it won't be long before the media gets wind of the story. Nia's face will be everywhere in the coming days, and there will be eyes on those closest to her.

The elevator arrives. I take one last look at the flier and toss it in the trash before stepping inside.

CHAPTER 7

CHRIS

We arrive at Byron Clarke's apartment first thing in the morning. He has agreed to meet with us, and I'm anxious to get whatever information we can from him. Nia has officially been missing for twenty-four hours, and things are beginning to look bleak.

Crime scene technicians spent the night processing her car for evidence. The initial report has already been released, and a large amount of blood was uncovered from the driver's side of the car. There is no way to tell for sure if it is Nia's blood until we get the test results back, but the discovery itself is enough to let me know that we're running out of time.

Byron's apartment is on the second floor of his building, down a maze of hallways. When we reach the door, it swings open before I have a chance to knock. The young man from Nia's Facebook page is standing in front of me. He's about 6'1" and sports a drop fade haircut. A thick beard covers the lower half of his face. His eyes look tired like he hasn't slept in days.

"Byron Clarke?"

"Yes, that's me." He looks at me and then glances over my shoulder at Cramer.

"I'm Detective Chris Evans, and this is my partner Detective

Cramer," I say, flashing my badge. "We're from MPD. We spoke earlier on the phone."

Byron opens the door wide and steps back. "Yes, come in."

The apartment is small and cluttered. The common area is dimly lit, with the only light coming from the small kitchen. The room smells of old food and cheap cologne. A large pot sits uncovered on the stove, and a pile of dishes is sitting in the sink, waiting to be washed. Byron runs past me to a sectional couch and begins tossing aside a pile of unfolded laundry to make room for us to sit.

"Sorry about the mess," he says. "I haven't had much time to straighten up—you know, with everything going on. Have a seat." He takes a seat in a small recliner and clasps his hands on his lap. "Do you guys have any updates on Nia?"

"We haven't been able to locate her," Cramer says. "We were hoping you could shed some light on things for us."

"I don't really know what to say," he says. "She's never done anything like this before. I spent all day yesterday driving around the city looking for her. I'm really worried something has happened."

"When was the last time you saw her?" I ask.

Byron appears to think for a moment. "I saw her on Thursday morning before class. We had coffee together at the café on campus."

"And have you talked to her since that time?"

"We texted throughout the day on Thursday, but I haven't heard from her since she left for her probate practice that night."

"Do you have any idea where she may be? Any special places she liked to go that you may have missed when you first searched for her?"

He shakes his head. "No, I looked everywhere that she would've gone. And it's not like her to up and leave without telling anyone."

"And you were the one who discovered her car parked at her residence?"

"Yeah, I was the one who found it. That's when I called her parents because I had a feeling that something was wrong."

I don't tell him about the blood that was found in the car. Byron seems genuinely concerned about Nia, but we can't rule him out—not yet, at least.

"Something bad has happened," he says. "I just know it!"

I can see him beginning to panic, and I raise my hand to calm him. "We don't know that yet. For all we know, maybe she wanted to get away for a while. But we need to find her soon."

Byron sits back in the recliner. He quickly wipes away a single tear that has fallen down his face.

"Where were you Thursday evening until the time of the probate yesterday afternoon?" I ask.

"Um, I got home about 8 p.m. on Thursday after I left the gym. I was here all that night."

"And you never left?"

He shakes his head. "No, I was here until the next morning when I left for class."

"Can anyone account for that?"

"My roommate, Drew Bradley. He was here too."

"Have you and Nia had any problems lately in your relationship?" Cramer asks.

"No, not really. We're actually in a really good place right now."

"No fights or disagreements recently?"

"Not lately, no. I mean, we've had our issues in the past like any couple, but nothing out of the norm."

"You said that you and Nia are in a good place right now," I say. "Has that not always been the case?"

Byron exhales and looks down at his hands. "A couple of months ago, we did go through a rough patch."

"What happened?"

"I cheated on her. Nia found out, and she broke up with me."

"Was it with someone from the university?"

He nods. "It was stupid—I know. But it only happened a few times. I apologized to her and broke it off with the other girl, but it took Nia a while to get past it. She said she wanted a break, and I told her to take as much time as she needed."

"Before that, how long were you two together?"

"We started dating last summer. Nia started as a freshman for the summer semester, and we met around that time."

"And you're a freshman as well?"

"No, I'm in my third year."

"So, how long were you guys separated during the break?" Cramer asks.

"About three months. She eventually came around, though, and we decided to give it another go. I mean, I love her ... I didn't want to lose her."

As Byron recounts to us the relationship problems between him and Nia, I think back to all the photos of the couple from Nia's social media. From the outside looking in, one would never know that there had ever been any strife in the relationship. To the social media world, Nia looked to be happy and in love—but there was another side to the story.

Suddenly, the front door opens. Another young man enters the apartment. He is slightly taller than Byron and has a muscular, athletic build. The jogging pants and matching shirt that he's wearing are drenched in sweat. He kicks off his shoes near the front door and pauses when he sees us sitting in the living room.

"What's going on?" he asks, eyeing Byron. "Is everything ok?"

"Are you Drew?" Cramer asks.

He nods and puts his keys down on the kitchen counter. "Yeah. I'm Drew."

"These are the detectives working on Nia's case," says Byron.

"I'm Detective Evans," I say. "This is my partner Detective Cramer. We're from MPD."

Drew shakes my hand. His grip is strong. "Have you guys found Nia?"

"No, not yet. We were hoping to get some information that may help from people that know her. Would you mind speaking with us for a few minutes?"

"Yeah, of course. Whatever I can do to help."

I turn to Byron. "Hey, Byron, would you mind giving us a few minutes alone with your roommate? We just have a few questions for him."

"Yeah, sure. I'll just be in the other room." Byron goes into the next room and closes the door, leaving us alone with Drew.

"I'm glad you guys are here," Drew says. "Everyone is really worried about Nia."

"Can you tell us when you last saw her?" I ask.

"The last time I saw her was earlier this week on campus. I'm pretty sure it was Tuesday."

"And how did she seem?"

"She seemed ok. I didn't notice anything unusual."

"So, I take it you know Nia pretty well since she dates your roommate?"

"Yeah, she's over here a few times a week visiting Byron," he says. "She's younger than us, but she's a nice girl."

"Do you know where she might've gone?" Cramer asks.

"No, I don't. Everyone was looking for her yesterday."

"Byron gave the impression that she's not one to just up and leave like this," I say. "Would you say that's true?"

"Yeah, this has never happened before that I know of. And for her not to show up yesterday was just strange. The girls were excited about their probate."

"The girls? You mean the sorority members?"

"Yeah. They were the first to notice that Nia was missing when she didn't show up yesterday. My girlfriend is the chapter president of the sorority, and she said that they spent all morning calling and texting Nia but got no answer."

"May I ask your girlfriend's name?"

"Her name is Diana. Diana McNamee. She was at the show yesterday."

I make a note of Drew's girlfriend in my notepad. "Is there anything at all that you can think of? Any small detail may be helpful."

"I can't think of anything else. Like I said, when I saw her, she seemed fine."

The door to the next room opens slowly, and Byron peeks his head out. "Everything ok?"

"Yeah, everything's fine," I say. "We're just wrapping up." I reach into my pocket and hand Drew two business cards. "If you guys think of anything else, please give us a call."

"Will do," he says. He hands Byron one of the cards.

"One more thing, Drew," I say. "May I ask where you were Thursday evening into Friday morning?"

"I was here."

"All night?"

"Yes, sir. We both were."

I look back and forth between him and Byron. Drew looks down at the floor and fumbles nervously with the business card. "I see. Well, that's all for now. I'm sure we will be following up in the next few days if we don't locate Nia. If anything else comes up in the meantime, you know where to find us."

When we leave, Cramer waits until we are a safe distance down the hall from the apartment before finally speaking.

"Well, what do you think?"

"I don't know," I say. "They were cooperative."

"But?"

"But ... something seemed off about him."

"About the boyfriend?"

I shake my head. "Not Byron. His roommate."

———

We stop at a small diner downtown after leaving Byron's apartment to grab a quick bite to eat. The Saturday morning rush is already underway, and the diner is full of people. A small television behind the counter is tuned to the morning news. Nia's disappearance is the top story of the day. Several patrons stop to stare at the screen and whisper amongst themselves as they share their theories on the case.

My eyes are turned to the screen, but I don't hear anything that's being said. Instead, I keep going back to the interview with Byron and Drew.

Cramer watches me from the other side of the booth. "You alright? You've been quiet since we left that apartment."

"Yeah, I'm good. Just something about that Drew kid that was a little off to me."

"Yeah, tell me about that."

"I don't know," I say. "I have a feeling he's hiding something."

Our waitress Sherry emerges through the swinging doors that lead to the kitchen, toting two large plates of food. She places the plates down on the table in front of us and refills our drinks. "Here we go!" she says. "Anything else I can get you right now?"

Cramer smiles hungrily at his food. "Nope. I think we're good for now."

"Yeah, everything looks great," I say. "Thanks, Sherry."

She smiles and rushes off toward the front of the restaurant to seat another table. The line in the waiting area is hanging out the front door as several large parties wait to be seated.

"So, what bothered you about him?" Cramer asks. He stuffs a spoonful of food into his mouth.

"His body language," I say. "He avoided eye contact at some points during our conversation. I just got the impression he wasn't being completely honest—like he was nervous about something."

"Well, some people don't like talking to the police. Maybe that's what it was."

"Could be, but I doubt it."

My cellphone rings. "It's Jacobs."

"I wonder what it's about," he says. "Maybe they've found something."

I connect the call. "Hey, Jacobs, what's up?"

"Hey, Evans." His voice sounds strained. Everyone is tired and running off little to no sleep.

"Everything ok?"

"Well, I've been working on the information requests all morning like you asked. We finally got her bank records. Unfortunately, it doesn't seem like there's been any activity since Thursday morning."

"And where was the last activity?"

"It looks like she made a purchase at a café on the MSU campus."

I think back to the conversation with Byron. The charge that Jacobs is referring to seems to match up with his story of grabbing coffee with Nia Thursday morning. "So, no ATM withdrawals or anything like that recently?"

"Nope. That was the last transaction. There's been no activity on any accounts since."

"What about her phone?"

"We've been unable to track it. Wherever it is, it's been turned off, or it's dead."

"And the vehicle? Any update on that? Have the techs been able to uncover anything more?"

"We're still waiting on the lab results for the blood, but we should have that soon. We're being allowed to use the fed lab for DNA testing for this case, so hopefully it won't take too much longer. Other than that, the car is clean."

"Ok, well, that's good. For now, see if you can get in contact with the property management company at her apartment complex. I want access to any cameras that may be on the property where she lives. Since the car was parked there, it's safe to assume that whatever happened occurred after she got home. Maybe the cameras will show us something."

"Alright," he says. "I'll get on it and see what I can find and let you know. Give me a ring if you need anything else."

"Well, what'd he say?" Cramer asks once the call ends.

"There's been no bank activity since Thursday morning on Nia's accounts," I say. "Her phone is untraceable as well."

"Well, that's not a good sign. What about the car?"

"So far it's clean besides the blood that was found in the driver's seat. We're still waiting on the lab results. Shouldn't be too much longer since the fed lab is doing the processing."

I force myself to take another bite of my food, but I no longer have an appetite. Even though it's still early in the case, I can't help but feel frustrated at the lack of progress we've made. Now that the media has gotten word of her disappearance, the pressure to find Nia is mounting.

Sherry returns to our table carrying two refilled drinks. "How's everything going over here? Anything else I can get for y'all right now?"

"No. We're almost done here, Sherry. Do you mind bringing the check?"

"Sure thing!" She clears the plates from the table before disappearing into the kitchen.

"So, you ready to go and talk to the sorority members?" Cramer asks.

I take one last sip of my drink. "Yeah, I think it's time we have a sit down with these girls. After all, they were the last to see her."

CHAPTER 8

TORI

The ringing of my cell phone jolts me out of my sleep. The sound is muffled, and it takes me a few seconds to realize that it's my phone ringing. I sit straight up in my bed and begin frantically tossing the covers. The ringing grows louder, and I finally find the phone tucked between the headboard of the bed and the wall.

"Hello!" I barely recognize my own voice.

"Hey, is this Tori?"

"Yeah, who is this?" I check the clock on my nightstand. I don't know when I finally drifted off to sleep last night, but I can already see that it's daylight from my bedroom window. I shield my eyes from the brightness. My head is spinning, and I can feel the first signs of a headache.

"Hey, it's Tre! I got your number from Byron. I hope that's ok."

"No, no, it's fine," I say, muffling a yawn. "Is everything ok? Any news on Nia?"

"Um, I'm not sure if anyone told you, but we found her car yesterday at her place."

"What?" I try to keep my voice level, but I can feel myself getting annoyed. I had specifically asked Byron to call me as soon as he heard anything. I can't help but wonder if he didn't call me on purpose.

"It's all over the news this morning," he says. "Byron called her parents after we found it to let them know. She's been declared missing with the police."

"Oh, my God!" My heart feels like it has dropped into my gut, and I can feel my hands beginning to shake. If Nia had decided to leave town for some reason, she would've needed her car. The fact that it was found at her apartment doesn't make sense.

"You there?"

"Yeah, I'm here." I swallow hard as I try to hide the trembling in my voice. "Sorry ... it's just ... it's just a lot."

"Sorry to spring that on you so early, but I thought you should know."

"No, that's ok! I've been worried out of my mind all night waiting on an update."

"Well, that's not the only reason I called."

"Oh? What's up?"

"A few of us are meeting up on campus soon. Nia's sorority sisters had some fliers printed up late last night, and we are going to post them around the campus. I was wondering if you'd like to come?"

"Of course," I say. "I'd love to help."

"Cool. We should be there in about an hour. You can meet us at the courtyard."

"Sounds good! I'll see you soon." I hang up the phone and rush into my bathroom to get ready. My head is pounding now, but I ignore it. All I can think about is Nia and joining in the search to find her.

I take a quick shower and untwist my hair before walking into the kitchen. Aunt Lyn is sitting at the kitchen counter nursing a cup of coffee as she watches the news. The reporter on the TV is standing in front of the police station giving a live update on Nia's disappearance. She looks up from the TV and forces a smile, but I can see the worry in her eyes. I'd told her about Nia's disappearance when I arrived home from the probate, and she had been just as shocked as me. Nia visited me at the house often, and Aunt Lyn had taken a liking to her, even inviting her over for dinner a few times a month.

"No news yet?" she asks.

"Not yet." I pour myself a small cup of coffee. "I just found out that her car was found yesterday. Her parents have reported her missing to the police."

"I saw. I know they're probably worried sick."

I can feel her watching me, and I know she's already probably thinking the worst. Aunt Lyn is like that—always more tightly wound than she needs to be. She is a lot like my mother—something I learned quickly after moving in with her. "Are you headed out?"

"Yes, for a bit. Some people are meeting on campus to start hanging fliers for Nia. I'm going to go and help out for a few hours." I drain the last of the coffee from the mug and place it in the sink. "I'll be back a little later."

I am halfway out of the kitchen when she calls out to me. "Have you talked to your mom?"

I turn to face her. "Oh my God! Don't tell me she called you too?"

She circles the rim of her mug with her finger. "You should probably call her Tori."

I can feel my face growing hot. "I talked to her just last night! I told her I would call once I hear something."

"You know how she is," she says. "She's just worried about you. You and Nia are always together. You may need to check in a little more often right now, at least until this all blows over."

"But—"

"Call your mom," she says, cutting me off. "Don't make her worry."

I can tell by the tone of her voice that I don't really have a choice in the matter. "Ok, I'll call her."

As much as I hate to admit it, I know Aunt Lyn is right. The last thing I need is to send my mom into a frenzy by not calling and updating her. She'll be on the next flight up without a second thought if she even begins to suspect that I'm in any kind of trouble. She'll only make an already hard situation even worse. I make a mental note to call her as soon as I'm done on campus.

———

When I arrive on campus, Tre and a large group of students are congregated in the courtyard. Most of Nia's sorority sisters are present as well. They're hard at work, passing out fliers and speaking with volunteers.

Tre comes over to meet me. "Hey! Thanks for coming!"

"No problem," I say, looking around at the large group. "What can I do to help?"

"Well, we need to post these fliers around campus and in the surrounding neighborhood. We're hoping someone may recognize her." He hands me a large stack of fliers with Nia's face printed on the front. A tip line phone number has been provided for people to call in with information. "We've already got some posted near the dorms. I thought maybe I could go with you, and we could start on the south end of campus and work our way in."

I'm happy that he's decided to accompany me, but I don't let him see it. I've managed to keep my attraction to him under wraps for months, and I don't want to give myself away. Tre has always been nice to me, but I also know that I'm not the only one who feels this way about him. He's well-liked amongst the women on campus, but he doesn't seem to let it get to his head. It's part of what makes him even more attractive.

As the rest of the fliers are distributed amongst the group, Tre walks with me to the south end of the campus. We begin the slow process of posting fliers on buildings and in the common areas. As time passes, more volunteers begin to show up. Before long, Nia's face is on every building, door, and lamppost on the campus.

"Thanks again for coming," he says.

"It's no problem. I'm actually glad you called. I want to help in any way that I can."

"Well, we definitely needed the help. Sometimes it's easy to forget just how big this campus is. I'm glad all of these people showed up."

"I just pray someone recognizes her from these fliers and calls in with some information."

"Yeah, me too. And hopefully her dad's position will push the police to really take the case seriously."

I nod in agreement. Nia's dad has served as state congressman for the last five years and is one of the first MSU graduates and African Americans to be elected to state office. Now that Nia is missing, I can only pray that Tre is right and that Mr. Bryant's position will help speed the investigation along.

"How's Byron?" I ask, shifting the conversation.

"I haven't really had a chance to talk to him much with everything that's happened," he says. "I texted him this morning, though. He said that the police were stopping by today to talk to him."

"Do you think the police think he had something to do with her disappearance?" Even though I don't particularly like Byron, I don't think he's hiding anything. Just because he has a wandering eye doesn't mean that he's capable of harming Nia.

"I hope not," he says. "I know Byron. He may not have been the best boyfriend in the past, but he loves Nia. He wouldn't do anything to hurt her."

There is a low chime from his cell phone, and he pauses to answer it.

"Sorry. This thing has been ringing nonstop all morning." His expression changes as he stares at the phone screen.

"Is everything ok?" I ask.

He finally looks up at me. His eyes are wide, and I know immediately that something is wrong.

"What's wrong? What is it?"

"I—I just got a text from Byron. The car ..."

He stops mid-sentence and glances back down at the phone.

I press him. "The car? What about the car?"

"It just hit the news. The cops found blood in Nia's car."

I suddenly feel sick. "Blood?"

"Yeah, and they had it tested."

My skin feels cold and clammy even though I'm sweating in the heat. "Is it hers?"

He nods. "The police just confirmed that the blood belongs to Nia."

CHAPTER 9

CHRIS

WE'RE ON OUR WAY TO THE KAPPA THETA THETA SORORITY house when Lieutenant Stokes calls with the news. It's not unexpected, but I've been dreading it, nonetheless. The results from the blood uncovered in Nia's vehicle has been confirmed as a match to the missing student. There is still a possibility that she could still be alive, but the odds are slim. The idea that she left voluntarily is unlikely. It's evident that she has been the victim of some sort of foul play.

Cramer turns onto a quiet residential street near the campus and slows the car to a crawl. "I figured the blood was hers."

"I think we all knew, but we needed to be sure," I say. "There's still a chance she's just injured."

I see him roll his eyes. "You can believe that if you want. We both know how this is gonna end."

I lean forward in my seat and peer out of the passenger side window. The house up ahead has the Greek letters for Kappa Theta Theta hanging neatly above the front door. "This must be it."

Cramer turns into the long driveway and shuts off the engine. There's no one outside, but there are several cars parked in the driveway. "Doesn't look like there's much going on here," I say.

"Well, there are a few cars here, so someone has to be home. Come on. Let's see what we can find out."

We find the front door propped open, and voices can be heard coming from inside. Cramer is about to knock when an elderly woman emerges from behind the door. She appears startled to see us.

"Oh! I'm sorry!" she says. "I almost ran right into you!"

"It's ok, ma'am," I say. "We were just about to announce ourselves."

"Can I help you?" She looks back and forth between us with curious eyes that seem to bulge behind her large-framed glasses.

"Yes, ma'am, I'm Detective Evans, and this is my partner Detective Cramer. We're from MPD."

"Are you here about Nia?" she asks, her eyes growing wider.

"Yes, ma'am, we are."

"Oh, please tell me you've found her. We've been so worried!"

"We're working some leads, but unfortunately we haven't been able to locate her just yet."

The woman's face drops. The wrinkles she's tried to conceal with a heavy layer of makeup pop through. "I'm sorry," I say. "I didn't catch your name?"

"I—I'm sorry, how rude of me," she says, shaking my hand. "My name is Maggie Price, but everyone calls me Ms. Maggie. I'm the chapter advisor here for the sorority."

"Nice to meet you, Ms. Maggie. Sorry to show up unannounced like this. I know things must be difficult right now."

She waves her hand dismissively. "Oh, that's perfectly fine. I'm just glad you're here. The girls have been putting fliers up all morning at the campus, and we've been waiting on an update. I must admit the police haven't been very forthcoming so far with us."

I look past her into the house. "Did we catch you at a bad time?"

"No, not at all. We're just here picking up the last few boxes of fliers, but that can wait. Please come in."

She opens the door wide, which leads into a spacious foyer. The air is pleasantly cool inside, a welcome relief from the stifling heat. She beckons for us to follow her into a large sitting area.

"Please, have a seat," she says. "Can I get you anything?"

I take a seat on the couch and glance around the room. It's expensively decorated, like something out of a home décor magazine. Kappa Theta Theta paraphernalia covers the walls. "No, ma'am, we're fine. You mentioned that the sorority members are at the campus?"

Ms. Maggie takes a seat on the opposite end of the couch. "Yes, they've been out there most of the morning. The girls had fliers printed up late last night and are trying to get as many posted as possible. Shawna just had another batch printed up so that we can start posting some around town next."

"Shawna? Is she one of the girls?"

"Yes, she's in the back room." Ms. Maggie stands slowly to her feet. "I can go and get her if you'd like."

"In a minute," I say. "We'd like to speak with you alone first if that's ok."

"Of course." She takes her place back on the couch and clasps her hands in her lap. I watch her from across the room. She has an air of gentility to her—a certain gracefulness that commands respect. Her silver hair has been curled in loose ringlets that fall just past her shoulders. Her starched light-yellow pantsuit matches her manicured nails.

"So, you said you're the advisor for the sorority?"

"Yes," she says proudly. "I've been the advisor here for almost thirty-five years."

"And what are your responsibilities?"

"I look after the girls," she says. "I'm pretty much responsible for making sure things run smoothly here. I also keep after the house."

"Were you in attendance the evening that Nia went missing?"

She shakes her head, her curls bouncing. "No, I don't usually come to the rehearsals. At my age, I rely heavily on the senior girls to help with those things. The chapter president has been overseeing the rehearsals."

"And that would be Diana McNamee, correct?" I ask, recalling my earlier conversation with Drew.

"Yes, that's right."

"And we were told in the initial report that the rehearsal took place at Groveland Park?"

"Yes, sir, that's where the girls usually practice."

"In the days leading up to Nia's disappearance, did you notice anything peculiar about her behavior?"

"She seemed fine," she says. "I haven't noticed anything out of the ordinary with Nia. She's a good girl. But then again, she has to be. You do know who her father is?" Ms. Maggie leans forward and searches our faces, her large eyes protruding behind her glasses.

"Yes, we're aware of her relation to the congressman," I say.

"Well, I should hope so." She leans back and crosses her hands on the tip of her cane. "Nia wouldn't just up and disappear like that. I've known her family for a long time. They raised her right."

"Do you know of any issues that she was having with anyone in particular?" I ask. "Has she ever received threats or anything like that?"

"Oh God, no! I've never known Nia to have any issues with anyone. She's a sweet girl. I can't even imagine someone wanting to harm her."

"So, you have no idea where she may have gone or of anyone that she may have left with?"

She shrugs. "No, I don't. And I highly doubt that she would up and leave with someone without telling anyone."

"Why do you say that?"

"Because the girls were so excited about their probate show. It's all they've been talking about for the last few weeks. People flew in from all over to be there. We even had past chapter members in town. She knew how much it meant to everyone, especially her line sisters. The idea that she just up and left without speaking to anyone just doesn't make sense."

"May we ask where you were that evening?" Cramer asks.

Her back stiffens, and she turns to look at him. The question has rubbed her the wrong way, but she keeps her composure. "I was right here. All night."

There is a light knock at the door. A young woman peeks her head inside the room.

"Oh, I'm sorry," she says, glancing at us and then back at Ms. Maggie. "I didn't know you had company."

Ms. Maggie waves her inside. "Oh no, it's fine. These are detectives from MPD. They're here about Nia."

"Are you Shawna?" Cramer asks.

The young woman lingers just outside the room. She's tall and slender, with long braids that hang down her back. "Yes, I'm Shawna. Have you guys found Nia?"

"Not yet," I say. "We're trying to speak with everyone connected to her to get a better idea of what happened that night and her state of mind."

Shawna steps into the room and stands close to Ms. Maggie. She stares awkwardly at the floor as if she's nervous.

"Ms. Maggie, do you mind if we speak privately with Shawna for a few minutes?" I ask. "Just to get her statement?"

Ms. Maggie hoists herself up from the couch and walks toward the door. "Sure. Take your time. I'll call and check on the girls at the campus. Let me know if you all need anything." She steps out of the room and closes the door behind her, leaving us alone with Shawna.

"Thank you for speaking with us," I say. "I know everyone probably has a lot of questions right now."

"It's no problem," she says. "How can I help?"

"Well, we'd like you to tell us about the night Nia went missing. Walk us through what happened. You all last saw Nia Thursday evening at the probate rehearsal, which took place at Groveland Park?"

"Yes, that's right."

"What time exactly did that start?"

"It started at 11:00 p.m. on Thursday, and we ended around 1:30 a.m."

"Do you guys usually practice at that time of night? Is that normal?"

"Yeah, we do. And we always go to that park. We've never had an issue before."

"Did anything seem different about Nia?" Cramer asks. "Did she seem worried or upset about anything?"

"No, not that I can think of. Everyone was a little stressed about the show the next day, but I didn't notice anything out of the ordinary with her."

I look around the room again at the dozens of photographs of past and current members of the sorority chapter covering the walls. "How many people were in attendance that night?"

"There were twelve of us. The ten girls who were on the line and Diana and me."

"Ms. Maggie tells us that Diana was also in charge of things?"

"Yes ... well, we both were. I'm the chapter vice president. We were both working with the girls."

"So, would you say that the practice was uneventful?"

"Yes, pretty much. We had the girls run through the show a few times. After that, we all headed home."

"What about clothing? Do you remember what Nia was wearing when you last saw her?"

"We all were dressed in the same thing that night for rehearsal," she says. "Black tights, a black top, and black jackets."

I make note of Nia's clothing in my notepad.

"Oh, and she had on a necklace," she says.

"A necklace?"

"Yeah, a little silver locket she always wears. We have a rule of no jewelry at practice, but she always has it on. The only reason I remember is because I had to remind her to remove it that night."

"And did she?"

"Yeah, she did," she says. "When we finished practice, I saw her slip it back on when we were packing up to leave."

I note the necklace in my notes. "So, after the rehearsal, Nia left with the group?"

Shawna drops her eyes and stares at her hands in her lap. She looks uncomfortable. "Well, no. Nia didn't leave when we left."

"Well, do you know when she left?"

"I'm not sure," she says. "After practice, Diana pulled her aside and asked her to hang back for a minute. I didn't stick around, so I don't know what happened after that."

"So everyone else in the group left at the same time except for Nia and Diana?" Cramer asks.

"Yes. When I left, Diana and Nia were the last two still there. I figured they would be right behind us."

"Any idea why Diana would've asked Nia to stay behind?" I ask. "Does she normally do that?"

"I don't know what was going on. She just said she needed to speak with her in private."

"Was there anything going on between them? Any bad blood?"

"No, nothing like that. I mean, they're not best friends, but they're not enemies either. They're cordial to each other."

"And what about Diana?" Cramer asks. "Did she seem upset about anything that night?"

She hesitates. She knows something but doesn't want to say it.

"Shawna, any detail you have may be helpful in helping us find Nia," I say. "I know this is difficult, but we need to know everything that happened that night."

She sighs and looks up at me. "Diana did seem a little off that night at practice."

"Off? How so?"

"She seemed upset about something and was really distracted the whole time we were there. I didn't think anything of it, though. It's been a long few weeks leading up to the probate, and I think everyone was just tired. I just assumed everything had taken a toll on her. This is her first year as president."

"Did you hear from Diana after leaving the park that night?"

"I didn't see her again until the next morning before the show. She seemed a little better—that was until Nia didn't show up. When we couldn't reach Nia, she got worried. In fact, she was the one who started calling and texting her to find out where she was."

"Has Diana been on campus this morning with you all?" Cramer asks. "We'd like to speak with her."

"No, I haven't seen her today. I texted her a few hours ago to let her know we were heading out there, but I haven't heard back yet. I know she's still a little upset about how the show went yesterday, you know, with Nia not showing up and all."

Cramer gives me a concerned look. If Diana is the last known person to have seen Nia, then we need to speak with her as soon as possible to get her side of the story. The fact that she has been a no-show all morning has me worried that she could be in the wind if she is somehow involved.

"Is there anything else that you can think of that may be helpful? Any other details about that night?"

"No, not that I can think of," she says.

"Well, I think we have all we need for now. We'll leave our cards here for the other young ladies when they return from campus. If you can see that they get them, we'd appreciate it. We would like to speak with everyone as soon as possible to get as much information as we can, especially Diana."

"Sure, I can do that," she says. "Whatever you need."

"If you think of anything else, please do not hesitate to reach out. And we will be in contact soon to speak to the rest of the members."

Shawna leads us out of the sitting room and back into the foyer. Once outside, we find Ms. Maggie sitting on the front porch.

"So, what now?" She moves away a stray curl that has fallen into her face.

"Well, we have every officer in the city searching for Nia," I say. "We hope to have some updates soon as we work on tracing her last steps. In the meantime, we left several business cards with Shawna for the other members. As soon as they have a moment, please have them give us a call so that we can speak to them individually."

She leans on her cane as she slowly stands. "I'll see that they get them as soon as they get in."

"Thank you, ma'am. We'll be in touch."

Back at the car, Cramer waits until we are out of earshot before speaking. "So, what do you think?"

"I don't know," I say. "They seem truthful enough. But this whole situation with the chapter president has me thinking."

"Yeah, something isn't adding up."

"I don't want to wait around for her to show up. I think we should try and find her ourselves. What if she—"

I'm cut short by an incoming call on my cell phone. The shrill ringing startles me in the enclosed space of the car. The lieutenant's phone number flashes on the screen. "It's Stokes."

Cramer rolls down his window and reaches into his pocket for a cigarette. "Well, see what he wants."

I take a deep breath to collect myself before answering. "Hey, Lieutenant."

"Whatcha got on the Bryant girl?" There is no beating around the bush with him. Stokes skips the pleasantries and jumps straight to business.

"Well, we just spoke to her sorority advisor and one of her sorority sisters. Their stories are consistent with the information that we already have. But we did learn that Nia didn't leave with the rest of the group that night. She stayed behind with the chapter president, Diana McNamee."

"Diana McNamee? Have you spoken with this girl?"

"Not yet, sir. Her sorority sister says she hasn't been able to reach her today. I was just talking with Cramer and suggesting that we try and make contact with her. We already have Jacobs working on retrieving the surveillance video from the management company at the property where Nia lives. Hopefully there will be some footage that may give us something. But right now, Diana seems like our next best lead since she's the last person that was seen with Nia."

"Well, Nia's parents have just arrived at the airport, and they should be at the station soon. I'd like you and Cramer to come in and interview them."

"Ok. But what about the girl, Diana? Shouldn't we see if we can locate her?"

"Since you and Cramer are heading the case, I think it would be good for you both to conduct the initial interview with the parents and see what information they can provide," he says.

"I understand, sir. But right now, I think our main priority should be locating—"

"Evans, right now your priority is to interview the parents." His voice is stern as he cuts me off. "Don't worry, I will handle getting someone to get in contact with the girl. You two just focus on the parents right now."

Even though I don't agree with the command, I bite my tongue and decide not to press the issue further. Lieutenant Stokes has been over our division for the last year, and I would be lying if I said that we always see eye to eye. I don't agree with dropping everything to conduct an interview, especially when there are dozens of other officers who are available to do it. But now isn't the time to let our personalities get in the way.

"Yes, sir, we'll head over."

"Good! I'll see you two shortly."

Cramer looks at me out of the corner of his eye. He takes a long drag on the cigarette and tosses it out of the window.

"We gotta head back," I say.

"What about the girl?"

"Stokes says he will work on getting someone to locate her. Right now, he wants us to head back to the station."

"For what?"

"The Bryants just arrived in town. He wants us to be there to interview them."

"Can't someone else do that?"

"That's what I said. But he's insisting that we do it since we're heading the case."

He shakes his head and reverses the car out of the driveway. "The parents are not who we need to be focused on."

He mumbles something else under his breath, but I don't hear. I take one last look at the sorority house as we drive off. I'm convinced someone within the organization knows what happened to Nia Bryant. We just have to figure out who.

CHAPTER 10

CHRIS

BACK AT THE STATION, NEWS MEDIA VANS CROWD THE parking lot. Reporters and camera personnel are everywhere, waiting like prey for anyone willing to give them a statement on the case.

"I swear these people are like vultures."

"You know how it is," Cramer says. "Everyone wants to be the first to break the story." He maneuvers carefully through the crowded parking lot, taking care to avoid the crowd of people huddled near the front entrance of the station.

"Let's go in through the back," I say. "I really don't feel like fielding questions that we don't have the answers to right now."

Cramer drives around to the back of the building. To my relief, the back entrance is empty and offers a clear path into the station. We rush inside the building before we can be seen.

We find Lieutenant Stokes near the information desk in the main lobby. He is pacing the floor nervously as he peers out the front doors of the station at the crowd of reporters camped outside. He looks relieved when he sees that we've arrived.

"Oh good, you're here," he says, rushing toward us. "The parents just arrived a few minutes ago. I have them all set up upstairs."

We follow him to the second floor, where the interrogation rooms are located. Inside one of the rooms, a man and woman wait anxiously. They are seated at the far end of the conference room table. I immediately recognize the man as Congressman Dwight Bryant. He stands and walks around the table to greet us. I've never met him in person, and he is much taller than I expected. He is dressed conservatively in a pair of khaki slacks and a teal, short-sleeved linen polo. His salt and pepper hair gives him a distinguished look.

Cassandra Bryant is seated in the chair next to his. She has stunning features, with large brown eyes that are framed by long, wispy eyelashes. Her skin is taut and smooth, giving her the look of a twenty-something-year-old instead of a woman in her forties. I do a double take as my eyes meet hers. Nia is the spitting image of her mother. For a moment, it feels like I'm looking at the missing girl herself.

The congressman greets us, his booming voice echoing through the small room. "Detectives! I'm Dwight Bryant, Nia's father."

I shake his hand. "Pleasure to meet you in person, Congressman Bryant. I'm Detective Chris Evans. This is my partner Detective Albert Cramer. We're lead on your daughter's case."

"I'll leave you all to it," says Stokes from the doorway. "Let me know if I can be of assistance." He shuts the door, leaving us alone with Nia's parents.

"Let me be the first to say that we know how stressful this has to be on both of you," I say. "But I want you to know that we have every available officer focused on finding your daughter."

"None of this makes sense," says Congressman Bryant. "Nia has never done anything like this before. She is very responsible. She wouldn't just up and leave."

"And that's the consensus we've received from everyone we've spoken to thus far. And that's another reason why we are taking her disappearance very seriously. This seems very out of character for her."

Mrs. Bryant begins to sob softly, covering her face with her hands. Her husband reaches over and strokes her back as he tries to comfort her. "My wife is beside herself with worry. We both are."

"We will take whatever information you can give us about your daughter," Cramer says. "Any details you have will certainly be helpful."

"What have you found so far?" Mrs. Bryant asks between sobs.

"Well, ma'am, we've spoken to quite a few of her associates," I say. "From what we've been told, she was last seen at her probate rehearsal late Thursday evening into Friday morning. After that, no one can account for her whereabouts."

"But her car was found at home?"

"Correct. It was parked there, and the keys were found inside. Our CSI team has processed it for evidence, and I'm afraid that blood was found."

"Yes, Lieutenant Stokes called us and informed us before we arrived. And you're sure it's Nia's?" asks Congressman Bryant

"It's a positive match, sir."

"So, you think Nia drove home after practice, and that's when she disappeared?"

"Yes, that's what it looks like. But there is no evidence that she ever made it inside. We've had her home checked, but so far, nothing out of the ordinary has been uncovered."

"Can you pull any cameras?" he asks. "Something that may show her last movements?"

"We've already requested the camera footage from her apartment community. We also have detectives requesting and pulling footage from nearby businesses. Of course, some of the footage may take some time to obtain, but we are confident we will get what we need."

Congressman Bryant glances anxiously around the room. I can tell that our conversation so far has done nothing to reassure him. "Something isn't right. Something has happened to Nia. I just know it."

"Detectives, you must understand," says Mrs. Bryant. "We talk to our daughter every day. Nia would never not answer her phone or my text messages. When she went off to school, we made sure that she understood how important it is for her to keep in contact with us. She knows better than to just take off like this."

"When was the last time you spoke to her?" Cramer asks.

"I talked to her Thursday night before she left home for rehearsal," says Mrs. Bryant.

"And how did she sound?"

"She sounded fine. Maybe a little stressed, but I assumed it was because of the probate the next day." She takes a tissue from the Kleenex box in the middle of the table and wipes her eyes before continuing. "I wanted to be here ... we should've been here."

"What kept you away?"

"I had a conference in D.C. this weekend," says Congressman Bryant. "With the election coming up next year, we needed to make an appearance."

"Was Nia upset about you all missing her probate?" I ask.

"She was a little disappointed, but she understood. This is my fifth year as congressman. She knows how things go with the job."

Mrs. Bryant shakes her head. "We should've been here, Dwight. This would've never happened if we'd come."

"What about people from her past?" I ask. "Anyone worth noting? Any ex-boyfriends?"

"She's been dating Byron since the summer," says Congressman Bryant. "Before that, she had a few interests in high school, but nothing too serious. Byron is her first serious relationship."

"Do you know anything about her relationship with Byron? Did Nia seem happy with him?"

"Byron is a good kid and comes from a good family," he says. "We've never had any reason to question his intentions."

I glance at Mrs. Bryant, but she doesn't look at me. The look on her face catches my eye. She knows more about the troubles between Nia and Byron than she has let on to her husband.

"Well, he's been cooperative thus far," I say. "But in these situations, we have to look at everyone."

"And what about you guys?" Cramer asks.

Congressman Bryant looks at him. "What about us?"

"Well, we have to look at all factors. And considering your political status, it's not unheard of for people to make threats toward politicians and their families. Can you think of anyone who may be targeting you? Has your office received any threats?"

"No, not that I'm aware of."

"So, what do we do now?" asks Mrs. Bryant. "Just sit here and wait?"

"We are working around the clock on this," I say. "I hope we can give you more answers soon. In the meantime, why don't you go get checked in at your hotel and get settled, and we will update you in a few hours. I know you all have probably been traveling all morning."

"Thank you. That's probably a good idea," says Congressman Bryant. He stands and shakes our hands again. "Thank you both for what you're doing. We really appreciate it."

"Oh, no problem at all, sir," I say. "And don't worry. Nia's case is top priority. We won't stop until we find her."

The Bryants gather their belongings, and Cramer escorts them out of the room. I stay behind. When he returns, he shuts the door behind him. "So, what do you make of the parents?"

"I don't think they're involved," I say.

"Yeah, I agree."

"The problem is, we still didn't get much out of them; nothing that we don't already know, at least."

"Diana McNamee is going to be the key to finding out what happened that night," he says. "She is who we need to be talking to."

"Yeah, I know. But we need to find her first."

Chapter 11

Evie

I take a sip of the wine. The smooth, chilled liquid warms my body as it flows through me. My eyes are glued to the TV, taking in every word. Nia's story is on every station, clogging up the airwaves and capturing everyone's attention. The community is now fully engaged, and her face is everywhere.

I turn the volume up on the TV. A clip airs of the Bryants walking into the police station, their heads bowed as they are escorted up the front steps by a team of stone-faced police officers. The reporters swarm them, sticking microphones into their faces as they bombard them with questions.

I catch a glimpse of Cassandra Bryant's face; her tear-filled eyes turned toward one of the cameras. She no longer looks like the confident woman that always stands proudly next to her husband at social events and political functions. Today she looks helpless and frail, her life hanging in the balance.

Congressman Bryant holds his wife's hand, leading her up the steps as he tries to ignore the mob of reporters. He is used to this type of attention, a master at deflecting questions. His entire career has prepared him for this moment, whether he realizes it or not. I watch them closely, studying their every move. They are understandably distraught, thrown headfirst into every parent's worst nightmare. The panic has set in, and they are desperate. They will do anything to bring Nia home.

CHAPTER 12

TORI

TRE'S HOUSE SITS ON A QUIET CUL-DE-SAC IN AN UPSCALE
neighborhood. The large, stately homes are overly extravagant with their
well-manicured lawns and overpriced cars parked in the driveways. It's
picture-perfect—too perfect.

The sun is low in the sky when I arrive. A slight breeze drifts in
through my car window, cooling my face. A middle-aged woman jogs
past my car, taking advantage of the last bit of sunlight on her evening
jog. I watch her through my rearview mirror as she passes. Her long
black ponytail swings as she runs, her body moving in one fluid motion
with each step. I watch her until she disappears around a corner.

The world around me is quiet, and I feel a sense of calm. For a
moment, things seem normal. Children have been called in from
outside, and families are sitting down to dinner. I imagine them gathered around the table, recounting the events of their day while sharing a
meal. I wish for normal again, for the time when Nia was here.

The news of the blood discovery is all anyone has been able to talk
about. A cash reward has now been posted for information leading to
Nia's whereabouts. Teams of volunteers have taken to the streets,
conducting searches in wooded areas and abandoned buildings. The
thought of searches unnerves me. I want Nia to be found, but not

under these circumstances. I've been glued to my phone all day, waiting for her to call me and say that she's fine—that this whole thing has been blown out of proportion. But the call hasn't come. It is almost the end of day two, and we are all fearing the worst.

My cell phone rings. It's my mom, and I have a mind to send her to voicemail. I'd kept my promise to Aunt Lyn and checked in as soon as I had finished up on campus, but that hasn't stopped her from calling every couple of hours. The news of Nia's disappearance has hit the major news networks, and she's been able to keep up with the story even from out of state.

I finally answer on the fourth ring. "Hey, Ma, what's going on?"

"I'm just checking on you," she says.

"I'm fine. Everything is ok. You don't have to keep checking in, you know?"

"Have you heard anything new?"

"Not since I last talked to you an hour ago."

"I just spoke to Lyn. She said that they are conducting searches now. They even had a dive team checking the lakes in the area."

"Yeah, they are."

"I know you said you're fine, but I really think I should come up to be with you right now."

"No, you don't need to do that."

"I know you don't think I need to, but I would just feel better if I was there with you."

"I told you I'm fine. You don't have to worry about me. I know how to handle myself."

She is silent for several seconds before she finally speaks again. "Well, where are you now? Are you at home?"

I glance out of the window at the large house on the other side of the gate. "I'm at a friend's house."

"A friend? What friend?"

"Someone Nia and I have class with. We're meeting up to work on a social media page for Nia … to help spread the word."

"Tori, it's really getting late—"

"It's only 7," I say, cutting her off. "I won't be out late. Besides, I already told Aunt Lyn."

She isn't happy with the idea of me being out, but she doesn't push the subject. "I know you want to do what you can for Nia. Just don't stay out too late."

"I won't." I quickly hang up the phone and text Tre to let him know that I'm outside. I know I only have a few hours before she calls and checks in again. Nia's disappearance has sent her anxiety into overdrive, and I'm exhausted from trying to reassure her on top of dealing with everything else. The sooner I get home, the better—for her and for me.

There is movement on the side of the house, and Tre appears near the front gate. I climb out of my car and walk up the driveway toward him.

"Hey! Thanks for coming," he says.

From inside the gate, I have a full view of the property. "When you said you lived in Magnolia Springs, I knew it would be nice. But I wasn't expecting this. You have a really nice house."

"Thanks!" he laughs. "But it's my uncle's place. Come on back."

He leads me through a side gate into a spacious backyard. The grounds are well-kept, with potted plants running along the perimeter of the house. A small patch of grass near the back gate has been turned into a garden. The spring weather has been good to the soil, and tomatoes and large heads of lettuce sprout up from the ground. Basil and other herbs grow from small terracotta pots. A small wind chime hangs from the lanai awning. It makes a subtle tinkling sound in the gentle breeze.

At the very back of the property is a small single-story guest house. "This is me," he says, pointing to the house.

"Wow! You have all of this to yourself?"

"Yep! This has been my home away from home for the last few years. My uncle offered me the place to stay when I moved here for school. They don't use the guest house much, so it kind of worked out."

I glance back at the main house. "He won't mind that I'm here, will he?"

"No, my uncle and his wife are cool. Besides, my uncle isn't even here. He's out of town for work."

A wicker patio set has been set out on the small porch connected to the guest house. A box of pizza lies open on the table. The cup of coffee from this morning is the only thing I've taken in today, and I'm suddenly starving.

He motions for me to sit down. "Have a seat. I hope you're hungry."

"I am." I take a seat across from him, but I don't immediately go for the pizza. "I haven't had anything except for coffee and water today. I just haven't felt like eating. I've been so worried about Nia."

He pushes the box of pizza toward me. "Well, dig in."

I grab a small slice and take a bite. My eyes wander around the yard. "So, what does your uncle do exactly?"

"He's an architect, and he travels a lot for work. He's actually been in Japan for the last few weeks overseeing a project." He leans back in his chair and studies me closely. I can feel myself blushing. I try to think of something to say, anything to keep the conversation going.

"So, are you from here?" I ask.

He shakes his head. "No, I was actually born and raised in Charleston. I just came out here for school."

"What made you decide on MSU?"

"It's kind of a family tradition, I guess. My grandpa went to MSU. So did my uncle, who owns this place."

"So, your path was already decided in a way?"

"Eh. Yes and no. I've always wanted to go to an HBCU for college, so it just made sense to come here."

"Yeah, MSU was my first choice," I say. "I had a few offers from some in-state schools back home, but I'm happy I made the decision to come. It's a nice change."

"Yeah it is." He scoots his chair back from the table. "Hey, I'm going to grab a beer. Do you want something to drink?"

I pause, unsure of what to say. It won't be the first time I've dabbled with alcohol since starting college. With everything that has happened today, I need something to take the edge off.

"Sure, I'll take one."

He disappears into the house and returns a few minutes later with a couple of beers. He places one on the table in front of me.

"So, what about you?" he asks.

"What about me?"

"Tell me about Tori. We have class together and see each other around campus, but I don't know much about you."

"I don't know that there's much to tell," I say. "I'm from Fort Lauderdale. It was just me and my mom growing up. I had a pretty average childhood—nothing exciting."

"So, no brothers and sisters? You're an only child?"

"Yes. My dad died when I was three, and my mom never married after that, so it was just her and me."

"Oh man, I'm sorry to hear that."

"It's fine. I don't even remember when it happened. I don't know much about my dad aside from pictures. My mom doesn't really like to talk about it much."

"Well, I'm sure that was hard on her, raising a kid on her own and all."

"She did the best that she could. I'm all she has, and she never lets me forget it. It's one of the reasons why I felt guilty moving so far away for school."

He stops eating and gives me a confused look.

"Sorry, that came out wrong," I say. "I love my mom; she can just be a little much. I felt smothered growing up, and I still do sometimes. But I know she means well."

"So, she's overprotective?"

"Yeah, you can say that."

"Coming here must've been nice then," he says. "You're getting your first taste of freedom without having your mom constantly looking over your shoulder."

"Well, I wouldn't say that exactly. I have an aunt who lives here. That's the only reason my mom even entertained the idea of me applying to MSU and moving out here."

"So, your aunt is your mom's eyes and ears for the next four years?"

"Pretty much. I moved in with her at the beginning of this semester. I stayed on campus in the fall, so I got to experience dorm life for a short time before my mom insisted that I move in with my aunt. She said she felt better knowing that I was staying with family. It's been ok so far. It was a little awkward at first, but we're getting used to sharing a space."

"Awkward? How so?"

"Well, we're close now, but it wasn't always that way. She's my dad's sister, and most of his family lives across the country, so it's hard to stay in touch. I saw her a few times as a kid, but I was too young to remember. She always sent me money every year for birthdays, but that's about it."

"Oh, so she's the rich aunt?" he jokes.

"I wouldn't say rich," I laugh. "She got divorced a few years ago. She lives alone, so there's plenty of space for me. And honestly, I think she likes the company."

I pop open my beer and take a sip. The bitter liquid is strong, and I wince at the taste. It burns going down. "So, what about this page?" I ask, steering the conversation back to Nia. "Do you have any ideas for how you want to set it up?"

"So, I've pulled some pictures from Nia's profile page," he says. "I have all of the phone numbers and contact information that people can use to call in tips. I want to have it up and running tonight if possible. The sooner we start sharing it, the sooner people can start following it from their accounts. The more followers, the better."

"This is still so weird," I say. "I can't believe Nia is missing. It's like the type of thing you see on TV."

"I know. I never thought this would happen to someone that I know. I remember when I met Nia and her parents when I volunteered for freshman orientation week. She was so nice. Now she's gone."

"I just wish I knew what the police were doing."

"Well, they were already at the sorority house earlier today asking questions."

"Really? So they finally talked to the girls?"

"Yeah, that's what I heard."

"I mean, that makes sense. Nia was with them the night she disappeared. Maybe they saw or know something."

He disagrees. "Nah, if they did, they would've told the police. They wouldn't withhold that type of information."

"Yeah, I guess you're right. I'm just happy to know that the police seem to be taking it seriously."

"Yes, me too. But they did tell the police that Diana was the last person seen with Nia."

"Wait! Diana McNamee?"

He nods. "Yes, that's what everyone is saying. She and Nia stayed behind at the park after everyone left."

"Diana came up to me before the probate and asked me if I had seen Nia," I say. "That was how I found out that she hadn't shown up. Did the police talk to her? Was she able to tell them anything?"

"We don't know what she knows because no one has been able to reach her since the show yesterday."

My heart drops. "What do you mean? Not even Drew?"

"I spoke to Drew earlier. He's been trying to reach her all day. She's not home. But now that the police know, I'm sure they are looking for her as well."

He goes into the house to grab his laptop, and I push away the plate of pizza. My appetite is suddenly gone again. Diana seemed concerned when we'd spoken yesterday at the probate, but now I can't help but wonder if she's involved; especially since I know something that Tre doesn't know.

A million thoughts are running through my head, but I have more questions than answers. Diana is the only one who truly knows what happened, but now she seems to have disappeared as well. Then something occurs to me—something that I haven't considered until just now. What if Nia isn't the only one? What if there's more than one girl missing?

Chapter 13

Chris

Lieutenant Stokes sits quietly across the table from me, his head buried in his hands. His untouched cup of coffee has gone cold, but he doesn't seem to notice. He circles his temples nervously with his fingers.

"Everything has gone to shit, Evans."

I look up from my cup of coffee. It's my fifth one today.

"We have no leads on this girl and no definite suspects," he says. "On top of that, I got a call this afternoon. The FBI has taken an interest in the case. If we don't get something soon, this won't be our case anymore."

The only other person in the employee lounge is sitting several tables over, preoccupied with a basketball game playing on the TV.

"We just need a little more time, sir," I whisper. "I know we're close to something."

"If this were any other case, I wouldn't be worried. But we're dealing with a politician's daughter here." He picks up his cup of coffee and finally takes a sip of the lukewarm liquid. "Did you and Cramer uncover anything from the surveillance tapes we've obtained so far?"

I shake my head. "We've spent all afternoon reviewing them. There are no visuals of Nia or of any suspicious activity."

"I just don't understand," he says. "You'd think we would have uncovered something by now."

"I know. We were really hoping the surveillance footage would show us something."

"Have you all had a chance to talk to the remaining sorority members?"

"We have, all except for Diana McNamee. The sorority advisor, Maggie Price, gave them our contact information. They all came in willingly to provide statements. Their stories are consistent, and they all have alibis that check out. We just need to speak with Diana now."

The lounge door opens, and Jacobs appears in the doorway.

"What is it?" asks Stokes.

"We've got something, sir."

He jumps up from the table and rushes out of the lounge. I gulp down the rest of my coffee, toss my cup into the trash, and follow them across the hall to the squad room. When I arrive, Jacobs, Lieutenant Stokes, and the head of our IT department, Andy Gesky, are huddled together. They are peering over Andy's laptop, studying something closely on the screen.

"Hey, Evans, come look at this," says Jacobs.

"What is it?"

"We got the surveillance tape from Nia's residence."

I stand next to Jacobs so that I can get a good view of the computer screen. "Does it tell us anything?"

Andy shakes his head. "Not really, and it's really grainy."

"Well, what can we see?"

"See for yourself." Andy presses play on the video. The image is in black and white and is slightly distorted. Nia's car can be seen entering the gate at her apartment complex at exactly 2:23 a.m.

"What'd I miss?" Cramer stands in the doorway of the squad room. His eyes look heavy, and I can tell that the long hours are beginning to wear on him.

"Come take a look at this," I say, moving over so that he has a better view of the video.

He slides on his glasses and squints as he stares at the computer screen. "Finally got the tape, huh?"

"Rewind it, Andy," I say. "Go back to the clip where Nia's car comes through the gate."

Andy rewinds the video, and we all lean in close to the screen as the video restarts. "Can you slow it down?"

He presses a button on the keyboard, and the video slows to a crawling pace. Nia's Honda Accord rolls into view again as it enters the guard gate.

"That's her car," says Cramer.

"So we know she made it home," I say. "Do we have any camera footage from inside the property? Maybe from the street she lives on?"

"That's the problem," says Andy. "We requested that, but most of the cameras on site are not functioning."

"Seriously?"

"Yes, I double-checked."

"And no exit camera either?" asks Cramer.

"No footage from there either. I checked with the management company. It wasn't functioning on the night she disappeared." He ejects the disc from the computer drive and shuts the laptop. "I'm going to see if I can clean it up a bit and see if there's anything else we can use that maybe we're not seeing."

"Alright," I say. "Keep us updated."

Andy packs up the computer and leaves the squad room with Lieutenant Stokes. I was hoping that the surveillance tapes at Nia's residence would shed some light on what happened to her that night, but they didn't show us much of anything.

"No sightings yet?" I ask Jacobs.

"Nope," he says. "No reports of anyone matching her description."

"What about the phones? Any tips or leads coming in worth looking into?"

"No, nothing on the phones either. And I don't know how much we're going to get tonight. It's getting late."

A uniformed patrol officer knocks on the squad room door and peeks his head inside. "Detective Evans?"

"Yeah?"

"I have a young lady in the lobby to see you."

I check the time on my phone. I'm not expecting anyone, and we've already completed our planned interviews for the day. "Who is it?"

"She says her name is Diana McNamee. She—"

I don't let the officer finish. I make a break for the door, pushing past him. I can hear Cramer on my heels following close behind.

When we arrive downstairs, the officer points to a young woman sitting in the waiting area. "Over there," he whispers. "I told her to have a seat."

Diana sits slouched in the chair. She looks up when she hears us approaching.

"Hi, Miss McNamee. I'm Detective Evans, and this is my partner Detective Cramer."

Diana flashes a card in her hand. "You wanted to speak with me?"

"That's correct. Thank you so much for coming in. We've been trying to reach you."

Her eyes are red and swollen. I can tell she's been crying. "Do you mind if we speak to you for a moment in a private room? We just have a few questions for you about Nia Bryant."

I almost expect her to decline. To my surprise, she grabs her purse and throws it over her shoulder. "Fine, we can talk. Not like I have much of a choice anyway."

We lead her out of the lobby and up the stairs to the second floor. When we reach the interrogation room, Diana takes a seat at the far end of the table, putting as much distance between herself and us as possible.

"Can we get you anything?" I ask.

"No, I'm fine." Her tone is snipped. She lowers her eyes and stares at her hands in her lap.

"So, as you probably already know, Nia Bryant has not been seen or heard from in almost forty-eight hours. We were wondering if you could tell us about the last time you saw her."

"I last saw her at the probate rehearsal." Her voice is low. She keeps her eyes pointed to the ground, avoiding our gaze. I lean forward so that I can hear her better.

"Did anything happen during the rehearsal that was out of the ordinary?"

"No, not really."

"What about after?" asks Cramer.

Diana raises her eyes and finally looks at us.

"We were told by a source that you asked Nia to stay behind after the rehearsal ended," I say. "What was that about?"

"Yeah, I did," she admits. "I asked her to stay behind ... so that I could talk to her."

"After the rest of the group had left?"

Diana doesn't answer, but I continue to press her. "What exactly did you need to speak with her about that required a private conversation after everyone else had already gone home?"

She rests her head in her hands, and that's when I see it. The outside of Diana's right hand has dark, red scratches that stretch from her wrist to her knuckles. The scratches look fresh, the skin around them slightly swollen. She notices me staring at her hands and instinctively drops them back in her lap. Cramer and I exchange looks, and I can tell that he has noticed it too.

"Diana, can you tell us why you asked Nia to stay behind?" Cramer asks. "We're just trying to understand what happened."

"Do you really wanna know the truth?" Her voice trembles as tears build in the corners of her eyes. "Everyone thinks Nia is this sweet, innocent girl, but she's not."

She inhales deeply and slowly blows the air out of her mouth. She's shaking, but it isn't out of fear; she's angry about something. Then the truth hits me. I turn to Cramer, but his eyes are glued on the young woman as tears begin to run down her cheeks. Soon she is sobbing, and all I can think of is our earlier conversation with Drew Bradley. I had been suspicious of Byron's roommate all along ... and now I think I know why.

CHAPTER 14

CHRIS

"Nia has been sleeping with my boyfriend, Drew."

The words come tumbling out of Diana's mouth in between sobs. They replay over and over again in my head, like a bad song you can't seem to forget. Everything suddenly makes sense—the strange feeling I'd had when interviewing Drew, his avoidance of eye contact, the guilty body language. Drew is more connected to Nia than he let on in our initial interview. They are more than just casual friends—they are lovers.

Cramer slides a box of tissue across the table to Diana. "Do you need a minute?"

"No, I'm fine," she says, wiping her eyes.

"I'm sorry to hear about Nia and your boyfriend," he says.

She rolls her eyes. "I don't know how I didn't see it. It's been happening all this time right under my nose."

"Did that have something to do with why no one could reach you earlier?" I ask.

"I know it looks bad, and I'm sorry about that. I just needed to get away from everything for a bit."

"May I ask where you were?"

"I drove up to Myrtle Beach and stayed the night in a hotel. I just needed to clear my head. I didn't want to talk to anyone, so I turned off my phone. I haven't told my sorority sisters about what happened, and I definitely didn't want to talk to Drew."

Myrtle Beach is about an hour and a half drive from Magnolia. It's close enough for a day trip but just far enough to escape to if you need a break from life. From what we've just learned, I can't blame Diana for wanting to run away from it all.

"So you're telling us that you were at a hotel all this time?" Cramer asks. "In Myrtle Beach?"

"Yes," she says. "You can check with the hotel. I don't have anything to hide."

"So, did you know Nia had been declared missing?" I ask.

"Shawna, my sorority sister, texted me last night and told me that Byron found her car with her keys inside and that he had called her parents. By that time, I was already on the road."

"And you're just coming in now? You didn't want to help find her?"

She shrugs. "To be completely honest, I didn't really care at first. I was so mad over what happened, and I still am. Honestly, a part of me thought she took it upon herself to run away. She has to know that the other girls will find out sooner or later about what happened with Drew. I thought she was embarrassed about the whole situation and just skipped town."

"Does Drew know that you know about his relationship with Nia?" Cramer asks.

"Yeah, he knows. I confronted him about it as soon as I suspected something was going on, and he admitted to it."

"What about Byron? Does he know?"

"Byron doesn't know," she says. "At least I didn't tell him. But it's going to kill him when he finds out."

She dabs at her eyes, and I notice the scratches on her hand again. "What happened to your hand?"

She drops her hand into her lap and looks down at the table. "It's nothing."

"That's not what it looks like. Looks pretty painful to me. Does it have anything to do with Nia?"

She waits a few seconds before answering. "Look, it's not what you think."

"Why don't you tell us what happened."

"Nia and I got into it that night out at the park. That's how I got the scratches, ok?"

"Got into what?" Cramer asks. "Can you be more specific?"

"Just like I said … we got into it. I lost my temper, and I pushed her. It was nothing serious, though."

Cramer and I exchange glances.

"I know what you're thinking," she says. "I swear I didn't hurt her."

"No one is saying you hurt her," I say. "But we do need you to tell us exactly what happened."

She straightens in her seat. "Ok. It happened when I confronted her about Drew. I told her that I knew that they had been seeing each other, and I asked her how long it had been going on. She told me that they've been seeing each other a few months. I told her that before she crossed that stage the next day at the show, she had to promise never to see him again."

"And what did she say?" Cramer asks.

"She told me that she isn't going to stop seeing him … that it isn't that easy. That's when she told me that she's pregnant."

Her words catch me off guard. "Nia is pregnant?"

"Yes. At least that's what she told me."

"Did she say who the father is? Is it Drew?"

"According to her, yes."

"Do you think she was being truthful?" Cramer asks.

"She and Byron broke up a few months back," she says. "It wasn't a secret. We all knew they weren't on good terms, so they took a break from dating to work on things. She told me that she's eight weeks pregnant, and as far as we all know, she and Byron only recently got back together a few weeks ago. She told me that Drew was the only person that she was sleeping with during that time … so it has to be his baby."

"So, you believe her?"

She nods slowly. "I do. I haven't told anyone, but for the last few months, Drew has been distant with me. I didn't know what was going on with him, but now it makes sense. His attention was on Nia."

"So, what happened after she confessed this to you?"

"I don't even remember doing anything," she says. "I must've blacked out or something. The next thing I knew, she was on the ground."

"Did you push her?"

"I think so. She fell back hard against a tree. I know I shouldn't have done it, but I wasn't thinking. I just reacted. That's when she came at me and pushed me. I went to grab her, and she scratched my hand."

"And what did you do after that?"

"Nothing," she says. "That's just it. I didn't touch her after that."

Cramer looks doubtful. "You expect us to believe that you didn't do anything after she scratched you?"

"Oh, trust me, the thought definitely crossed my mind. But if Drew wanted her, I wasn't about to play myself and fight over a guy. So I told her she could have him, and I left."

Cramer looks at me and rolls his eyes.

"I know how it sounds, but it's the truth. I didn't hurt her! And she was fine when I left."

"So, when you left the park, did you notice anything unusual? Any strange vehicles parked nearby or anyone following you guys as you left the parking lot?"

"Well, no, not that I noticed," she says. "I saw Nia walking to her car when I pulled off. I didn't see anyone around or notice anything strange."

"Wait, back up," I say, holding up my hand. "When you left the parking lot at Groveland Park, you saw Nia walking to her car?"

"That's right."

"So you never saw her physically leave?"

Diana thinks for a moment. "No ... I guess I didn't. I just assumed she left."

"Did you stop anywhere before going home?"

"No, I went straight home. I got there a little after two."

Cramer taps me on the shoulder and motions toward the door. "Step outside with me for a minute, would you?" We excuse ourselves and go out into the hall. He closes the door and begins pacing the floor. "Are you buying this?"

"It's one hell of a story," I say.

"And the scratches on the hand? I don't know, man. This girl had motive and means. And she just gave us a reason as to why her DNA could be underneath Nia's fingernails."

"For now, we have to take her at her word until we can find something concrete."

He leans back against the wall. "Something just doesn't seem right."

"I know, but there's something else we didn't think about."

"What's that?"

"We always assumed that Nia went home that night because her car was found there. But Diana just told us that she didn't see her physically leave the park."

He shrugs. "Yeah, so?"

"So, what if she never left the park? What if whatever happened took place there?"

"But what about her car? How would it have gotten to her place?"

"That's what we need to find out," I say. "We've been so focused on gathering surveillance from around her home and the businesses in the vicinity. But maybe we need to be looking harder at the last place where she was physically seen."

"You think someone else drove the vehicle back to her place?"

"It's possible. We didn't get a look at the driver from the surveillance video from when her car entered the community. The gate is remote activated, so whoever was driving didn't even have to roll down the window. So we can't say for sure that Nia was behind the wheel."

"But the park was one of the first places that was searched. There was nothing there."

"Groveland Park is hundreds of acres, Cramer. Something could've easily been missed."

He exhales sharply. "You're right."

"It's worth revisiting," I say. "I think we may need to have another look. We may even need to bring out the hounds as well. There's a possibility that she could still be out there."

CHRIS

I MAKE THE CALL TO THE LIEUTENANT. IT'S BEEN OVER AN hour since we were all huddled together in the squad room watching the surveillance footage.

"Evans, slow down," he says. "What's going on?"

I pause to catch my breath. "Sir, we need to search the park again. Tonight."

"For what? What have you guys found?"

"We finally spoke to Diana McNamee. She came into the station willingly, and she was able to give us some information."

"Like what?"

"Well, for one, she claims that Nia has been sleeping with her boyfriend. And she also claims that Nia revealed to her that she's eight weeks pregnant the night she went missing."

"Pregnant?"

"Yes sir, that's what she said. She believes her boyfriend is the father of Nia's baby. And to make matters worse, Diana claims things got physical between her and Nia that night. There are some scratches on her hand."

"What do you mean?"

"According to her, she got upset when she found out about the pregnancy, and she lashed out at Nia. She pushed her. One thing led to another, and Nia scratched her during the altercation. But she swears she didn't injure her and that Nia was fine when she left."

"You think she's credible?"

"The story is pretty hard to believe. But she admits that she never actually saw Nia leave the park. She pulled out of the parking lot before Nia left. The last thing she can confirm is seeing Nia walking to her car."

"So, you think something may have happened at the park? There was already a preliminary search done out there. The teams didn't find anything."

"Yes, sir, I know. And the fact that the car was found at her apartment led us all to believe that whatever happened occurred after she got home. But what if we missed something from the park?"

He seems to consider the possibility. "Let me make a few calls. I'll have the evening sergeant pull a few guys from the road to take a look out there."

"Thanks, Lieutenant. I just don't want to take any chances with this case, especially if she's still alive."

"Let me see what I can do. Stand by for my call."

The line goes dead in my ear. Cramer has just wrapped up the interview with Diana and joins me in the squad room. "Did you call Stokes?"

"I just got off the phone with him."

"Well, what'd he say?"

"He's going to make some calls to get some guys to look around out there tonight."

"Well, it looks like it's gonna be another long night," he says, fishing a cigarette out of his pocket. "I need a smoke. I'll be right back."

He slips out of the squad room and heads for the back of the building. I decide to help myself to another cup of coffee while he's gone, but I notice that the message indicator on my desk phone is blinking. There are two missed calls and a message waiting. I dial into my voicemail and listen as Congressman Bryant's voice plays on the answering machine. There is a hint of desperation in his voice as he requests a callback for an update on his daughter's case.

I listen to the message all the way through before hitting the callback button. The phone only rings once before he picks up. He's been waiting for my call.

"Good evening, Congressman Bryant. This is Detective Evans returning your call."

"Ah yes, Detective. I was hoping you'd call back."

"I'm sorry I missed you earlier. I was in an interview when you called. Is everything ok?"

"Are there any updates yet? Any word on my daughter?"

"We were able to gather some additional statements regarding the night she went missing, but nothing that has changed the course of the investigation." I hold off on telling him about the information we'd just gathered from Diana McNamee. Even though he is Nia's father, we need to tread lightly in order to avoid divulging too much information that could hinder the investigation.

"Cassandra and I are going out of our minds right now," he says. "We can't eat. We can't sleep. This has just been a nightmare."

"Well, I know it's difficult, but try to get some rest. We have everyone here working your daughter's case, and I hope to have more soon. I will call you in the morning to let you know if anything comes up overnight."

"Thank you, Detective. We'd appreciate that."

"Of course. I'll be in touch."

I hang up the phone and lay my head down on my desk. I decide to hold off on the cup of coffee. Most of the team is out right now, and the squad room is quiet for the first time in two days. My eyes are heavy with sleep, but all I can think about is Diana. I want to believe that what she's told us is the truth, but there are too many coincidences to ignore. If anyone has a motive to harm Nia, it's her.

———

"Evans! Evans!"

I blink my eyes several times, trying to make sense of where I am. Cramer stands above me, his hand on my shoulder as he jolts me awake.

"What time is it?" I ask, looking slowly around the squad room.

"It's almost 10 p.m."

I rub my eyes to bring them into focus. "I must've dozed off."

"Yeah, well, at least you were able to sneak in some rest," he says. "Looks like we're going to need it."

An unsettling feeling comes over me. "Why? What's going on? Is everything ok?"

He shakes his head. "No, it's not. Jacobs just called. They've found a body."

CHAPTER 16

TORI

THE SOUND OF THE TELEVISION BREAKS THROUGH MY SLEEP. I can sense immediately that something is wrong. The first thing I feel is the headache. It's excruciating, radiating through my temples and creeping into my neck. I shift my body as I try to relieve the strain in my neck, but I realize that I'm not in my bed. As my eyes begin to focus, I see the outline of Tre's silhouette on the opposite couch, his long body crammed into the small space. I try to sit up, but the pain in my head lands me back on my back. A vodka bottle lies empty in the middle of the coffee table, and suddenly the events of the night before come rushing back.

I grab my cell phone from where it's lying on the floor next to the couch. There are over ten red notifications in my call log and about a dozen unanswered text messages from Aunt Lyn and my mom.

I sit up again. My head is pounding, but I throw my legs over the side of the couch and force myself to stand. The room is dark except for a small sliver of sunlight that has filtered in through the blackout curtains that are drawn over the front window. I feel around frantically for my shoes that have slipped underneath the couch.

"Leaving so soon?" Tre is awake and is sitting up on the couch, watching me. He yawns loudly and stretches his arms up over his head.

"I didn't mean to wake you," I say. "But yeah, I gotta run."

He turns on a small lamp sitting on the end table next to the couch. I find my shoes and slip them onto my feet. "Are you alright?" he asks. "Is something wrong?"

"My mom and aunt have been ringing my phone off the hook. I guess I should've just stuck to the beer last night and held off on the hard stuff. I fell asleep without realizing it, and I didn't check in. I know they're probably worried."

"Yeah, you did have quite a bit last night. It kind of surprised me that you could drink that much."

"Yeah, I usually don't. It's just with everything going on ... I don't know. I guess I just wanted to drown it all out."

"Have you called them back yet?"

I shake my head. "I just saw all of the missed calls and texts. I'll call them when I get to my—"

Something on the TV catches my eye. Tre turns to look at what has gotten my attention. A red breaking news banner is scrolling across the bottom of the screen. I have to read it twice to make sure my eyes aren't playing tricks on me. Tre finds the remote and turns up the volume. According to the update, a woman's body has been uncovered in Groveland Park. A young news reporter is reporting live from the scene laying out the latest updates:

"Late last night, we received reports that officers at Magnolia Police Department uncovered a woman's body from the area right behind me here at Groveland Park," says the reporter. The camera zooms in on a heavily wooded area in the background. *"Police have roped off the area as a crime scene and are working on identifying the victim. Officers here at the scene behind me are not providing many details at the moment as the investigation is still ongoing, but they have informed us that foul play appears to be involved. Stay with Channel 6 for the latest on this developing story as it unfolds."*

My legs suddenly feel weak, and I lower myself slowly onto the couch. Tre looks over at me, stunned. When I finally find the courage to speak, my voice is a whisper. "You think it's her?"

He doesn't have time to answer. His cell phone chimes from a text message that has just come through. "It's a text from Byron."

"Does he know something?"

He shakes his head as he reads the text message. "The police haven't confirmed if it's her or not. He's heading out to the police station now."

"What should we do?"

"I'm going to meet him there. I want to be there—you know, just in case."

"I'm coming with you." The words are out of my mouth before I have a chance to think.

"Are you sure?" he asks. "I thought you had to get home?"

The truth is, I do need to get home. I've already stretched my boundaries with Aunt Lyn by staying out overnight without checking in, but right now, that is the least of my worries.

"I'll deal with that later," I say. "Right now, all I'm worried about is making sure that body they found isn't Nia."

Chapter 17

Evie

I stand near the edge of the crowd, my eyes fixed on the roped-off area behind the police barricade. There are dozens of patrol cars lining the road. The reflection of their red and blue lights dances off the trees as the sun rises overhead. People are whispering amongst themselves, rattling off theories while trying to probe the officers for information. I stand quietly, not daring to speak to anyone.

The black lycra jogging suit that I'm wearing fits like a stretchy glove, hugging every inch of my curves. To the unobserving eye, I look like the average park visitor, showing up in the wee hours of the morning to get in a morning jog—only I am here for a different reason altogether.

A body was found last night. The people around me are busy speculating whether it's Nia. The crowd is on edge, anxiously awaiting confirmation, praying that by some stroke of luck that it isn't her—that some other unfortunate soul has perished in the park.

The medical examiner's van drives through the park entrance, its tires crunching on the gravel. I watch closely, following it until it's no longer in sight. I shift my gaze back to the crime scene. A sudden rush of adrenaline pulses through me. I can feel my skin tingling—a hot, prickly heat coursing through my veins.

"Isn't this just awful?" The older woman in front of me whispers loudly to her jogging buddy.

The other woman nods in agreement. "I wonder who it could be?"

"Do you think it's that girl who's gone missing from the university? The one that's been all over the news?"

The woman shakes her head. "God, I hope not."

I slide my sunglasses onto my face and slip quietly away from the crowd, the whispers of the two women growing faint as I retreat. A safe distance away, I turn and take one final look back at the park. The news reporters are now gathered around the barricade, pushing their microphones in the officer's faces as they try to solicit statements. The officers appear flustered, with too many things happening at once. No one notices me. No one knows I'm there. I fade into the background ... and wait.

CHAPTER 18

CHRIS

THE SCENE AT GROVELAND PARK IS CHAOTIC. OFFICERS swarm the area, and more continue to arrive as news spreads of the found body. Crime scene technicians move stealthily around us, their white jumpsuits swishing as they walk back and forth. Yellow caution tape has been used to rope off the area. Patrol officers are stationed at the park entrances, holding off the growing crowd of spectators. The early morning hours are usually the busiest at the park. Keeping the area clear has proved to be difficult as curious onlookers continue to descend upon the area, hoping to get answers.

After the call came through confirming the discovery of a body, Cramer and I rushed to the scene. When we arrived, we were escorted to where the body lay. She had been left in a remote area near the south entrance of the park at the bottom of an embankment. The area is well hidden from view, nearly impossible to see from the walking trail that snakes through that part of the park. The decomposition has already begun, and Nia no longer looks like herself. Her body is bloated and discolored. Flies swarm the gaping wounds where she's been stabbed repeatedly. The smell of death makes my nose sting. There's blood everywhere, and I have to turn away from the body to keep from getting sick.

Cramer walks up to me and puts his hand on my shoulder. "You doing ok, kid? You don't look so good."

"Not really," I say. "I was hoping it wouldn't end this way."

He looks down at the body before looking away again. "No one wanted this, Evans."

"Who could do something like this? She had to have been stabbed over twenty to thirty times. It was overkill."

"It was clearly personal," he says, staring off into the woods behind me. "My money is on Diana. It's the only thing that makes sense."

I see movement near the top of the embankment. A white van appears through the thick trees. "The medical examiner's office was called?"

"The Lieutenant put in a call. He requested that their office come out to have a look at the body as it is before she's transported to the morgue. Why?"

The medical examiner's office is rarely asked to come to crime scenes, so seeing Rosalind is the last thing I expected to happen today. Besides a few texts, we haven't spoken since our last conversation two nights ago. Nia's case has been my focus for the last forty-eight hours, and everything else has taken a backseat.

"Nothing," I say. "I just saw the van, so I was just wondering."

He stares at me for a moment. "Ok, well, I'll go up and meet them to escort them down. You wait here with the body."

It isn't long before he reappears, Rosalind following close behind as they make their way down the embankment to the body. A young intern trails a few feet behind them, carrying a large black case. When they finally reach the bottom of the embankment, our eyes meet. I can feel Cramer watching me as he tries to figure out what's going on.

"Hello, Detective Evans," she says, giving me a quick head nod. It's been a few weeks since our last date, and she has dyed her hair since that time. It looks nice on her.

"Hey, Doc." I keep it professional, not wanting to draw any attention to us.

Cramer turns to Nia's body and motions for Rosalind. "Well, here she is, Doc. Just as we found her."

Rosalind walks slowly toward the body and shakes her head. "They told me it was bad—but I didn't expect this. Poor girl."

"Yeah, this is one of the most gruesome crime scenes I've ever seen."

She takes out a pair of gloves and slips them carefully onto her hands, kneeling in the wet brush. She gently pulls at the fabric of what is left of the shirt covering Nia's body.

"Multiple stab wounds," she says out loud. "Easily upwards of thirty —primarily in the torso and neck region. Of course, we won't know what type of knife until we get her back to the office to do a more thorough evaluation."

She continues her review of the body and uses her hand to tilt Nia's head slightly to the side to examine her neck.

"Can you tell the time of death?" I ask.

"Well, rigor has set in. The corneas of the eyes are opaque, and there is already quite a bit of decomposition. Rough guess, I would say, about forty-eight hours ago."

Her assistant walks slowly around the body, snapping pictures of the crime scene. Rosalind lifts Nia's arms and examines the skin beneath her fingernails. "We'll swab her. Maybe she took a swipe at whoever did this to her."

Our conversation with Diana comes to mind and I think about the scratches on her hand. I'm sure we'll find her DNA on Nia. The altercation between them just further implicates her in Nia's death.

"I think she's safe to be moved," she says, slowly removing the gloves from her hands. "I'd like to have my guys get her over to the office now so that we can get started on the autopsy."

She motions to two men who are waiting at the top of the embankment. They carry a large black body bag and a stretcher. When they reach the body, they begin the painful task of carefully moving Nia's corpse for transport.

"Whoever did this really did a number on her," she says. "Have you all told the parents?"

"Not yet," Cramer says.

"I heard the father is a congressman. It's going to be a media circus for sure."

"It's already been a nightmare. It's only going to get worse."

"Well, I hope to have some answers for you soon."

"We appreciate that. Thanks for coming out."

"Of course," she says. "I'll be in touch." She turns to me and smiles. "Nice to see you again, Detective Evans."

She walks back up the embankment with her team. We watch as they load the body into the van. Cramer waits until she pulls out of the parking lot before speaking. "Is it just me, or is there something going on between you two?"

"It's just you," I say.

Back at the parking lot, the crowd at the park entrance has doubled in size. More news vans are on scene, and reporters have set up their cameras as they prepare to live stream with updates. I look out at the commotion near the entrance. Something above the trees catches my eye. Above the parking area are three lampposts that provide lighting during the night hours. Attached to the tops of the lamps are surveillance cameras that are pointed down on the parking lot.

"Did you see those?"

Cramer looks up and squints his eyes against the sun's rays. "Well, what do ya know? I wonder if those cameras actually work?"

"Only one way to find out." I spot Detective Jacobs and wave him over.

"What's going on?" he asks.

"Have we requested footage from those cameras yet?"

Jacobs looks up at the cameras and shakes his head. "I don't think so. Things have been so crazy; I don't think we've gotten around to it."

"Can we see about getting those ASAP?"

"I'll put in the request," he says. "It's the city, so it may take a while, but I'll let you know as soon as we have something."

"Alright, thanks."

I take a seat on the curb behind one of the patrol cars. Cramer sits down next to me and lights up a cigarette. "My money is still on the McNamee girl," he says.

I look back at the thick trees that line the area where Nia's body had been found.

"Yeah, there are too many things that point to her to ignore," I say. "She had the means and the motive, but she had to have known that killing her would be a risk. She had multiple witnesses that saw her stay behind with Nia. Why would she risk that if she wanted to kill her?"

He takes a long drag on the cigarette. "I don't know. Maybe she didn't plan to kill her. Maybe things went south."

"I guess it's a possibility. I just don't know."

"What happened out here that night was a crime of passion," he says. "Whoever did this was someone that girl knew."

Chapter 19

Tori

The speed limit through downtown is forty-five miles per hour, but Tre is doing close to sixty as we speed toward the police station. My head throbs and I feel nauseous. Tre hasn't said a word. His eyes are fixed on the road as he swerves through traffic. I know he's probably thinking the same thoughts that I'm having about the found body.

When we reach the police station, the scene outside is chaotic. News vans are everywhere, and a large group of reporters is gathered around the front entrance. As we drive slowly through the parking lot, Tre spots Byron's car parked at the end of the back row.

"Looks like Byron already made it," he says, pointing to the red SUV.

We park and rush toward the front of the building, pushing past the reporters and camera people. Once inside, the outside noise fades away. The lobby is spacious and modern-looking, nothing like the dingy police stations you see on TV. I spot Byron. He's sitting in a small waiting area just past the information desk, his head buried in his hands.

"There's Byron," I say, pointing in his direction.

Tre walks over and puts his hand on his shoulder. "Hey, man. Any news?"

"They're not telling me anything," says Byron. "Still no word if it's her or not."

"Damn! I was hoping maybe you'd heard something since I last talked to you."

"I've been calling the detectives assigned to the case, but I just keep getting their damn voicemails. I've left three messages already this morning. You would think someone would call me back." He stands and starts pacing the floor. "I just need to know if it's her! This waiting is killing me!"

For once, I feel sorry for Byron. Nia's disappearance has been hard on him. His clothes look grungy like he hasn't showered in a few days. His eyes are plagued by dark circles. He doesn't even look like himself.

My phone vibrates, and I fish it out of my purse. It's Aunt Lyn calling again. I still haven't checked in, and I know she's probably panicking. I step away from Byron and Tre before picking up the phone.

"Hey, auntie."

"Tori, where are you?" Her voice is frantic, and I brace myself. I know she's probably going to give me a piece of her mind.

"I'm at the police station. I'm sorry I didn't call—"

"Wait, the police station? Why are you at the police station?"

"The police found a body last night out at Groveland Park. I came to find out if it's Nia."

The news of the body seems to have caught her off guard. "A body?"

"Yes. It's all over the news."

"Have you heard anything?" she asks.

"Not yet. We just got here."

"We?"

"Um yeah, I'm here with a friend. We all have class together." I decide not to tell her that Tre is a guy, at least not now. I don't want to dig myself into a deeper hole than I'm already in.

She sighs. "How long will you be out? Your mother is about to blow a gasket. You should've called."

"I know, and I'm sorry. I promise I'll come home as soon as I'm done here. I just want to find out what the police know."

"Ok," she says. "Be careful and keep me updated." She sounds concerned, but her tone is firm. Even though she is letting it slide for now, I know that I'm not quite off the hook for not coming home last night.

"I'll call you as soon as I know something."

There are raised voices coming from the station entrance. I say goodbye to Aunt Lyn and quickly hang up the phone. A middle-aged man and woman have just rushed inside the station and are at the information desk demanding information from the on-duty officer.

Byron begins waving his arms in their direction. "Mr. and Mrs. Bryant! Over here!"

Mrs. Bryant looks up and runs over to Byron. They embrace, and she cries softly into his shoulder. I stand back as they console one another, unsure of what to say. I've never met Nia's parents in person. Now that they're standing in front of me, I feel like an intruder, even though I am with their daughter every day.

After Mrs. Bryant is done greeting Byron, she walks over to Tre and gives him a hug. "We haven't seen you since you Nia was in orientation, Tre. How are you?"

"I'm doing ok." He turns and motions in my direction. "This is Tori. I don't know if y'all have met. She's friends with Nia."

Mrs. Bryant smiles at me, her eyes brimming with tears. "It's so nice to finally meet you, Tori. Nia talks a lot about you. Thank you for coming."

I force a smile. "Nice to meet you as well."

"Have they told you all anything?" Mr. Bryant looks at the three of us, his eyes desperate for answers.

Byron shakes his head. "No, not yet. I've been calling, but no one has called me back yet."

"I spoke to Detective Evans a little while ago," says Mr. Bryant. "He should be here any minute. He didn't say much over the phone, though."

The front entrance door opens again. Several officers walk into the building dressed in black polos and slacks. They have shiny badges draped around their necks.

Mr. Bryant runs toward the door. "Detective Evans! Detective Cramer!"

Mrs. Bryant and Byron follow close behind while Tre and I hang back. Nia's family speaks to the officers in hushed voices. The officers have somber expressions, and I have a bad feeling that it's not good news.

"What's happening?"

Tre shakes his head. "I don't know. I can't hear what they're saying."

Suddenly, a loud, piercing scream echoes through the lobby. Mrs. Bryant collapses into a heap on the floor. My breath catches in my throat. I stand there frozen, unable to move. Mrs. Bryant's loud wails fill the air, attracting the attention of everyone in the lobby. I can feel the warm sting of tears in my eyes. I didn't hear their conversation with the officers, but deep down, I already know the truth.

Nia is dead.

CHRIS

MRS. BRYANT'S BLOODCURDLING SCREAMS RING IN MY EARS, drowning out everything around me. She crumples helplessly to the ground, her legs giving way beneath her. Congressman Bryant crouches down on the floor next to his wife, tears pouring down his own cheeks as he becomes emotional at the news of his daughter's death.

"I'm so sorry for your loss," I say. The words seem scripted—a hollow attempt at reassurance. I'd said the same words to Zakari Stanton's parents months ago. I feel a sense of déjà vu.

Congressman Bryant's entire body shakes as he sobs, his broad shoulders bouncing up and down with every breath. "Do you know what happened?"

"Let's step into one of the interview rooms. We can talk more privately there."

My eyes fall on Byron. He's in shock at the news. I place my hand on his back. His breathing is shallow, coming out in short gasps.

"I'm so sorry about everything, Byron. Really I am."

His eyes search my face as the gravity of the news sinks in. I lead him over to the waiting area and help him into an empty chair.

"Is it true?"

A man's voice comes from behind me. A young couple is standing nearby. I hadn't noticed them before, but I can only assume that they are with the family.

"Yes," I say, nodding my head slowly. "The body discovered in the park is Nia Bryant."

The young woman begins sobbing loudly, burying her face in her hands. The young man places his arm around her shoulders and leads her over to the chair next to Byron.

"I'm so sorry," I say. "We were all hoping for a better outcome."

"What happened?" The young man turns away from the young woman and wipes a tear from his eye.

"We don't know yet," I say. "The investigation is still ongoing."

"I can't believe this," he says. "I can't believe she's gone."

"I take it you all knew Nia as well?"

"Yes," he says. "We all go to school together."

"I know this is a rough time right now, but would you all be willing to speak with a detective while you're here?"

"Yeah, sure, I guess." He glances over at the young woman. "Are you cool with that, Tori?"

She wipes her eyes with the backs of her hands and nods.

"Thank you," I say. "We'll have someone out to speak with you all shortly. Sit tight."

Cramer and I escort Nia's parents out of the lobby and into an interview room. Once inside, I close the door to give us some privacy. Congressman Bryant helps his wife into one of the chairs. She's crying inconsolably, her loud wails filling the small room and spilling out into the empty hall.

"Can I get you all anything?" I ask awkwardly.

Congressman Bryant turns to face me. "We just want to know what happened. Just tell us what happened to Nia."

"Well, we're still trying to figure out what happened," I say. "But there was foul play involved."

"Why would someone kill my baby?" wails Mrs. Bryant. "Who would do that?"

"That's what we're going to find out. We will know more once we get a report from the medical examiner."

Congressman Bryant stares absently at the table, tears staining his aged face.

"I know we've asked you this before, but is there anyone—anyone that you can think of who would want to harm Nia?"

"No!" he says. "That is why none of this makes any sense. Nia didn't have enemies."

"And nothing out of the ordinary associated with your office?" asks Cramer. "No threats or any strange phone calls?"

"No, I've told you! Nothing like that has happened."

There's a knock at the door. Lieutenant Stokes pokes his head inside the room. His thick eyebrows are set in a frown. The permanent worry lines that cover his face seem more pronounced this morning. "Excuse me, Detectives; I'm sorry to interrupt. Evans, can I see you for a moment?"

"Sure." I excuse myself and step outside, closing the door behind me. Even through the closed door, I can still hear Mrs. Bryant's cries of grief.

"Were the parents able to provide you with anything?" he asks, pacing the hall.

"No, sir. They continue to maintain that they have no idea who would've done this. The body has already been transported to the morgue, though. Hopefully, the autopsy will tell us more."

"And what about this girl who was last seen with her?"

"Uh, yeah, Diana McNamee. We haven't spoken to her since our last conversation, but of course, we are going to need to revisit her story."

"I agree. We need to re-interview everyone who knew Nia—friends, family, everyone. Talk to the boyfriend and his roommate again as well. Get detailed statements and pull their phone records. I want to know their every move over the last few weeks."

"Yes, sir."

"This case has gone from bad to worse, and I need you and Cramer to be extra diligent and follow up on every lead. The media is going crazy out there. There are a lot of eyes on us right now."

"We'll do our best, sir."

"Good! Just keep me informed on what you find."

He turns and disappears back down the hall. I turn to go back into the interrogation room when my cell phone rings.

"Hello, this is Detective Evans."

"Detective Chris Evans?"

"Yes. Who's calling?" The man's voice on the other end of the line is unfamiliar to me.

"I don't know if you remember me," he says. "My name is Drew Bradley. You left your card yesterday when you came over to ask about Nia."

I lean against the wall, dropping my voice. "Oh yes, I remember. How can I help you, Mr. Bradley?"

"I just heard ... I heard you found her."

"Yes, I'm sorry to inform you that we uncovered Nia's body in Groveland Park."

I can hear muffled sobs on the other end of the line. "I'm sorry for your loss," I say. "I know you knew her well."

After several minutes, he finally speaks. "Can I—can I come down and speak with you?"

"Yeah, of course," I say. "Is something wrong?"

"I—I don't know. I didn't know who else to call."

I take a few steps down the hall, moving further away from the door. "What's wrong, Drew?"

He takes a deep breath, and his voice is barely a whisper. "I think I know who killed Nia. And it's all my fault."

CHAPTER 21

CHRIS

LESS THAN AN HOUR AFTER OUR PHONE CONVERSATION, Drew arrives at the station and agrees to a formal interview. I am eager to find out what he knows and if it will bring us any closer to finding the person responsible for Nia's death.

Drew sits quietly across from us, staring blankly at the wall. He's still reeling from the news, and I wonder if he's in the right state of mind to even go through with the interview. He looks like he's in a trance, his eyes focused on nothing.

"Drew?"

He finally looks at me. His face is confused like he's forgotten where he is.

"You told me on the phone that you had some information about Nia's case?"

"Yeah, I do," he says. "I think I know who might've killed her."

"And who do you think killed Nia?"

He throws his head back and looks up at the ceiling. "Damn, I hate to even think that she would. But now, after everything that's happened, it's the only logical explanation."

"Who?" Cramer asks.

Drew straightens and looks across the table at us. "I think it was my girlfriend, Diana."

"And why do you think she did it?" I ask. "Do you have any proof?"

"No, I don't have any proof. But I have a strong feeling."

"Why would Diana want to harm Nia? What led you to come to this conclusion?" Even though we already know the background story surrounding Nia and Diana, I don't let him know that upfront. We need to hear his account from his own point of view to compare it with what we've already learned.

Drew stares down at his hands in his lap and takes a breath before answering. "Because I was secretly seeing Nia. It's my fault she died."

"Why do you say it's your fault?" Cramer asks.

"Because if we hadn't been together, she would still be alive."

"Did Byron know about your relationship with Nia?" I ask. "I mean, you guys are roommates. It would be hard to keep that a secret for long."

Drew shakes his head. "He doesn't know. Nia and I tried our best to keep things on the low, but it got complicated."

"How so?"

"Look, I didn't mean for things to happen the way that they did with Nia. Things just kind of got away from me. Before I knew it, we were in too deep."

"So when did this all start? Take us back to the beginning."

He sighs. "It started a few months ago. Nia and Byron broke up after Nia found out that Byron had cheated. She came over one night when he wasn't home and told me that she was there to get some things that she had left in the apartment. So, I let her in."

He pauses for a minute before continuing, almost as if he's hesitant to reveal all the details. "Byron had gone home for the weekend, so I had the place to myself. When Nia showed up, I didn't think anything of it. But once she was inside, she started crying and venting to me about her relationship with Byron. I didn't know what to say, so I just listened. Byron is my best friend, but I couldn't help but feel bad for her. She didn't deserve what he did to her."

"So what happened next?"

"The next thing I knew, she was kissing me. I probably should've stopped her, but I didn't. To be honest, I've always been attracted to Nia, but I never acted on it. I mean, she was dating my best friend. I never knew that she felt that way about me. But that night, it became clear to me that she did."

I peer at him from across the table. "One could argue that she was acting out—getting back at Byron in some strange way by coming onto you."

"That's true," he says. "I had never seen that side of her before. She was grabbing on me and kissing all over me. I didn't know what to think. I just reacted."

"So, did you two sleep together that night?"

"Yeah, that was the first time. After that, it just continued. We would just find ways to see each other."

"And you're sure Byron has no idea that you two were sleeping together?"

"Like I said, we were very careful. I felt bad, and I still do. Byron and I have been roommates since freshman year. I didn't mean to intentionally hurt him. But Nia ... she was different."

"In what way?"

He lowers his eyes. "I don't know—Nia just understood me. When I was talking to her, I felt like she was listening. She made me feel like a person—like a man. I haven't felt like that in a while."

"So, I take it things weren't going well in your relationship with Diana?"

He rolls his eyes up toward the ceiling. "Diana and I have been together since we started college. Things were good at first, but the last year has been rocky. Diana is cool, don't get me wrong, but I don't think she's ever truly known me. She likes to give off this façade like we're the perfect couple. But in private, she can be cold. Nia accepted me the way that I was. She didn't try to change me to fit this persona of what she wanted the world to see. I fell in love with her."

"So, Diana found out what was going on?" Cramer asks.

"Yeah, she did. That's when everything started going downhill."

"When did she find out?"

Drew appears to think. "It was this past Tuesday. Nia came over when Byron was in class. Diana also had class during that time, so we thought we would have the place to ourselves for a few hours. She came over in the middle of the day, and one thing led to another. We had sex."

"So, this was rather recent?"

"Yes, it was only a few days ago. Diana's professor didn't show up to class, and she ended up getting out earlier than usual. That's when she came over to my place."

"And that's when she saw Nia?"

"Yes. She drove up to my apartment and saw Nia leaving. Neither one of us even noticed that she was there. After Nia left, I went to shower. Just as I was about to get in, I heard a knock at the door. I thought it was Nia, figuring she had left something behind. I opened the door and saw it was Diana."

"What happened next?"

"Diana questioned me about it. She wanted to know why Nia was in the apartment when Byron wasn't home. I was caught off guard. I didn't know what to say. But Diana knew something was up."

"Did you let Nia know that Diana had found out about your relationship?"

"Yeah, I did. I called her right after it happened. I wanted her to know because I knew her probate was coming up. She and Diana see each other almost every day. I didn't want to cause problems between her and her sorority sisters."

"So, you think Diana killed Nia because of her secret relationship with you?"

He shrugs. "I guess, yeah. It's the only thing that makes sense to me. She found out about us, and a few days later, Nia is dead. It's just too coincidental."

"Well, how do we know you aren't throwing all the blame on Diana to keep the attention off of yourself?" I ask.

He frowns for the first time. "You think I did something to Nia? Why would I hurt her?"

"You tell me. You had a lot to lose, too. Maybe Nia wanted more from you. Coming clean would've hurt your friendship with Byron and would've probably ruined your reputation around campus."

"That's crazy!" His voice begins to rise. "I would never—"

"You and Byron are part of the same fraternity as well. How would your frat brothers react if they knew that you were having sex with Nia?"

His jaw clenches as he stares angrily at me. My words have struck a nerve, and I know I'm taking a risk. He can call off the interview at any point, but I need to get the truth out of him.

"So, what was it?" I ask. "Did Nia want to take things to the next level? Maybe you didn't, and one thing led to another."

"It wasn't like that. I told you already; I loved her. I came here to try to help, and now you're accusing me!"

"We have to look at every possibility," Cramer interjects. "And we have to pay close attention to those that were close to the victim."

He crosses his arms defiantly in front of his chest. "Well, it wasn't me."

"Tell us again, when was the last time you saw Nia?" I ask.

Drew looks down at the floor. There's a noticeable shift in his demeanor. After several seconds of silence from him, I ask the question again. "Drew? When was the last time you saw Nia?"

He finally looks up. "I saw her the night before the rehearsal. She spent the night with Byron at the apartment that night."

"Did anything happen between you two?"

"Yeah," he sighs. "We got into a huge argument."

"What were you arguing about?"

"She came to my room after Byron had already gone to bed. She told me she needed to talk to me."

"What did she need to talk to you about?"

"Nia told me that she was pregnant, and she said it was my baby."

"And what did you think?" I ask. "Did you think it was your baby?"

"Like I said, Nia and Byron had broken up. She told me that there was no way that Byron was the father. I was the only person she had been with during that time. She had already gone to the doctor and was about eight weeks along."

"Well, that must've been a shock to hear," I say. "How did you take the news?"

"That's what I feel so guilty about." His voice trembles as he fights back tears. "I was angry. I lashed out at her."

"So you weren't too happy about the idea of a baby in the mix?"

"No, I wasn't. I panicked. A baby was going to complicate things even more. There was no way we could keep things a secret anymore, especially with Diana already onto us."

"So, what happened between you and Nia that night?"

"Like I said, we argued. Before I knew it, she was crying. I said some things I shouldn't have. I knew I hurt her feelings, and I tried to apologize. She didn't want to hear it, though. After that, she went back into Byron's room and slammed the door in my face. That was the last time I spoke to her."

"And you're sure Byron was asleep when this conversation between you and Nia took place?"

"As far as I know. I'm pretty sure he didn't hear anything."

I lean forward in my chair and bring my face close to his. "So let me get this straight—you and Nia were secretly seeing each other, and she tells you that she's pregnant. She claims the baby is yours. You admit to being upset at the news and arguing with her. Then the next day, she's murdered. Do you see where I'm getting at?"

"Like I told you before, I didn't have anything to do with Nia's death," he says. "I would never hurt her."

"You know what I think happened? I think you didn't want anything more than sex from Nia. Y'all were having a good time and sneaking around, and then she got pregnant. I think you panicked, and you killed her."

"No, you've got it all wrong!" he yells, slamming his hand on the table.

"I think you killed her to shut her up! You knew she wasn't going to get rid of the baby, and then your secret would be exposed to everyone."

"I told you I didn't kill her!"

"Well, if you didn't, then who did?" I'm yelling now, my frustration with Drew boiling over.

"I don't know!" he snaps. "I told you everything that I know. But it wasn't me!"

"Where were you between the hours of 11 p.m. on Thursday evening and 2:30 a.m. on Friday? Because when we initially spoke, you said you hadn't seen Nia since Tuesday. Now you're saying you saw her the day before her rehearsal."

"Ok, I lied when I first spoke to you guys. I panicked. Byron was there, and I didn't want to say too much about what was going on between Nia and me."

"Well, you can see how we're having a hard time believing anything you're saying right now. You haven't been truthful from the beginning, so it's hard to take you at your word."

"I'm telling the truth now." Drew holds up his right hand as if he's taking an oath. "I swear everything I've told you today is the truth."

"Then where were you between the hours of 11 p.m. on Thursday evening and 2:30 a.m. on Friday?"

"I was home all night like I told you the other day. After I left classes that day, I went straight home."

"And no one can account for your whereabouts except for Byron?"

"Yes, but he'll tell you that I was there."

"Do you know anyone else who may have wanted to hurt Nia?" Cramer asks.

"No! Nia got along with everyone. The only person angry at Nia was Diana, and that was only after she found out about our relationship."

"Well, we did speak to Diana in detail yesterday," I say. "But as my partner said, we are exploring every possibility. With that in mind, we will take what you've shared with us today and follow up."

He looks from me to Cramer. "So, I can go?"

"For now, yes," I say. "We can't hold you. I'm sure there will be more questions later, but for now, you're free to leave."

Drew breathes a sigh of relief and relaxes for the first time since starting the interview.

"Before you leave, though, would you mind providing us with a DNA sample? It'll help us to rule you out if you weren't involved."

He sits back in the chair and rolls up his sleeves. "Do what you gotta do. I'll do whatever I need to do to prove that I didn't do this."

———

After obtaining a DNA sample from Drew and releasing him, I return to the squad room and escape to my desk. It's barely noon, but it feels much later in the day. I know it's because I haven't slept in days, but I won't be heading home anytime soon. I re-read my notes from Drew's interview. Even though he had been cooperative, I can't discount the possibility of his involvement. The fact that he lied when we first spoke to him is a huge red flag—one that I'm not willing to overlook.

"What you got there?" Cramer asks as he takes a seat across from me.

"Nothing. Just reading over my notes from Drew's interview."

"Turns out you were right about him," he says. "He's been lying since the beginning. I don't know if we can trust what he says."

"That's what's bothering me," I say. "Coming in and speaking with us could've just been his way of getting ahead of the storm that's about to come down on him. I think he just wanted to get the heat off himself."

"Yeah, but the kid was scared too. Maybe he did just panic when we first spoke to him."

My desk phone rings, and I see from the caller ID that it's the Medical Examiner's office.

Cramer cranes his neck over the glass partition that separates our desks. "Who is it?"

"It's the medical examiner. Maybe she has something." I pick up the receiver on the third ring.

"Hey, it's me," says Rosalind. "You got a minute?"

"Yeah, sure. What's going on?"

"I just wanted to call and give you an update on the Bryant girl."

I use my free hand to grab a pen out of my desk drawer. "What do you have?"

"Well, we just got her up on the table, but I'm pretty sure I know the type of knife you need to be looking for. From what I'm able to tell so far, it looks like a butcher knife was used in the attack. You need to be looking for a knife with a ten-inch blade."

She talks fast as she rattles off details. "She was stabbed with a lot of force. There are bruises on her skin where the knife's hilt made contact. Whoever did this ... they went deep."

"Interesting. Anything else?"

"Yes, there's more. Just from the initial examination, I can tell you that most of the wounds are localized mainly around her abdomen. She has several wounds on her arms, but most of the wounds are confined to the abdominal area. The wounds on her arms are most likely defensive wounds that she sustained during the attack."

I think back to our interviews with Diana and Drew. As far as we know, they are the only two people who knew about Nia's pregnancy. The way Rosalind is describing the stabbing doesn't seem like a coincidence.

"There would've been a lot of blood associated with this attack," she continues. "The killer wouldn't have gotten away clean. There definitely would've been blood transfer."

"Which explains how it probably ended up in Nia's car," I say.

"Exactly. I can give you a call once we know more, but I wanted to get you a description of the murder weapon ASAP. Sorry it wasn't more descriptive, but it seems like she was stabbed with your average, everyday kitchen butcher knife."

I close my notepad. "We can work with that. There's one more thing, though. Will you be able to determine if she was pregnant at the time of her death? We've gotten statements from two witnesses that she may have been."

"I haven't gotten that far yet, but I can let you know. Do you think that had something to do with why she was targeted?"

"I'm not sure yet. We're still trying to piece everything together. But with the way you say she was stabbed, I don't think it's a coincidence."

"Hmmm, you may be right," she says. "Well, I'll keep at it and call as soon as I have more."

"Thanks, I appreciate it. Talk to you soon."

Cramer walks around to my desk. "What did she say?"

"She said it was a standard butcher knife used in the attack. Approximately ten inches. And she said a lot of force was used. There are bruises on the skin from where the hilt of the knife made contact."

"A standard butcher knife," he groans. "That's gonna be hard to narrow down without some type of physical evidence."

"Also, she said most of the wounds are confined to the abdominal area. I can't help but think about the fact that Nia was reportedly pregnant. It makes me think the killer knew something."

"Again, all signs are still pointing to the McNamee girl," he says. "I don't see a random stranger going to this extreme."

"Well, we're going to have to find something that ties her to this."

Cramer places both his hands on my desk and leans in toward me. "So, you ready to take another run at her?"

"I have an even better idea." I turn on my laptop and wait as it boots up.

"What are you doing?"

"I think we've established enough probable cause. It's time we get a search warrant."

Chapter 22

Tori

I don't know how long I've been in the interview room. Thirty minutes? An hour? I've lost all sense of time as I sit across from the detective, my mind in a daze. I can see her lips moving, each word being spoken slowly as she tries to get a response out of me. I try to open my mouth and speak, but no sound comes out. Everything around me feels warped, moving in slow motion as my body tries to catch up with my mind.

"Miss James?" Her voice sounds far away, almost muffled. I bring my eyes to meet hers and try to open my mouth to respond. She stares at me, her perfectly arched eyebrows knitted together in a worried frown. She places her hand on mine and gives it a gentle squeeze.

"Are you ok?" she asks. "Can I get you anything? Maybe some water?"

Her voice breaks through the fog. I shake my head.

"I know this is a difficult time, and I know this is the last thing you probably want to be doing right now, but we would really like to get any information that you can offer about your friend Nia."

I turn my eyes away from hers. The tears begin flowing again at the mention of Nia's name.

"When was the last time you saw Miss Bryant?" she asks, handing me a Kleenex.

I try to think back to when I last saw Nia, but my mind is scattered.

"It's ok," she says, sensing my anxiety. "I know this is difficult. Take your time."

She's an older woman, at least ten years older than my own mother, if I had to guess. Despite her commanding uniform with the badges and the black gun attached to her hip, she has a warm, comforting smile. There is something motherly about her, and I begin to feel more at ease as my mind clears.

"I saw her on Thursday afternoon," I say finally. "She came by my house after she missed our statistics class."

"Ok, and did she seem normal? Did she appear to be in distress or anything?"

"I don't know. She didn't seem like herself."

"In what way?"

"She looked really tired and out of it. I asked her what was wrong. I wanted to know why she'd missed class. She'd never done that before."

"And what did she tell you?"

I don't answer right away. My last meeting with Nia has been haunting me ever since she went missing, and I'm hesitant to reveal too much. Even in death, I still want to protect her.

"Miss James, is there something you'd like to disclose that may help the investigation?"

"I want to help," I say. "I do. I just don't know if it's my place."

She leans closer to me, her face only a few inches from mine. "Miss James, your friend is dead. At this point, keeping secrets isn't helping anyone."

Even though I don't want to face the truth, I know that she's right. Nia is dead. She's never coming back.

I take a breath. "When she came over that day, she was crying. I had never seen her like that before. She and her boyfriend had just gotten back together, and I thought he had done something."

"What made you immediately go to him?"

"Well, he's cheated on her before, so that was my first thought."

"And was that it?"

"No, it had nothing to do with him. She asked me if we could talk in private, so we went to my room. That's when she told me she was pregnant. Then she told me that she had been secretly seeing Drew Bradley."

The detective writes as I talk. "And who is Drew? Do you know him?"

"Yes, he's her boyfriend's best friend."

The detective looks up at me. "So, this Drew guy, was he the father of her baby?"

"Yes, that's what she said. She told me she was about eight weeks along and that during her breakup with Byron, Drew was her only partner."

"Ok. Anything else?"

"Yes, there's more. Drew is dating one of Nia's sorority sisters. Diana McNamee. She told me that Diana had found out about them."

"About her and Drew?"

"Yes. Nia was freaking out. She was nervous about the rehearsal. I think she was scared to face Diana."

"Had Diana done anything to frighten her? Was she threatening her in any way?"

"Not that I know of. But I think Nia just got in over her head with everything. I told her not to go to the rehearsal, but she said she had to."

"And that was the last time you spoke to her?"

"Yes. I wish I had talked her out of going. None of this would've happened if she'd just stayed away. That's everything that I know. That was the last time I saw her."

The detective hands me another tissue. Now that everything is out on the table, I feel like a huge weight has been lifted off my shoulders.

"Has she ever expressed to you any concerns about any other individuals?" she asks. "Was there anyone else that you can think of that she was having issues with?"

"No, not that I know of. Nia was popular on campus and seemed to get along with everyone. I've never seen her have any issues with anyone."

The detective shuts her notepad and pats my hand. "Well, you've been most helpful. This is information that may be useful."

"What happened to her?" The question has been burning on my

tongue ever since Nia's death was confirmed, and I've finally gotten up the nerve to ask.

The detective looks at me, and her smile fades. "We're still investigating."

"And it wasn't an accident?"

She purses her lips. "No, I'm afraid not."

I cover my mouth with my hand and sit back against the chair. I'm speechless. My hands begin to shake, and I clasp them together as I try to control myself.

"Well, thank you for staying to speak with me." The detective takes out a card and writes a phone number on the back. "This is my card, and I've also written down the phone numbers of the detectives heading the case, Detective Evans and Detective Cramer. If you think of anything else, please don't hesitate to give us a call."

I tuck the card into the inside pocket of my purse. The detective leads me out of the interview room.

"So, what happens next?" I ask when we reach the main entrance.

"Well, we are following up with everyone that knew her. We will be speaking with all of her acquaintances over the coming days. We're hoping someone knows something or saw something that may lead us to who killed her."

I look outside at the crowd of reporters. Despite the detective's attempt to appear confident, I know that finding the person responsible isn't going to be an easy task. Nia had so many connections that sifting through everyone that knew her could take months.

She places her hand on my shoulder. "Don't worry. We're going to find who did this."

I muster up a smile before walking out of the station. As much as I want to believe her, I have a feeling that it isn't going to be that simple.

Chapter 23

Tori

Tre is waiting for me outside behind the group of reporters. I have to squeeze through the crowd to make it down the steps. He takes me into his arms and gives me a long hug. I can feel him breathing deeply as he tries to hold back his tears.

"Did they talk to you?" I ask.

"Yeah, they did," he says. "Byron is still in there with them. I'm waiting around for him to make sure he gets home ok."

His eyes float up toward the entrance. Byron has just walked out of the front doors. He walks slowly down the station steps, gripping the railing tightly. He looks like he's in shock, his eyes unblinking as he maneuvers through the thick crowd of reporters. Tre rushes up the steps and takes him by the arm and leads him the rest of the way down.

"Are you ok, Byron?" I immediately regret asking the question as soon as the words leave my mouth. *Nia is dead. Of course he's not ok.*

He doesn't answer and continues to stare straight ahead with a blank expression.

"I can't let him drive home like this," says Tre. "I'll drive his car. Do you mind driving my car and following me to his place so we can make sure he gets home ok?"

"Yeah, sure," I say. "I'll follow you over."

Tre hands me his keys and ushers Byron toward his car. I trail them out of the parking lot, taking extra care to avoid the news vans parked along the curb. Tre turns out onto the main road, and I follow him as we head toward Byron's apartment.

We have barely gone a mile when I get a call. It's my mom. With everything that has happened, I haven't gotten around to returning her calls from last night. I can already feel that the conversation is going to be stressful before I even pick up the phone.

"Hey, Ma."

"Tori, where have you been? Why haven't you been picking up your phone?"

"I know you've been calling. I forgot—"

"Well, if you know I've been calling, why haven't you returned any of my calls? I've been worried sick! Lyn couldn't even reach you."

"Ma, Nia is dead." It's the first time I've said the words out loud, and even I can't believe what I've just said. Saying that Nia is dead just doesn't seem real.

There is a long silence before she finally speaks. "What? She's dead?"

"Yes, they found her body this morning. I just left the police station. It's her."

"Oh no, Tori!" she whispers. "I'm sorry. I'm so sorry. Do you know what happened?"

"The police are still trying to figure it out," I say in between sobs. "They're saying it wasn't an accident."

"Someone killed her? Do they know who?"

"No, not yet."

"I can't believe this," she says. "I really thought that they'd find her. I just knew she was ok."

"Me too. I can't believe she's gone. I just don't understand who would do this."

Tre makes a right turn into an apartment complex, and I follow as we turn off the main road.

"I'm going to see if I can take a few days off from work," she says. "I know you say you're fine and you don't need me, but I think it would be best if I were there, Tori."

Normally, I would try to persuade her not to come—to let me

handle things on my own. I've always made it a point to prove to her that I can handle myself—but Nia's death is too much—even for me.

"Ok," I say. "Only if you can …"

"I'll find a way," she says. "You just hang in there until I get there, ok? I love you."

"I love you too."

Tre parks in front of Byron's building, and I pull in next to him. As he helps Byron out of the car, I notice movement in the rearview mirror. Drew has just arrived as well. I haven't seen him since Friday at the probate, and he looks almost as bad as Byron as he gets out of his car and stumbles across the parking lot.

I unbuckle my seatbelt and climb out of the car. Tre turns around and finally spots Drew.

"Where the hell have you been, Drew? I've been calling you!"

Drew looks up and stops in his tracks. He looks like a deer caught in headlights, his eyes wide as he looks back and forth between us.

"I've been calling you for the last hour," says Tre. "Have you heard about Nia?"

"Yeah, I heard …"

Drew stops mid-sentence as something behind us catches his eye. I turn to see what he's looking at. Diana is walking quickly in our direction, her face a scowl as she barrels toward us. I jump out of the way as she pushes past us and walks up to Drew.

"What are you doing here?" Drew asks, his voice shaking.

"Tell them, Drew!" she yells. "Tell them!"

"Tell us what?" asks Tre. He looks confused, and I take several steps back. My last conversation with Nia replays in my head again. I suddenly feel sick.

"What are you doing here?" Drew asks Diana again.

Diana tilts her head and smirks. "I think it's time you tell Byron what's really been going on."

Byron looks up at the mention of his name. He seems more alert, like a fog has lifted. He creeps forward toward Drew, but Tre grabs his shoulder.

"Don't do this!" Drew says to Diana. "Not right now! Please!"

"Why not now?" Diana asks. "Don't you think everyone deserves to know the truth? After all, this is all your fault!"

"Man, Drew, what is she talking about?" Byron finally speaks, his voice hoarse.

"Tell him!" Diana says. "Tell him before I do!"

"What does she mean, this is all your fault?" Byron is clenching his fists now, glaring at Drew. "What did you do?"

"I—nothing," Drew stutters, taking several steps back.

"Then what the fuck is she talking about?"

Drew looks down at the ground and stuffs his hands into the pockets of his shorts. We all stare at him, waiting for him to speak.

Diana turns to Byron and shakes her head. "He's not gonna tell you, Byron. He's too much of a coward to come clean."

"Tell me what?" Byron asks, frustration rising in his voice.

"Diana, don't!" Drew yells. His voice bounces off the walls of the nearby apartment buildings, but it's too late.

"Drew was sleeping with Nia behind your back." Diana spits the words out with disgust like they've left a bad taste in her mouth.

Byron's face goes pale. Diana's words hang in the air. I hold my breath, my eyes darting from Byron to Drew. No one dares speak.

Drew looks up at Byron with guilt-ridden eyes. "I'm sorry, bro. I didn't mean—"

"You're sorry?" Byron inches forward, and Tre tries to grab his arm, but he wriggles away. "All this time, you've been screwing my girlfriend behind my back?"

Drew is at a loss for words. Byron takes another step forward until their faces are just inches from each other. Drew tenses. He looks Byron square in the eyes; hands clenched into fists at his sides. A small crowd gathers around us. Several people have pulled out their cell phones and are now pointing them in our direction, recording the altercation.

"Did you kill her?" Byron's voice is barely a whisper, and I have to strain to hear.

"What?" Drew exclaims. "No, I didn't kill her! I loved her; why would I—"

A loud gasp escapes my throat as Byron raises his fist and punches Drew in the face, knocking him off his feet. Byron moves fast, pinning

Drew to the ground as he begins punching him repeatedly. I want to scream, to yell for help. I want someone to stop them, for this nightmare to end—but when I open my mouth, no sound comes out.

Tre rushes toward them and tries to pull them apart, but Byron has a tight hold on Drew as he pummels his face with his fists. Diana steps out of the way as several people rush to break up the fight. She looks smug, almost as if she's enjoying the commotion.

Tre is yelling as he tries to separate them, but his words sound muffled. I feel like my body is in another space, unable to move or react. Tre grabs Byron under his arms and finally pulls him away, throwing him against a nearby car. Drew stumbles as he tries to gain his footing. Blood drips down his face and onto the front of his shirt.

"What the fuck were you thinking?" Tre says to him. "Nia? Really?"

"Get the fuck out of my face!" Drew pushes Tre now, knocking him to the ground. Tre scrambles to his feet and rushes toward him, his fist raised in the air. I move now, my feet bounding against the pavement as I jump in between them.

"Stop it!" I shout. "Just stop it! Tre ... calm down! People are watching!"

Tre looks around and notices the crowd that has gathered around the parking lot. I take him by the arm and pull him away until he is a safe distance from Drew and Byron.

Drew glares at Diana as he wipes the blood from his nose. She still has that sick look on her face, like she's enjoying the action. I suddenly feel a surge of anger building up inside of me. This is all her fault ... her doing.

"You happy now?" Drew says to her. "You got what you wanted?" He walks back to his car and peels out of the parking lot, blowing his horn as he rams past the crowd of people.

Byron picks himself up from the ground and limps slowly up onto the curb as he makes his way toward his apartment.

Tre gives me an apologetic look. "I'm sorry you had to see that."

"No, it's ok. Just make sure Byron is ok."

"Wait here," he says. "I'll be right back."

I glance around the parking lot. The crowd has dispersed, all except

Diana. She is standing a few feet away from me, and our eyes finally meet.

"What happened between you and Nia?" I ask. "What did you do to her that night?"

My chest rises and falls with each breath. I am convinced that she killed Nia, and I fight the urge to do to her what Byron just did to Drew. She doesn't speak—doesn't even acknowledge my presence. Instead, she turns on her heels and begins walking back in the opposite direction. I watch her as she walks away, never taking my eyes off her.

Chapter 24

Evie

I'VE SPENT MOST OF THE DAY CAMPED IN FRONT OF THE TV, waiting for the news to break. A young reporter appears on the screen and stares grimly into the camera as she prepares to report the news that everyone has been dreading:

"This just in. We have just received word that the body of the woman found last night in Groveland Park is indeed that of missing college freshman Nia Bryant. Authorities have not yet released a cause of death but have confirmed that the young woman is believed to have been a victim of foul play. Our sources say ..."

I mute the TV and turn my attention to my laptop propped open on my lap. The world is now finding out what I've already known for days—Nia is never coming home. But now that the word is out, something else has caught my attention.

I lean in close to my computer screen and press play on the video, increasing the volume to the maximum. At first glance, all I can make out is a crowd of people. The person recording the video moves closer to the center of the crowd, and that's when I spot them. Byron and Drew are front and center and appear to be in the middle of a heated exchange. Even with my volume at its maximum level, I can't quite make out what they're saying. I search the crowd and spot Diana standing close by, her arms crossed in front of her chest as she watches the altercation.

Suddenly, Byron makes a move and punches Drew in the jaw, knocking him to the ground. Byron wastes no time and moves quickly, straddling Drew and punching him repeatedly. The crowd grows rowdy, and another young man rushes toward them and tries to break up the fight. Meanwhile, Diana makes no move to help her boyfriend. In fact, she appears amused—a cunning smile spread across her lips.

I pause the video and look back at the TV. The reporter is still on the screen. Her lips are moving, but there's no sound with the TV muted. The frozen image on the laptop screen gives me a perfect view of Byron's face—his eyes wild with rage. His right arm is raised up in the air, poised to land another blow to Drew's face. I close the laptop and sit back in my bed, resting my back against the padded headboard.

I know immediately what led to Byron's outburst. It's no secret to me that Drew and Nia have been sleeping together behind Byron's back for months. I've been watching them for a while, studying their patterns and learning their routines. It was happening right under Byron's nose, and yet he never picked up on it. The fact that he's been in the dark all this time doesn't completely surprise me, though. Byron has always been wrapped up in himself, not paying much attention to those around him, including Nia. The idea of his woman entertaining another man probably never crossed his mind, even though he has slept around multiple times himself. Byron never expected Nia to hook up with someone else, to give him a taste of his own medicine. He'd always managed to stay two steps ahead—but he'd underestimated Nia.

I open my laptop again and pull up the fake social media page I've created. I type Nia's name in the search bar. I've been following her on social media since shortly after we first met, but of course, she never knew. I knew better than to use my real name and information. To her, I was just another one of her thousands of followers.

I click on her profile picture and stare at the smiling photo. Nia was the definition of perfect—beautiful brown skin, bright brown eyes, and a picture-perfect smile with subtle dimples. She looks innocent and pure —certainly not the type of girl who would sleep with her boyfriend's best friend. But there was another side to Nia—a side that most people didn't know.

The girl that had been featured in dozens of articles, the all-American sweetheart that everyone loved, was just a front. Nia was calculating and manipulative—setting fire to anyone that burned her, and that included Byron. When his infidelity came to light, it wasn't enough to end the relationship. Nia set out to break Byron—and she fixed her sights on the person closest to him. It was something that had been ingrained in her, an inherent trait that ran deeper than anyone knew. Nia would always find a way to get what she wanted, and I know better than anyone just how much damage a person like that can do.

CHAPTER 25

CHRIS

The judge grants our request for the search warrant. We arrive at Diana's apartment just before nightfall with two uniformed patrol officers. Cramer knocks loudly on the front door and announces us. We stand back and wait, and I hold my breath. For a split second, I wonder if she's left town again, slipping away before we can question her.

The lock turns, and I tighten my fingers around the search warrant. The door slowly opens, and Diana appears in the doorway. I'm relieved that she's home. To my surprise, she doesn't seem alarmed that four cops are standing on her doorstep. In fact, it looks as if she's been expecting us.

"I knew it was only a matter of time before you showed up," she says, rolling her eyes. "Look, I feel bad about what happened to Nia, but I've already told you everything that I know."

"Well, that's not why we're here." I hold up the search warrant for her to see. "We have a warrant to search your residence and vehicle."

Her face drops. "What? No! You can't just look through my things!"

"Actually, a judge says that we can." I hand her the warrant.

Diana unfolds the paper and carefully reads the warrant before turning her attention back to us. "Do I need to call a lawyer or something?"

"That won't be necessary," Cramer says. "But that is your choice. We are just going to look around and make sure there is nothing here connected to Nia Bryant's death. The sooner we get this done, the sooner we'll be out of your hair."

Diana takes one last look at the warrant and then hands it back to me. She reluctantly steps aside and allows us to enter the apartment. We find ourselves standing in a small living room. The apartment is neat and quaint, the perfect size for a college student. The walls in the living room are a deep shade of blue offset by the neutral greys of her furniture. A live plant stands in the corner of the room. It gives the living area an earthy feel.

"So, how does this go?" She shifts nervously from one foot to the other.

"The warrant gives us permission to search your residence as well as your vehicle," I explain. "You don't have to do anything at this time. If we have any questions about what we find, we'll let you know."

I can tell the idea of us searching through her things makes her uneasy, but she doesn't protest any further. She finally stands aside, and we spend the next twenty minutes searching every room of the apartment, looking for anything that could be linked to Nia's murder. I take my time, scouring every cabinet, compartment, and space that could be used to hide evidence. Cramer works quietly beside me as we sift carefully through Diana's belongings.

After checking the living area and second bedroom, we move to the master bedroom. It's the largest room in the apartment and takes the most time. We search every drawer and every dresser. Cramer tears through the attached closet, tossing aside shoes and searching through bags. I've executed dozens of search warrants in the past, but this one feels different. There's so much riding on this case that it's hard for me to relax.

When I finish searching the bedroom, a sinking feeling comes over me. We've found nothing connected to Nia's murder. Diana's apartment is clean. If she did have evidence of the crime hidden here at some point, it is long gone by now.

Cramer emerges from the walk-in closet. "Nothing in the closet. Found anything?"

I shake my head. "Nothing."

"We've gotta be missing something," he says.

"There's nothing here. If there was something at some point, she's gotten rid of it."

"Well, we still need to check the vehicle," he says. "I'll take a look."

He rushes out of the bedroom, and I hear the front door close as he heads outside to Diana's car. I decide to check the kitchen and make my way down the hall. Diana hasn't moved during the search and is still seated on the small loveseat. I can feel her eyes on me, watching my every move.

I pull my gloves up closer around my wrists as I look around the kitchen. A cutting board and knife set are on the counter next to the refrigerator. The largest knife in the set sits in the outermost holder, its thick handle towering over all the others. I remove it from the wooden knife block and hold it up to the light, turning it over carefully in my hand. It's a standard kitchen knife, just like the one Rosalind had described; however, I can tell that it's not the right size. It's slightly smaller than the knife that was used in the attack. I place it back in the holder and continue searching the kitchen. Everything appears to be in order, and I'm disappointed that the search hasn't yielded anything useful.

Cramer calls from outside. I muster up the nerve to answer. If he hasn't found anything during the vehicle search, then we will be back at square one.

"I need you to come outside." He's breathing heavily, and his voice is unusually low and raspy.

"Is everything ok?" Diana and the two patrol officers watch me from the living room.

"Just come outside. Now."

I make a break for the door, abandoning my search of the kitchen. Diana and the other officers follow me outside to the parking lot. Cramer is standing behind Diana's car with the trunk open. He's found something.

"What is it? I ask. "What did you find?"

He reaches into the car and pulls something out of the trunk. His hands are trembling as he holds an object out in front of him. Whatever it is has been wrapped in a tattered piece of black clothing. I look closer and realize that it's a black jacket, the same type of jacket that Nia was said to have been wearing when she disappeared. I carefully pull back the tattered edge of the jacket, revealing a sharp-edged butcher's knife. The knife is stained red, and I'm hit with the metallic scent of blood. The uniformed officers are now standing next to me. They fix their eyes on Diana as she sinks to the ground in shock.

"Call it in," I say. "Tell everyone to get here. Now."

CHAPTER 26

CHRIS

IT DOESN'T TAKE LONG BEFORE EVERY COP IN THE CITY IS ON the scene, descending like a swarm of flies on Diana's apartment. Crime scene techs are called out, and the knife is tested to confirm the presence of blood. The luminol test is positive, and the knife lights up like a Christmas tree. Forensic testing will have to be done, but I know in my gut that it's Nia's blood.

Diana has been detained and is sitting in the back of a patrol car. She immediately goes on the defense, denying her involvement in Nia's murder.

"I don't understand," she says. "None of that is mine."

"Diana, a bloody knife was found in your trunk," I say. "The jacket that the knife was wrapped in has Nia's name stitched on the inside. Do you really expect me to believe that you weren't involved?"

"I'm telling you the truth!"

A couple walking their dog stops to see what's going on. I lower my voice. "Diana, calm down. Let's talk through this."

"Don't tell me to calm down!" she says in a hushed whisper. "You guys are trying to pin this on me! You cops are so shady."

"Then how do you explain the knife in your trunk? I'll be honest;

your story was hard to believe to begin with. This certainly doesn't help your case."

"Please! You have to believe me! I could never kill someone."

"We are going to take the items into evidence and have them tested. You and I both know they'll come back as a match to Nia. So why don't you just save us the time and tell us what happened."

"Do you really think I'm that stupid?" she yells. "Do you really think I'd kill Nia after everyone saw me with her and then keep the murder weapon?"

Her words catch me by surprise. I look her in the eyes, and I see something that I've never seen in her before. Fear. All the evidence points right at her, but could we be missing something? The more I think about it, I can't deny the fact that everything seems to have magically fallen into place. The knife and jacket were bound together like a perfectly wrapped gift, waiting in plain sight to be uncovered.

Diana sobs uncontrollably, and I am unsure whether to comfort her or to continue questioning her.

"Diana, I—"

I don't have time to finish. Cramer pushes past me and takes out a pair of handcuffs. "Lieutenant says to bring her in now."

He reaches inside the car and places handcuffs on Diana's wrists as he begins reciting her Miranda rights. "Diana McNamee, you're under arrest for the murder of Nia Bryant."

"No! You're making a mistake. I didn't do this!" Diana is screaming now. The couple standing nearby with their dog stare in disbelief as she is put in handcuffs.

"You have the right to remain silent," Cramer says. "Anything you say can and will be used against you in a court of law."

"Cramer wait," I say. But he doesn't hear me. He closes the car door, drowning out Diana's screams as she's driven away.

———

When we arrive at the station, reporters swarm the car. I help Diana out of the backseat and hold her head down as we escort her through the crowd.

Once inside, a female officer takes over and leads her to the back of the station to be booked. Cramer and I make our way to the squad room where Lieutenant Stokes is waiting, a huge smile spread across his pudgy face.

"Excellent work," he says, slapping us on the shoulders. "We finally got her."

Cramer smiles proudly and nudges me in the side, but I turn away from them. Diana's words weigh heavily on me. The more I think about the events at her apartment, the more I'm convinced that we're missing something.

"Evans?" Lieutenant Stokes gives me a strange look. "What's with you?"

"Nothing, sir. It's just that ... I don't know. Doesn't this all seem a little coincidental?"

"Coincidental?" he asks. "What do you mean?"

"Finding the knife and the jacket the way that we did. I don't know anyone who would be that careless to leave something like that in plain sight. Why would she kill Nia and keep the murder weapon?"

Cramer clears his throat nervously. The smile on Lieutenant Stokes' face fades.

"Evans, people aren't always as smart as you think," he says. "This isn't the first time we've seen someone be careless."

"Yeah, but not like this—"

"Evans, enough!" Stokes' roaring voice seems to shake the walls in the empty squad room. He takes a deep breath to calm himself and lowers his voice. "Diana McNamee had every reason in the world to want Nia Bryant dead. The discovery of the knife and jacket just solidified what we already knew from the beginning. It's a clear-cut case. She's good for this."

The tension is thick. The last thing that I want to do is ruffle the lieutenant's feathers any more than I already have. I decide to keep my thoughts to myself, putting a stop to the conversation.

He turns to Cramer. "I put a call in. The fed lab is going to process the DNA on the knife. They're putting a rush on it. We should have an answer in the next day or so."

"Sounds good," Cramer says.

"In the meantime, you two get some rest. It's been a long couple of days. I'll see you two in the morning at the arraignment."

He turns and walks out of the room, his heavy footsteps receding down the hall.

Cramer snaps his head around and glowers at me. "What the hell is wrong with you? What were you thinking saying that to the Lieutenant?"

"What was I supposed to do? Was I just supposed to let it go? You have to admit it all seems to fit a little too perfectly."

"Yeah, but we both know Diana is good for this. You said it yourself. Now you don't sound so sure."

"Something just doesn't seem right, Cramer. I feel like we're missing something."

He shakes his head and grabs his coat. "I don't know what's gotten into you, but I'm too tired for this. I'm going home. I'll see you tomorrow."

He walks out of the squad room before I can say anything, slamming the door behind him. It's the first time since becoming partners that he has ever reacted angrily with me, and I am beginning to regret voicing my doubts.

I grab my keys and my cell phone from my desk, ignoring the growing pile of paperwork that has taken over my workspace. The squad room door opens again, and I expect to see Cramer. I know he's probably circled back to give me a piece of his mind about the case. When I look up, I'm surprised to see that it's Rosalind standing in the doorway instead. She's still dressed in her grey scrubs from work.

"I heard you guys made an arrest," she says. "How about that drink?"

CHAPTER 27

CHRIS

ROSALIND AND I END UP DOWNTOWN. WE DUCK INTO A small bar that's a popular hangout spot for the locals, and I order us a round of drinks. Several people are dancing drunkenly on the dance floor, moving out of sync to the pop music that the DJ is playing from his booth on the second floor of the bar. They don't seem to have a care in the world, even though a dead student's body was just discovered a few miles from here.

The bartender sashays over and winks at me. She places our drinks down on the counter. I take my glass and clink it with Rosalind's. "Cheers."

She raises her glass in the air and downs the drink in two big gulps. She winces at the taste of the alcohol.

"Looks like we both had a long day," I say.

"It's been one hell of a day." She signals the bartender for another drink.

"How's the autopsy going?"

"It's slow, but we're making progress," she says. "I want to make sure we check every box on this case. After what happened, the family deserves to have answers."

The bartender returns with another drink. We sit in silence for several minutes, the pump of the music filling the void between us. I look towards the door and notice more people filtering into the bar. The seats around us are filling up fast, and Rosalind points to an empty booth near the back.

"You wanna move?" she asks, yelling over the loud music.

I leave two twenties on the counter to cover the drinks. We move to the back of the bar, squeezing past people as we make our way to the booth. Rosalind slides in first, and I sit down next to her, positioning myself so that I have a clear view of the door. The music is not as loud from where we're sitting, and I finally feel like I can think clearly. I take another sip of my half-finished drink. The liquor is strong, but I feel my body relax.

"What made you come by the station?" I ask.

"Well, since we didn't get to go out the other night, I figured we both deserved a drink, especially after everything that happened today."

"It has been a long couple of days. And it's not over yet. There's the trial and trying to piece together exactly what happened. This case is much more complex than we initially thought."

"Speaking of that, I ran a blood test to check for pregnancy like you asked."

"Were you able to determine if she was pregnant?"

She sips her drink, slower this time. "Yes. It was positive. She was pregnant."

I shake my head. "This entire situation is one twisted love triangle."

"Do you have an idea of who the father may be?"

"Yeah, we do. He willingly allowed us to collect a DNA sample. We can run it to confirm, though I'm not sure what difference it'll make now."

"Well, whatever she did, she didn't deserve to die over it."

"I just hate that it ended like this. Breaking the news to her parents today was rough. I'll never get used to having to tell parents that their kids are never coming home." I think back to the scene at Groveland Park and Nia's lifeless body covered in stab wounds. I take another sip of my drink as I try to push the image out of my mind.

"We have a hard job," she says. "It never gets easier."

"Don't I know it. I feel like I'm still dealing with the aftereffects of the Stanton case … and now this happens."

"I remember that case. You were the one who found him, right?"

"Yes, I was the first on scene. I know there's not much I could've done, but part of me still feels guilty that I couldn't save him."

"You did what you could," she says. "It's not your fault."

"I know, but it doesn't make me feel any less guilty. When I got the assignment for Nia's case, a part of me was happy. In a strange way, I thought that if I found Nia that I could somehow make up for what happened to Zakari."

"So now that Nia is dead—"

"I feel like I'm reliving it all over again."

A waitress wanders over and drops two menus down on the table in front of us. "Are we eating tonight?" she asks, tapping her neon-colored nails on the tabletop.

I shake my head and turn to Rosalind. "I'm ok with drinks. What about you?"

She looks up at the waitress and smiles politely. "No food tonight, thanks!"

"Well, can I top off your drinks?"

She hands the waitress her empty glass. "I'll just take a glass of Merlot, please."

"And I'll take another Jameson," I say.

"Sure thing. Be right back." The waitress picks up the menus and hurries behind the bar, her short skirt hiking up with every step. Rosalind sits quietly, watching the crowd of people on the dancefloor. Several minutes pass before she speaks.

"Maybe you should consider talking to someone about how you feel?"

"Talk to someone? What do you mean? Like a shrink?"

"Sure. Why not? It's perfectly normal, especially in your line of work. You see things that most people wouldn't be able to handle. It begins to take a toll after a while."

"I don't think it's that serious. I just need some time to process everything."

"That's the problem," she says. "How do you know you'll ever find the time to process it? This case is a perfect example. As soon as you finish with one case, there's another that needs your attention. First Zakari. Now Nia. They just compound on top of each other. Each case leaves something with you. Pretty soon, it'll be too much to carry."

I know that she's right, but I've never been one to lay my feelings out on the table to a stranger. Until recently, I've always managed to separate myself emotionally from my cases. I try not to get too involved personally, but these cases are different.

The waitress returns with our drinks and then disappears into the crowd. Rosalind picks up her drink and takes a sip.

"Just think about it," she says. "You don't have to make a decision tonight. But you may find it helpful."

"I'll think about it."

She seems satisfied with my response and looks out at the crowded dance floor. The crowd is thick, with people practically pressed up against each other. Our waitress maneuvers through the crowd, holding a large tray of food above her head as she makes her way to another table.

"So, who is this girl you arrested?" she asks, changing the subject.

"She's one of Nia's sorority sisters," I say. "She's been on our radar from the very beginning. But—"

I have a moment of hesitation. I think about the situation at the station earlier with Lieutenant Stokes. I remember how enraged he had been at me, and I don't know whether I should tell her my thoughts on the discovery and Diana McNamee's arrest.

"Chris?"

"It's nothing," I say. "It's just ... I'm having second thoughts about what we found earlier that led to the arrest. Something is nagging at me."

She looks at me over her wine glass. "Oh yeah? What is it?"

"There was bad blood between the girls."

"What kind of bad blood?"

"Nia was sleeping with Diana's boyfriend."

"Wow, really?"

"Yes. The boy who I said gave us the DNA sample is the suspect's boyfriend. Nia was adamant that he was the baby's father. As you can imagine, that gave her every reason to want Nia dead. She was the person last seen with Nia that night at the park. That gave us enough probable cause, and the judge signed off on a warrant for us to search her residence and vehicle."

"And that's when you found the knife?" she asks.

"Yes, matching the description of the one you provided in your report. It was hidden in her trunk underneath some other items thrown inside, but not so hidden that it looked like she was trying to hide it, if that makes sense."

She thinks for a moment. "Ok, I see what you're saying."

"It was wrapped in Nia's jacket that she wore to the park the night she went missing. It was all there, just waiting for us. It was very convenient—too convenient."

"So you're thinking it was placed there to throw you guys off?"

"I mean, am I crazy for thinking that? I mentioned it to Lieutenant Stokes, and he damn near bit my head off for even bringing up the idea. But really, Ros, what killer would hide a murder weapon in the trunk of their car and not get rid of it immediately?"

"Do you think you guys arrested the wrong person?"

"I'm not saying she wasn't involved, but I think we're missing something. Maybe she didn't act alone."

"So, what are you gonna do?"

"I'm not sure yet. Cramer didn't even want to entertain the idea. I'm stuck between a rock and a hard place."

"I agree. Something does sound strange about that."

I glance down at my phone and check the time. My eyes are heavy from no sleep, and the alcohol hasn't helped.

"You look tired," she says.

"I am. I haven't slept in two days."

"You're kidding?"

"Nope! I've been going non-stop since this case broke. I haven't even been home since I left for work on Friday morning. I've been showering and taking cat naps at the station."

"Well, you better get some rest," she says. "Your body will thank you for it." She checks the time on her phone but stops to read something that has just popped up on the screen.

"What is it?" I ask.

"Looks like there's a candlelight vigil being held tonight on campus for Nia." She turns her phone so that I can see the screen. The glare is bright, and I have to focus my eyes. A post from one of the local news stations is on the screen.

"This is the first I'm hearing of it. Has it started yet?"

She looks back at the phone. "It starts in thirty minutes. Why?"

I look at the time again. "Dammit."

"What?"

"We always try to have some type of police presence at these types of events. It's a good way to show support to the family. It also gives us a chance to observe the crowd and look for any strange behaviors."

"Don't tell me you're thinking about going. Chris, you just told me that you haven't really slept in days. You need to go home and get some rest."

"Someone needs to be there, especially with the attention this case has gotten."

"Why can't Cramer go? I'm sure he won't mind."

"Cramer went home before I even left the station. He's probably passed out in bed by now."

She looks at me disapprovingly. "I think you can sit this one out. You already have a suspect in custody. You've done enough for today."

I signal the waitress for the check and take out my wallet. "If I leave now, I can make it in time. I promise I won't stay long. I'll stop by and show my face, and then I'll leave."

She gulps down the rest of her drink and grabs her purse. "Well, fine. If you insist on going, I'm coming with you."

CHAPTER 28

TORI

THE STUDENT PARKING LOT IS ALREADY FULL WHEN I ARRIVE on campus for the vigil. I circle my car around the campus, driving slowly through the dimly lit streets. Even with the light coming from the lampposts lining the road, I have to strain my eyes to see in the dark.

"You really need some glasses, Tori," Aunt Lyn says from the passenger seat.

"I know. I mentioned it to my mom."

"Well, maybe it bears repeating. You're just doing more damage straining your eyes like that."

I turn back to the road so that she can't see me rolling my eyes. I'm glad she offered to come to the vigil with me, but the last thing I'm worried about right now is glasses.

She leans forward in her seat and points up ahead. "There's a spot right there."

I make a sharp left and turn into the parking spot. A group of students walk past the car and make their way across the street toward the main campus where the vigil is being held. I hesitate before getting out, my hand hovering above the door handle.

"Are you ok?" Aunt Lyn takes her hand and places it on my chin, gently turning my face towards her.

"I'm fine." My voice cracks, and I clear my throat. "It's just all so much. I'm still trying to wrap my head around everything."

"We don't have to go," she says. "If it's too much, we can stop right here and go home."

"No, I have to be here. I owe it to Nia."

She touches the side of my face, wiping away a tear that has escaped my eye. "Well, I'm here. And we can leave whenever you're ready. Nia would understand, Tori."

"Thank you for coming," I say. "I don't think I could've come alone."

She smiles at me, crinkles forming at the edges of her large eyes. "I'm glad I could come. Nia was a good girl. I'm going to miss seeing her around the house."

I turn away from her and wipe away the tears that are now streaming down my face. Aunt Lyn gets out of the car and walks around to the driver's side, and opens my door. "Come on," she says, reaching out her hand. "It's ok."

I let her help me out of the car. She wraps her arm in mine as we cross the street and walk toward the main campus. We get to the courtyard just before the vigil is set to begin. There are more people here now than there were at the probate a few days ago. The flames of burning candles light up the courtyard, forming a beautiful sea of light against the night sky.

Aunt Lyn squeezes my arm. "Are you ok?"

"Yes, I'm ok. Do you mind if we go toward the front? I'd like to get a little closer."

She adjusts the bouquet of flowers that she's holding in her arms. "Sure, whatever you want."

We make our way through the mass of people. I don't stop until we are standing just a few feet from the front of the crowd. I can see Nia's parents on stage, along with several members of the university administration. A large photo of Nia sits on an easel at the foot of the stage, dozens of bouquets of flowers piled underneath. Nia's sorority sisters are standing to the right of the stage, along with several Lambda Nu Phi members.

I spot Tre standing with Byron. He looks into the crowd, and I wave at him from where I'm standing. He smiles and beckons for me to come closer.

"It's ok," says Aunt Lyn.

I turn to face her. "Huh?"

"It's fine." She looks across the courtyard at Tre. "Go stand with your friends."

"Are you sure?"

"Of course, I'm sure. You all need each other's support right now. I'll wait here, and just text me if you're ready to leave before the vigil is over." She hands me the bouquet of flowers and nudges me softly. "Go on. I'll be fine."

I take the flowers and squeeze past the people standing in front of me and make my way over to Tre.

"I was wondering where you were," he whispers. "They just started. I thought for a second that you weren't coming."

"Parking was just a nightmare. I tried getting here sooner."

He nods toward the crowd. "Did you come with someone?"

"Yeah, my aunt," I say. "Nia used to come over to hang out at the house a lot, so I invited her to come."

Tre continues to stare into the crowd, lost in his own thoughts. I turn my attention to the stage where the president of the university is giving an opening statement. Now that I'm closer, I have a full view of everyone. My eyes go immediately to Nia's parents. Mrs. Bryant is sitting in a chair to the left of the podium, her body hunched over as she sobs into a wad of tissue. Mr. Bryant stands next to his wife, his hand gripping her shoulder as he stares out into the crowd. His body is rigid. He has a strange look on his face as if something has caught his attention.

Across the courtyard is the detective who I'd met earlier at the station. He's standing next to a woman who I've never seen before. She's dressed down in a pair of scrubs like the nursing scrubs my mom wears to work.

I turn back to the detective. A priest has just stepped up to the podium and is leading the crowd in prayer. Everyone bows their heads, including the woman he's standing with. The detective doesn't move, though. He keeps his eyes glued on the stage. I follow his gaze, keeping my head bowed. I look up on the stage again, and my eyes land on Mr. Bryant. Everyone around him has their heads bowed in prayer, including Mrs. Bryant. His head is raised as he continues to stare out into the crowd with that same strange look—like he's seen a ghost.

CHAPTER 29

EVIE

I INCH UP TOWARD THE FRONT OF THE CROWD, MY EYES locked on the stage. There are candles burning all around me, causing my face to glow in the moonlight. I reach the second row and stop. My breathing is shallow and my heart races with excitement. I keep my head low and wait as the president of the university gives his opening remarks.

The people around me are tearful, the sounds of their muffled sobs filling the space around me. I clasp my hands in front of me and lower my head a few inches more. I'm in full view of everyone on stage, but I don't want to be too obvious. I open my eyes wide and lift them up toward my eyelids, keeping my head bowed.

He's standing at the front of the stage, his hand resting gently on her shoulder. He looks around the crowd, and I wait, holding my breath. Finally, he looks in my direction, and I lift my head, giving him a partial view of my face.

His body freezes as our eyes meet.

The president of the university concludes his opening remarks and steps away from the podium. A priest walks up to take his place, raising his arms high up in the air as he calls for the mourners to join him in prayer. Everyone bows their heads as the priest begins to pray.

I slowly lift my head, exposing my entire face. I am no longer hidden. Everyone on the stage has their heads bowed to the floor—everyone except Dwight Bryant.

He's staring at me, his eyes wide with shock.

A smile spreads across my face, and I mouth the word slowly so that he can read my lips. "Surprise."

CHAPTER 30

CHRIS

THERE'S SOMETHING WRONG WITH CONGRESSMAN BRYANT.

Everyone around him is praying; their heads bowed, eyes closed. Instead of joining along in the prayer, he's staring into the crowd of mourners. The color has drained from his face. His skin appears ashen in the glow of the candlelight. He tightens his grip on Mrs. Bryant's shoulder. She raises her head and looks up at her husband. I can see her whisper something to him, but he doesn't respond. She glances out at the crowd before slowly dropping her head again as she continues to pray.

I look in the direction that he's looking, hoping to see what has caught his attention. No one is moving, and the crowd has gone quiet, with only the sound of an occasional sob breaking the silence. Then I spot her. A woman is standing near the front of the crowd watching the congressman. The darkness makes it difficult for me to see her face, even with the light from the burning candles. I take a step forward to get a closer look. Suddenly, she turns around and begins walking quickly through the crowd back toward the courtyard entrance.

I turn to Rosalind and tap her arm. "I'll be right back."

"Where are you going?"

"Just stay here. I'll be back in a sec."

She opens her mouth to protest, but I'm already walking in the opposite direction toward the entrance. The priest concludes the prayer, and everyone raises their heads. I lose sight of the woman and stop dead in my tracks, my eyes frantically searching the crowd. I wait several minutes before I finally give up and walk back toward the stage where Rosalind is standing. A man and a woman are now standing at the podium, each of them taking turns saying a few kind words in memory of Nia.

"Where did you go?" she asks.

"I thought I saw someone." I can't be sure of the identity of the woman, so I decide to keep it to myself, at least until I can figure out her connection to the congressman.

The vigil ends shortly after, and the crowd begins to disperse. People congregate on the stage to offer condolences to Nia's parents, and I wait patiently off to the side. I keep my eyes on the congressman as he greets the well-wishers. Despite his attempts to appear composed, I can tell that something has him spooked. He keeps looking toward the courtyard entrance.

When most of the people on the stage have left for the evening, he finally makes his way down the steps. Mrs. Bryant lingers behind, speaking privately with several of the university administrators.

"Everything ok, Congressman?"

Dwight Bryant notices me standing near the foot of the steps. "I'm not sure what you mean," he says.

I can sense his agitation as my eyes lock with his. Even though it's only been a little over twenty-four hours since we were first introduced, he looks like he's aged overnight. His skin is blotchy, and there are age lines on his face that I didn't notice yesterday. A layer of stubble covers his cheeks.

"You seemed a little on edge during the vigil," I say.

"Well, I'm sorry if I'm not skipping around today, Detective," he says sarcastically. "I did just lose my daughter."

"I didn't mean it that way."

"Then what did you mean?" He looks angrily at me and then glances back toward the courtyard entrance.

"Did you see someone today, Congressman?"

"Excuse me?"

"Did someone show up to the vigil today? Someone you weren't expecting?"

"I don't know what you're talking about!" He tries to keep a straight face, but I can tell that he's lying. Something or someone that he saw during the ceremony has him on edge.

There's movement on the stairs as Mrs. Bryant walks slowly toward us. She comes to stand next to her husband and interlocks her arm with his.

"Hello, Detective," she says. "Thank you for coming."

"My condolences again on your loss, Mrs. Bryant."

"Lieutenant Stokes called us before the vigil. He says you all have made an arrest?"

"Yes, ma'am, we have."

"Who is it?" asks Congressman Bryant.

"Her name is Diana McNamee," I say. "She's a member of the—"

Mrs. Bryant gasps. "Wait! Did you say Diana McNamee?"

Congressman Bryant turns to his wife. "Isn't that Pat's daughter?"

Mrs. Bryant slides her arm out from around her husband's and sits down slowly on the steps. She brings her hand to her chest and takes several deep breaths. "There has to be some kind of mistake," she says. "That can't be right."

I crouch down in front of her. "Do you know her?"

She raises her eyes and looks at me, blinking slowly. "Yes, of course I know who she is. She's my line sister's daughter."

CHAPTER 31

CHRIS

I ARRIVE AT DIANA'S ARRAIGNMENT THE NEXT MORNING TO find the courtroom crammed with people. Officers, reporters, court officials, and spectators have all shown up to see Diana go up in front of the judge. The morning is already off to a great start for the State, with results from the DNA test back from the lab. The blood on the knife has been confirmed to be a 100% match to Nia Bryant. With all the evidence mounting against her, the case against Diana is strong. The young prosecutor looks confident at the front of the courtroom.

I spot Cramer sitting in the back row. We haven't spoken since the incident yesterday at the station, and I make my way over to where he's sitting.

"You're here early," I say.

He moves his coat off the chair next to him and motions for me to sit down. "Well, I figured it was going to be a shit show, so I wanted a snag a spot. Here, I saved you a seat."

"Well, it's a good thing you came early. It looks like it's about to turn into a standing room only for whoever shows up after this."

"Yeah, looks that way," he says. "Did you get some rest?"

I shake my head. "Not really."

"Why not?"

"It's kind of my fault. I went for a drink last night after I left the station. I just needed to unwind." I don't tell him about meeting with Rosalind. I'm not ready to have to explain our relationship to him right now.

"Well, it's been a rough week. Did you stay out late?"

"I wasn't planning to, but there was a vigil last night for Nia. I made the last-minute decision to swing by. I thought it would be a good idea if someone from the department was present, you know?"

He nods. "Yeah, I heard about the vigil this morning."

"Well, it was ... interesting."

"Really? Why do you say that?"

"Well, for starters, Congressman Bryant was behaving strangely."

"Well, that's to be expected," he says. "The man just lost his only child."

"No, I get that, Cramer. But this was different. I think he saw someone at the vigil ... someone he wasn't too thrilled to see."

"Did he tell you that?"

"He denied it when I asked him about it, but I'm telling you something was off about him. I saw a woman in the crowd who was watching him during the service, but I didn't get a good look at her face. I tried to catch up to her, but she left before I could make contact."

"Could've just been a coincidence," he says. "Maybe it was just someone he thought he recognized."

"I don't know what to think. Whoever it was, the congressman is being really tight-lipped about it. Makes me wonder if he's hiding something."

"Hmmm, could be."

"But there's more," I say. "I spoke to him and his wife after the vigil. It turns out they have history with Diana's family."

"History? You mean they know each other?"

"Yes, quite well," I say. "Diana's mother and Cassandra Bryant are line sisters. They pledged together in college—the same sorority that Nia and Diana pledged."

"So the girls knew each other before all of this happened?" he asks.

"Well, that's what I thought too. But it turns out they didn't know each other. Apparently, after college, they all went their separate ways.

Patricia, who is Diana's mom, had Diana from a previous relationship. When it didn't work out with Diana's father, she got married to her current husband, who is in the military. They moved overseas and just returned to the States during Diana's senior year in high school."

"So Nia and Diana never met before college?"

"That's right. Cassandra Bryant told me that she kept in contact with her line sister via telephone and social media, but they haven't seen each other in years. She's never met Diana in person either."

"And then both their daughters were accepted to MSU?"

"Exactly. Cassandra Bryant says that when Nia accepted the offer from MSU last year that she called Patricia to let her know that Nia would be attending. She says that she encouraged Nia to reach out to Diana since Diana had already been here for a few years, but she says that the girls didn't seem to mesh."

Cramer shrugs. "Well, they are a few years apart. They probably had different interests."

"Yeah, except when it came to guys. They both had their sights set on Drew."

He straightens in his seat. "Man, this is deeper than we thought. It's bad enough to lose your child. But to find out that the killer is the child of one of your close friends? That's a hard pill to swallow."

The door to the courtroom opens, and the defense team walks in. Two lawyers march into the courtroom, followed by a middle-aged woman and man. Following slowly behind them is Maggie Price, the sorority advisor we met a few days ago. She hobbles on her cane and takes a seat next to the man and woman in the row directly behind the defense table. The woman turns her head as she sits down, and I catch a glimpse of her face.

Cramer nudges me in the side and whispers. "I think those are Diana's parents."

"Has to be," I say. "That woman and Diana look just alike."

On the other side of the courtroom, the Bryants have already arrived and are sitting in the second row behind the state attorney. Cassandra Bryant glances toward the defense table. She and Patricia lock eyes before she quickly looks away.

The side door to the courtroom opens, and Diana is escorted inside.

She has her head hung low, and shuffles as the chains wrapped around her ankles clink against the tile floor. The corrections officer leads her to her seat next to her lawyer and moves to stand against the wall. Diana turns around in her seat and begins talking in a hushed whisper to her parents seated in the row behind her.

The noise in the courtroom dies down when the door to the judge's chambers opens. The presiding judge over the case enters the courtroom, and Diana's lawyer nudges her gently to stand. The judge takes his seat on the bench and looks around the crowded courtroom. The bailiff calls the court to order, and the room goes silent.

The judge directs his attention to the prosecutor. "Counselor, what say you on charges?"

The prosecutor stands and motions toward the defense table. "Your honor, the State is charging Diana McNamee with murder in the first degree for the murder of Nia Bryant. We believe that she knowingly lured Miss Bryant out to Groveland Park before savagely stabbing her to death."

The judge turns his attention to Diana. "Miss McNamee, how do you plead?"

"Not guilty," Diana says, her voice low and shaky.

"What say you on bail?" asks the judge.

"The State requests remand. Given the nature of the crime and the political status of the victim's father, we believe it would be in the best interest of everyone involved if Miss McNamee remains in custody until her set trial date."

Diana's attorney, a short, gray-haired white man with fierce eyes, stands and addresses the court. "Your honor, with all due respect, the State has blown this completely out of proportion. The State Attorney is making it seem like my client is a career criminal with outside ties. Miss McNamee is a college student and has never gotten so much as a parking ticket. She is not a flight risk. I see no reason why she should not be allowed to return to her residence until her trial date."

"While she has no priors or outside connections that we are aware of, we have confirmed that she had the murder weapon in her possession," the prosecutor interjects. "That alone is enough to give you an idea of what this young woman is capable of. I think the citizens of Magnolia would sleep better at night knowing that she's behind bars."

"Your honor, my client has been made aware of the severity of this case," says Diana's lawyer. "She understands that she needs to remain within county lines and understands that she will be under close supervision. In my professional opinion, I do not think Miss McNamee poses a threat to the community."

The judge looks over at Diana and takes a deep breath. "I can understand the concerns of both sides. But I'm going to give you the benefit of the doubt, Miss McNamee. Bail is granted at $500,000."

The crowd erupts in chatter. The judge bangs his gavel and calls for order in the court. "Under this order, the defendant is to remain within county lines until the start of the trial and shall not engage in any criminal activity or have any contact with the victim's family. If this order is violated in any way, the defendant will be remanded to the county jail until trial."

"Thank you, your honor," says Diana's attorney.

"If there's nothing else," says the judge, "we can go ahead and adjourn pending trial." He bangs the gavel again. Diana turns around and hugs her mother and stepfather before she's ushered back out of the courtroom.

"You think she'll post bail?" asks Cramer.

"We'll see," I say. "They need to come up with ten percent. Most people don't just have $50,000 lying around."

I watch as the Bryants gather their belongings and rush toward the courtroom exit, pushing past reporters. Patricia calls out after them. "Dwight! Cassandra!"

The Bryants continue toward the door, steadfast. Patricia continues yelling across the courtroom, and several people stop and watch. The Bryants rush out of the courtroom without acknowledging her and disappear into the hall.

I make my way to the front of the courtroom to the defense table. Maggie Price has her hands on Patricia's shoulders and is trying to calm her down.

"Pat, it's ok. Let them go," says Miss Maggie.

"But Diana didn't do this," she cries loudly. "They're painting my daughter as a murderer, and she's not."

"They've been through a lot too, Pat. Let's just all calm down. We'll figure this out."

Patricia looks up and spots me standing a few feet away. "Who are you?"

Miss Maggie immediately recognizes my face. "You're the detective," she says. "You came by the sorority house a few days ago asking about Nia."

"Yes, ma'am, we've spoken."

Patricia sneers at me. "So, you're the one who arrested my daughter?"

"My name is Detective Evans, and yes, I was there, ma'am. My partner and I conducted the search warrant and discovered the murder weapon."

"This is all your fault!" she yells. "I don't know what you think you know, but you're mistaken. Diana didn't kill Nia!"

"Well, ma'am, the evidence—"

"I don't give a damn about the evidence!" she screams, taking a step toward me and pointing her finger at my chest. "I know my daughter! She didn't do this!"

Her husband comes up behind her and places his hands on her shoulders, pulling her back several steps. "Calm down, honey."

"Don't tell me to calm down, Clay!"

Miss Maggie turns to me. "Detective, there must be something you can do."

I shake my head. "I'm sorry. The evidence is telling a different story."

"But I know Diana," Miss Maggie pleads. "She's not capable of this. In fact, she was one of the first people to notice Nia was missing. She was on the phone all morning calling her."

"See?" Patricia yells at me. "Everyone knows my daughter wouldn't hurt a fly. You've got this all wrong!"

"She's right," Miss Maggie says. "All of the girls saw how concerned she was. Evie was there, too. She saw it all."

Patricia's jaw drops, and she looks over at Miss Maggie. "Evie? You saw Evie?"

"Oh yes, with everything going on, I forgot to mention it. But yes, Evie stopped by a few days ago and visited me."

I watch Patricia closely. She suddenly looks sick. Her husband grabs her arm and helps her into one of the empty seats.

"Evie saw everything," Miss Maggie continues. "She saw Diana and how worried she was. There has to be another explanation for all of this."

"Who is Evie?" I ask, keeping my eyes on Patricia.

"No one!" Patricia blurts out. "It's no one!"

Miss Maggie frowns at her. "Pat!"

Patricia raises her hands out in front of her and closes her eyes. "Miss Maggie, please! Just ... not today. Please!"

The old woman turns to me and shrugs. Patricia grabs her purse and jumps to her feet. She pushes past me, her husband close on her heels.

"Where are you going?" asks Miss Maggie. She hobbles behind them on her cane as she tries to keep up.

Patricia looks back. "To bond my daughter out of jail!"

She storms out of the courtroom, rushing past Cramer as he walks quickly in my direction.

"What's wrong?" I ask. He's breathing heavily, and his eyes are wild.

"We have a problem. We need to get back to the station now."

"Why? What happened?"

"I just spoke to Jacobs. It's the surveillance tape we've been waiting on from the city. We finally got it back."

"Ok. What's the problem?"

"You know what you were saying last night about something not adding up with the evidence?"

"Yeah. So?"

"Well, you may be right," he says. "The tape is telling a completely different story."

CHAPTER 32

CHRIS

I weave in and out of the morning traffic as I make my way back to the station. When I arrive, the large group of reporters that were camped out in front of the station for the last few days have finally left. Now that we have a suspect in custody, the focus is already beginning to shift to other pressing stories.

I pull my car around to the back of the building and hurry into the station. I take the back staircase to the basement, where the IT room is located.

Cramer, Detective Jacobs, and Lieutenant Stokes are already inside. They are standing around a double-screen computer in the center of the room. Andy is hunched over in front of the computer, typing loudly on the keyboard.

"What's going on?"

"Shut the door," says Stokes in a stern voice.

"We finally got the surveillance tape from the park service," says Jacobs. "Andy is pulling it up now so that we can see."

"I already got a look at it," Andy says. "I called the Lieutenant as soon as we got it."

"Ok," I say. "Let's see it."

Andy starts the video. The image is much clearer than the

surveillance video from the apartment complex. The camera is pointed down at the parking lot, giving us a perfect view of the area. The time stamp in the bottom right-hand corner of the screen reads 1:43 a.m. on Friday morning. The feed is from right around the time when Nia is presumed to have been killed. The room grows silent as we all lean in and watch the video.

There are several cars parked in the parking lot, including Nia's Honda Accord. A few minutes pass before there is movement on the screen, and several figures come into view.

I point to the screen. "Stop! There!"

Andy rewinds the tape back. We watch closely as some of the members of Kappa Theta Theta sorority come into focus. The girls are all dressed identically in black bottoms and black knit jackets, just as Shawna had described. The girls are seen getting into their vehicles and driving out of the parking lot.

"This must be the end of the rehearsal they attended," says Cramer.

"Can you back that up some?" I ask.

"Why? What's wrong?" asks Lieutenant Stokes. I can hear the irritation in his voice, but I ignore it.

"I want to see if we can count how many people left at this point."

Andy rewinds the tape back about thirty seconds. I proceed to count the figures on the screen. "There are ten girls."

"The young lady, Shawna, that we interviewed the other day mentioned twelve girls being in attendance that night," Cramer says.

"So we can assume that the other two that aren't on camera are Diana and Nia," I say.

Andy presses play, and the video progresses forward in slow motion. The figures on the screen get into their vehicles again and pull out of the parking lot. They disappear from the feed, leaving two cars parked in view of the surveillance camera.

"And all ten girls left," says Cramer. He looks up at me and shrugs. "That pretty much rules them out right there."

"And there's Diana's car there and Nia's car there," I say.

A few minutes pass with no movement on the screen. I can feel my heart racing. I know at this point that Nia's life is running down to the minute. I feel like I'm in the middle of watching a bad horror film.

Suddenly, there's movement again on the screen. A single figure moves across the parking lot. It's Diana walking quickly to her car, her face in full view of the camera.

"There's Diana," I say.

"Yeah, but where's Nia?" Jacobs asks.

Diana is seen getting into her car. She turns on her headlights as she prepares to leave the park. Another figure appears on the screen and is moving slowly across the parking lot. My heart skips in my chest. It's Nia Bryant.

"Pause it!"

Andy pauses the video, and the image on the screen freezes. Andy zooms in, bringing Nia's face into full view.

"That's Nia," I say.

Everyone is silent as we stare at our victim. She looks nothing like the girl in her photos. It's the first image I've seen of her where she isn't smiling. Instead, she looks distressed, like she's been crying. I look closer at the screen and notice a necklace around her neck.

"There's the necklace Shawna said she was wearing. Was there any mention of a necklace found at the scene?"

"No, not that I can recall," Cramer says.

Andy zooms out from Nia's face and returns the video to the original setting so that we once again have a full view of the parking lot. Nia can be seen walking slowly to her car, which is parked a few spaces down from Diana. Diana has now backed her car out of the parking spot and is seen driving off.

My heart drops. Her words from yesterday replay in my head. *Do you really think I'm that stupid? Do you really think I'd kill Nia after everyone saw me with her and then keep the murder weapon?*

I can see Lieutenant Stokes out of the corner of my eye. He looks like he's had the air knocked out of him. When I'd mentioned my concerns about the discovery, he'd shut me down without a second thought. But now it looks like I was right to question what we'd found. The surveillance tape clearly shows that Nia was still alive when Diana left the park.

The video continues to play, and Nia is seen opening the driver's side door of her car. She has one foot in and is preparing to climb inside when she suddenly stops. I hold my breath as I watch what she does next. Instead of getting into her car and driving off like everyone else, she has turned her attention back toward the park. There is no sound associated with the surveillance tape, but it seems like something or someone has grabbed Nia's attention. I check the corner of the screen where Nia appears to be looking in the video, but it's of no use. Whatever or whoever has caught her attention is outside the view of the camera. Nia closes the door of her car and walks back toward the park, and disappears from the frame.

"What the hell!" Cramer says. "Where is she going?"

I remain quiet, keeping my eyes on the screen. The minutes seem to tick by slowly as we wait in silence. There is no movement on the screen for almost ten minutes, and I can feel everyone growing restless. I keep thinking about the crime scene and Nia's lifeless body riddled with stab wounds. A chill runs up my spine as I realize that Nia is being murdered in cold blood at that very moment in the video.

"Look! There she is!" Cramer points at the computer screen. A figure comes into view again. It's moving quickly across the screen toward Nia's car.

Andy pauses the video so that we can get a better look. The figure on the screen has on black bottoms and a black knit jacket. The outfit is identical to what Nia was seen wearing earlier in the video. The figure appears to be a woman, but something catches my eye.

"Wait a minute! She didn't have on a hat when she first walked to the car!"

Andy zooms in on the woman, but whoever she is has her head tilted toward the ground. The visor from the hat shields her face from the camera.

"Dammit!" says Lieutenant Stokes. "Can't see her face."

I point at the computer screen. "But look! There's something in her hands." The woman in the video is carrying a black bundle in her hands as she walks toward Nia's car.

"It looks like a piece of clothing," says Cramer. "Probably the jacket we found the murder weapon wrapped in."

"She's also wearing gloves," I say. "Nia didn't have on gloves in the last frame. And she's not wearing a necklace either."

Andy resumes the video, and we watch as the woman opens the door and climbs into the driver's seat of Nia's car. "That isn't Diana," I say. "That woman is taller and has a slightly heavier build."

Lieutenant Stokes looks up at me, his eyes wide like saucers.

I turn away from him and watch as the woman drives out of the parking lot. "We were wrong. There was another woman there that night."

CHAPTER 33

CHRIS

WE RE-WATCH THE VIDEO SEVERAL TIMES. IT'S ALMOST AS IF we're expecting something different to happen—for our original theory to magically play out. But each replay only further confirms the truth—Diana wasn't there when Nia was murdered. Someone else had been there that night, and I'm positive that the unknown woman in the video is the real killer.

Lieutenant Stokes calls an emergency briefing. Me, Cramer, and Jacobs join the other detectives in the briefing room as we prepare to hear the next steps for the case. I take a seat in the front row and watch as the rest of the team files in quickly. Cramer sits down in the seat next to me. He looks frazzled, and I can tell that the recent findings from the surveillance tape have unnerved him.

Lieutenant Stokes takes his place at the front of the room. "Thank you all for being on time. I called this briefing to discuss how we all need to proceed from here on out with the Bryant case. For those of you who haven't heard, we've received surveillance footage from the night in question, and there are some new developments."

The room is silent. I listen intently, even though I know what's coming next.

"Upon review of the surveillance tape, it has been discovered that

Diana McNamee is most likely not the person who killed Nia Bryant," he says. "She is seen on tape leaving the premises before the murder occurred."

Several of the officers begin to whisper amongst themselves, and Lieutenant Stokes raises his hand to silence them. "Another person is seen leaving the park in Nia's car shortly after we believe she was stabbed," he says. "The suspect appears to be a woman, but we were unable to make a positive ID on her face."

One of the detectives sitting in the back of the room raises her hand, and Stokes motions to her to speak.

"But sir, what about the murder weapon?" she asks. "It was found in Diana McNamee's car."

"That's one of the questions we need to answer," he says. "It was in her possession, so she's connected to this somehow." He looks around the room at the small group. "For the sake of covering all our asses, we need to review all of the traffic cams from around Diana McNamee's apartment. We're missing something, and we need to see how she ties into all of this. Call the city and put in an urgent request for all the cameras on all the roadways that feed into the park as well. If we can establish a timeline on Diana, maybe it'll help us identify who this mystery woman is."

"We also need to re-canvass the park," says Cramer. "Someone had to have seen something."

"Yes, broadening our interview pool is going to be necessary at this point," says Stokes. "At first, this case seemed like it was open and shut, with everything pointing to Diana McNamee. But now we have to consider other possibilities."

I raise my hand to speak. "The woman in the video was wearing the exact same outfit that the girls were wearing that night. That can't be a coincidence. Whoever she is, she had inside knowledge into what was taking place that night."

"The organization certainly seems to be connected somehow. I know we've been talking to the current members, but we may need to branch out and talk to anyone who has ever come through that chapter."

He turns to Jacobs. "Jacobs, I would like for you to go back to Nia's apartment complex. Speak to the residents again and see if anyone saw this mystery woman. She drove Nia's car back to her apartment, so we need to find out if anyone saw anything that could help us."

Jacobs nods. "Yes, sir."

"Oh, and there's one more thing that may be of interest. In the video, Nia is seen wearing a necklace before she disappeared. However, when her body was discovered, there was no evidence of the necklace on her body or at the scene."

"Are we thinking that maybe it was taken during the stabbing?" asks a detective sitting a few rows behind us.

"It looks to be that way," he says. "Nothing else was taken that we can tell, and Nia still had her wallet on her when she was found. I don't think we're looking at a robbery, but we can't rule it out. If we find that necklace, we may find our killer or at least someone who knows what happened that night. If you all have any questions or concerns, bring them to me. If not, let's get to work."

The officers begin filing out of the room.

"I definitely didn't see this coming," Cramer says to me.

"Something was nagging at me the whole time about this case," I say. "I should've spoken up more."

"Oh, come on!" he says. "This isn't your fault. You tried to tell the Lieutenant, and he didn't want to hear it. I even dismissed the idea."

Everyone has already cleared the room, and we are now alone. "I should've done more," I say. "I should've listened to my gut."

"You did your best," he says. "Everything pointed to Diana. It was a foolproof case."

"You're right. I just don't like the idea of having an innocent person accused of something like this."

"Well, we don't know that she's innocent just yet," he says. "Let's work the case and find out what truly happened. Diana is tied up in this somehow; we just have to figure out how."

CHAPTER 34

TORI

THE TELEVISION SCREENS IN THE CAMPUS CAFETERIA ARE tuned into the afternoon news. My eyes are glued to the screen in front of me as I wait in line to place my food order. The current segment features an earlier recording of Diana's arraignment from this morning:

"The State has charged twenty-year-old Diana McNamee with the murder of MSU college freshman Nia Bryant," says the reporter. *"The victim was first reported missing last Friday afternoon. Detectives at MPD have confirmed that Miss McNamee was found to be in possession of the murder weapon, as well as an article of clothing that belonged to the victim. Miss McNamee was released late this morning after posting bail and has been ordered not to leave the city limits. A trial date has not yet been set— "*

"NEXT!" The cafeteria lady is staring impatiently at me as she waits to take my order. I walk up to the counter and order my food, ignoring her glares from behind the partition. The cafeteria is packed during the lunchtime rush, so I grab a seat outside at a small table on the back patio area. Today isn't as hot, and I decide to take advantage of the nice weather.

I take my statistics book out of my backpack and place it down on the table next to my unwrapped sandwich. The news of Diana's arrest has my stomach in knots. I no longer feel hungry, even though I haven't had anything to eat since yesterday. I take the sandwich and stuff it into my bag to take home for later now that my appetite is suddenly gone.

"What are you doing sitting way back here?" I look up to see Tre standing on the other side of the table. I wonder how long he's been standing there.

"Well, I was trying to grab a bite to eat and get some studying done. But now I'm not hungry." I point to my textbook that sits unopened on the table. "Studying isn't going so well either."

He pulls up a chair. His smooth, strong face looks tired and deflated. He sits quietly for several minutes, staring past me at the street that runs along the café.

"You ok?"

He shrugs. "I don't really know how I feel. There's just a lot going on right now."

News of Diana's involvement in Nia's death has reached the student body. Everyone is in disbelief, and the mood on campus is somber. I want to say something to reassure him, but I don't even know where to begin. I'm still trying to make sense of everything myself.

"To lose Nia was hard enough," he continues. "But now I feel like I've lost two friends. I've known Diana for years. I just never would've thought she'd be capable of something like this."

"I'm sorry," I say. "I know it's hard."

"And then this situation with Byron and Drew just complicates everything. People have started spreading rumors and speaking on things they know nothing about. I just don't know how this is going to turn out."

"How is Byron?" I ask.

"I stopped to see him this morning. He's pretty messed up over what happened to Nia. I've never seen him like this."

"What about Drew? Is he back at home?"

"He's staying with a friend for now. To be honest, it's probably for the best. Byron needs some time to cool off. It's not a good idea for them to be in the same house right now."

"Well, I take it they won't be roommates anymore."

"Most likely not." He pulls his statistics book out of his book bag and drops it down on the table next to mine. "And then, on top of everything else, we have this stupid exam in the morning."

"I know. You'd think Professor Stratman would give us a break and push the test back with everything going on," I say. "Nia was in our class. Don't they usually cancel classes in these types of situations?"

"I would think so," he says. "But since it's the midterm, I guess he can't change the date."

"It seems a little insensitive if you ask me."

"Have you studied any of the material yet?"

"I skimmed a few of the chapters at home this morning, but that's about it," I say. "It's a lot of information to cover. To be honest, I'm just not feeling it today. I have so many other things on my mind."

"Yeah, same here. But I can't afford not to pass this one. I didn't do so hot on the last test."

"Me too. This class has been a struggle for me. I need this grade to pass."

He looks out at the street again. "I'm going to head home to try and get some studying done there. Do you want to come? Maybe a change of scenery will do us good."

It sounds like a good idea. Everyone on campus is talking about Nia's murder, and I don't want to stick around. I grab my book bag and throw it over my shoulder. "Yeah, sure, I'll come. The last thing I need is to fail this exam, and I can't afford any more distractions."

He rolls his eyes. "Trust me if we fail, that won't be the worst thing to have happened this week."

———

Back at Tre's house, I have to force myself to study. My notes lay spilled out on the coffee table. Bright yellow highlighted sections line my textbook, and my eyes hurt from reading. The hours of studying have taken a toll, and my body feels tight from sitting in the same position. I stretch my legs out in front of me and glance out of the window. The sun has gone down, and the sky outside is dark by the time we're done.

"I can't believe it's so late," I say. "It's already after 8 p.m."

Tre has abandoned his textbook and is in the kitchen rummaging through the refrigerator. "Yeah, the day flew by. And I don't know about you, but I'm starving. I have a pizza in the freezer I can have ready in a few minutes if you want something to eat."

"Sure," I say. "That's fine with me."

He takes a box of frozen pizza out of the freezer and slides it into the oven. "What do you want to drink?"

I prop my feet up on the ottoman to give my legs a deeper stretch. "Something strong if you have it."

"Are you sure?" he asks. "You know we have an exam in the morning."

"Yeah, I'm sure," I say. "I need something to take the edge off. Between this midterm and everything going on with Nia, I'm so wound up."

He looks at me, concerned.

"I just have to make sure not to drink as much as I did the other night," I say. "But one drink won't hurt."

He shrugs and turns back to the refrigerator. "Ok, if you say so."

I turn on the TV to give my brain a break from studying. The evening news is on, and another breaking news alert is flashing across the bottom of the screen. A reporter is on screen discussing the story:

"Breaking news tonight in the investigation into the murder of Nia Bryant. New surveillance footage has just been released from the scene of the crime. The recently released video shows evidence that someone else may be responsible or involved in the murder of the young MSU college student. Take a look at the video footage released just moments ago."

"Tre, look at this!"

He comes to stand beside me. "What is it?"

"There's a video that was released from the park. Now they're saying there's a possibility it could've been someone else who killed Nia."

We watch the video closely. Someone dressed in all black can be seen walking quickly across the parking lot at Groveland Park toward a car that looks like Nia's. The person in the video appears to be a woman, but her face is hidden from view by a hat.

"According to sources at MPD, the individual in this frame of the video appeared after Diana McNamee had already left the premises and just moments after Nia Bryant was last seen on video heading back

toward Groveland Park. The attorney for Miss McNamee provided a statement earlier after the tape was released and is calling for all charges against his client to be dropped."

Diana's attorney comes on screen. He is standing on the front steps of the police station as he addresses a group of reporters:

"The release of this surveillance footage proves that my client was nowhere near the scene of the crime when the murder was committed. MPD detectives rushed to judgment in this case, and now the truth is coming to light. The person who killed Miss Bryant is still out there. My client has continued to maintain her innocence, and we will not stop fighting until all charges against her have been dropped."

The reporter is live again and continues her report: *"Detectives here at MPD are still not releasing many details surrounding the case but told me earlier that they are exploring every possibility at this point. They are asking anyone with information on the identity of the woman in the video to please come forward. And as always, anyone with information has the option to remain anonymous. Back to you in the newsroom."*

Tre sits on the couch next to me. "I never thought Diana did it."

"So, you do think it's someone else?"

"I know one thing—it's not Diana. I know her. She's smart. There's no way she would've been stupid enough to kill Nia knowing that everyone saw them together. And then to have the murder weapon in her possession ... it just doesn't sound like her."

"So, who do you think it is?"

The timer on the oven goes off, and he goes to retrieve the pizza. "I honestly don't know what to think. And to be honest, I don't think I can bear to think about it anymore tonight."

"What do you mean?"

He pushes my notes to the side and places the pizza down on the coffee table. "I know it sounds bad, but this is all becoming a little much for me. I don't know who to believe. I don't know who to trust anymore. For tonight, I just want to forget about everything. I have too much riding on this exam in the morning."

I take a slice of pizza from the pie and bite into it. It's the first time I've eaten today, and I can feel my appetite slowly returning.

"I get why you feel that way," I say. "It's been hard on everyone. We don't have to talk about it. For tonight, we can just let it be."

We finish the rest of the pizza in silence. After dinner, my one drink turns into three. It isn't long before Tre is fast asleep on the couch. The alcohol seems to have taken the edge off, and he's snoring softly. I finish the last of my drink and make my way to the bathroom. My head spins, and I know that I've drunk too much again despite my attempts to limit myself.

I decide not to make the same mistake again by not checking in. I close the door to the bathroom and dial Aunt Lyn's cell phone. When she picks up, I can tell from the tone of her voice that she's not in a good mood. She sounds irritated, and I know it's my fault.

"Hey, auntie." My words are slurred, and I close my eyes as I try to focus. "It's me."

"Tori, are you ok?" she asks. "Where are you?"

"Yeah, I'm fine. I just wanted to let you know I won't be home tonight. I've been studying all afternoon for my midterm tomorrow. I'm too tired to drive."

There's an uncomfortable silence. The longer I wait for her to respond, the more nervous I become.

"Auntie? Did you hear me?"

"You're tired?" she asks. "At 9:30?"

"Um yeah, I didn't get much rest last night." It's not a complete lie. I'd tossed and turned all last night, my mind restless with thoughts of Nia.

She sighs. "Tori, have you been drinking?"

The question catches me off guard, and I don't know what to say.

"Look, I've been trying to be understanding because I know we're all going through a lot right now," she says. "But you have to meet me halfway here. You wouldn't behave this way with your mother ... please don't do it with me."

"I'm sorry." It's the only thing that I can think of to say. I feel shame, like a child who has been chastised in front of their class.

"It's fine," she says. "We'll discuss this tomorrow."

Before I can respond, the phone goes dead. She has never been short with me, and I know it's because I'm pushing my limits with her. I know I'm going to get an earful when I go home tomorrow.

Back in the living room, Tre is still fast asleep on the couch. I take a blanket from the closet and turn off the lights before lying down. The room is shrouded in darkness except for the glow of the moon filtering in through the front window. I close my eyes and try to sleep, but all I can think about is the woman from the video. Who is she? And what had Nia done that had driven her to kill?

CHAPTER 35

TORI

I WAKE WITH A START THE NEXT MORNING TO THE SOUND OF loud knocking. My mind is still foggy from the alcohol as I try to make sense of where I am. The light streaming in through the living room window is bright, and it takes a few seconds for my eyes to adjust. Across the room, Tre is still fast asleep on the other couch.

Another loud knock.

I can hear a woman's voice on the other side of the front door. "Tre! Tre!"

My head spins as I force myself to my feet. It takes me a moment to gain my footing.

"Tre! Tre, wake up!" I whisper, tapping him on the shoulder. He begins to stir and looks up at me with sleepy eyes. "Someone is at your door."

The woman knocks again and calls out his name, louder this time. "Tre!"

"Oh shit! It's my aunt!" He jumps up from the couch, nearly knocking me over.

"Is she going to freak out about me spending the night?" I ask. "I thought you said it was ok if you have company?" My heart is racing—

my eyes are glued to the front door. The lingering effects of the alcohol cause my stomach to knot.

"It's fine," he whispers. "She's probably just checking to make sure I'm up. I'll be right back."

He unbolts the lock on the front door. I go into the bathroom and lock the door behind me. I wait quietly in the small bathroom, listening through the door to the muffled voices coming from the living room. I catch a glimpse of myself in the bathroom mirror and try to smooth down my hair. The twist-out that I had so carefully styled a few days ago is now a matted mess. I use my fingers and try to fluff out the curls as best as I can, but I know my hair is a lost cause.

After a few minutes, I hear the front door finally close. I turn the doorknob carefully and crack open the bathroom door just enough to see into the bedroom.

"It's ok," Tre says. "It was just my aunt."

I take a few steps out of the bathroom. "Is everything ok?"

"Yes, everything's fine. She's leaving for work. She was checking to make sure I was up. I told her about the midterm we have today."

"Oh shit! The midterm! What time is it?"

"It's 7:45 a.m."

"I should really be getting home," I say. "My aunt wasn't too happy about me staying out again last night."

"You're not in trouble, are you?" he asks. "I didn't even know you stayed. I was out like a light."

"I don't know. She made a big stink about it. She said she wants to talk when I get home."

He glances at the time again. "Well, at least eat something before you go. My aunt made breakfast. She always makes it a habit to cook before I have a big exam."

"Oh, that's sweet of her."

"Yeah, well, you're welcome to some if you want a bite to eat before you leave. I'm sure there's plenty. Besides, it'll do good to have something in your stomach after the alcohol from last night."

"Sure, I guess I should probably eat," I say. "I don't think I'll have time to stop and get anything before the exam."

I quickly pack up my books and notes that are still sprawled across the coffee table and toss them into my bag. When we step outside, the air is already humid even though the sun is barely up. I follow Tre across the backyard to the main house. The sliding back door has been left unlocked and leads directly into a brightly lit kitchen. It's an open-concept design, which makes the lower level of the house appear even more spacious. A traditional-style dining room table sits in the middle of the attached dining area. A crystal chandelier suspended overhead casts an inviting glow across the room.

"This house is even nicer on the inside than the outside," I say, running my fingers over the smooth marble countertops.

He laughs. "Yeah, my uncle has done a lot of remodeling, and his wife has expensive taste. They didn't spare any cost."

He portions out some of the leftover breakfast onto two plates. "Come on. I'll show you around. It'll take a few minutes for the food to heat anyway."

He leads me out of the kitchen and into the main hall, where he shows me around the first floor. At the end of the main hall, he stops outside of the last room and opens the door for me to enter. It's a small office with a single window that faces the backyard. The walls of the small room are lined with Lambda Nu Phi paraphernalia.

"Wow!" I say. "Did you do all of this?"

"Nope." Tre flips the light switch, and the room seems to come to life. "This is my uncle's office. I guess you can call it his man cave."

"I didn't know you guys both pledged the same fraternity, too."

"Yeah, he's a member of Lambda Nu Phi."

He leads me over to a large stone fireplace. On the edge of the mantelpiece is a framed photograph of a middle-aged man. "Is this your uncle?"

"Yeah. That's my Uncle Raymond. But we call him Ray."

I glance at him and then back at the photo. "Yeah, I can see the resemblance."

"That's what everyone says. He looks more like my dad than my uncle."

"I remember you telling me the other day that he went to MSU."

"Yeah, and he's lived here ever since," he says. "He actually crossed into the fraternity the same year as Nia's dad. We kind of found out by accident when I met her and her parents during her freshman orientation."

The mention of Nia's name causes a sudden sadness to sweep over me, but I push it aside as I continue to look around the room. The microwave beeps from the kitchen, signaling that the food has finished heating.

"I'll be right back," he says. "I'm going to pop the other plate in the microwave."

He leaves me alone in the room while he returns to the kitchen. I spot a framed photo of Tre and his uncle at Tre's probate show sitting on the mantlepiece. I hold it in my hands and run my fingers along the textured frame. Tre's uncle smiles proudly for the camera. His arm is wrapped tightly around Tre's shoulders as they hold up their fraternity sign.

I return the photo to its home and continue browsing over the other pictures when something catches my eye. Toward the very back of the mantelpiece is a smaller, unframed picture that is partially hidden between some of the others. I peer over the other photos to get a better look. It's a photo of Tre's uncle standing with Nia's dad, Mr. Bryant. The picture looks to be from their college days.

There is another person in the photo—a woman. Her face is blocked by the frame of another photo, but I can see the outline of the side of her head. I reach out to grab it but stop when I hear footsteps approaching. Tre appears in the doorway.

"Ready to eat?" he asks.

"Yeah, I'm starving."

"Well, it's ready when you are."

I turn and follow him out of the room. Suddenly, all I can think about is the breakfast waiting for me. I don't even think twice about the hidden photo.

CHAPTER 36

TORI

After breakfast, I rush home to shower. Aunt Lyn has already left for work by the time I arrive, and the house is quiet. We haven't spoken since last night, and I'm relieved to find the house empty. Now that she's gone, I have at least until the evening to get my thoughts together.

I take a quick shower and throw on a pair of jeans and a matching top. I throw my hair into a bun for now, smoothing it down with globs of gel until it's smooth and tight. In the kitchen, the coffee pot is still warm. Aunt Lyn hasn't been gone long. I start to pour myself a cup when I notice a light coming from her bedroom.

"Aunt Lyn?" My voice echoes loudly through the quiet house. The silence is eerie. The video from last night comes to mind, and I want nothing more than to get out quickly.

Her bedroom is at the end of the long hall. The door is slightly ajar, and I see that the light in her closet has been left on. I push the door open all the way and look around. The master bedroom is the largest room in the house and is also my favorite. Large bay windows run along the far wall that faces the backyard. The curtains, which are normally open, are drawn closed this morning.

The room is spotless, as is the rest of the house. I peer inside the walk-in closet. The small space is in the same immaculate condition as her bedroom. The clothes hanging from the rods are color coordinated, the shoes lined neatly on the closet floor.

I flip the light switch, and the closet is once again blanketed in darkness. I turn to leave, but my arm bumps a nearby shelf. A large bag topples to the floor and lands upside down. When I reach down to pick it up, something small falls out of the front pocket and lands at my feet.

I cover my mouth with my hand to silence my scream. My legs give out from under me, and I stumble back. The breakfast that I've just eaten begins rising in my chest, and I swallow hard as I try to keep myself from vomiting. I pick up the object from the floor and hold it up. Nia's silver necklace is clutched between my fingers, the pendant swinging back and forth like a giant pendulum.

———

I never make it to the midterm. It makes up the largest portion of my grade, but I can't bring myself to sit for an hour through a written test. Instead, I spend the next thirty minutes pacing the floor in my room. I can't think straight. My mind is running in circles, trying to make sense of what I've found. I don't call Aunt Lyn and confront her about the necklace. Something tells me that it's best that I keep this to myself—at least for now.

I finally get up the nerve to drive to campus. The midterm is a lost cause, but I make the drive anyway. This is a time when I would run to Nia with my problem. She always seemed to know what to do—but Nia is gone. I have to tell someone, so I go find Tre.

The midterm is still going on when I arrive, but some of my classmates have finished early. I pace back and forth in the hall outside of the auditorium, watching the door impatiently. They stare as they pass me in the hall, but I ignore them. I keep my hand in my pocket, my fingers gripping the tiny silver necklace. Dark thoughts are running rampant in my mind.

The auditorium door opens again, and Tre finally walks out into the hall. He spots me standing across the hall and walks over. "Hey, what happened? Are you ok? I didn't see you in the exam."

"I know. I missed it."

He looks at me, confused. "Why? What happened?"

I grab his arm and pull him into a quiet corner of the hall. When I'm certain that no one is watching, I reach into my pocket and reveal the necklace. He stares at it for a moment.

"Where'd you find that?" he whispers. "Isn't that Nia's necklace?"

I nod my head slowly as I try to keep my hands from shaking. "It was in my house."

"Your house? How did it get in your house?"

"I don't know; I don't know!" My voice is high. I feel myself beginning to panic.

"Calm down." He puts his hands on my shoulders. "Where in the house did you find it?"

"It was in my aunt's closet in a bag," I say. "It just doesn't make sense. Why would she have—"

He holds up his hand to stop me. "Wait! This was with your aunt's things?"

"Yeah. In her closet. I accidentally knocked over a bag, and it fell out of the pocket."

"Have you asked her about it?"

I shake my head. "Not yet. She had already left for work by the time I got home. And to be honest, I don't know if I should."

Tre seems to be deep in thought as he stares down at the necklace.

"What is it?" I ask. "What's wrong?"

He raises his eyes and looks at me again. "I've seen this necklace before."

"Of course you've seen it." I close my hand around the tainted silver and place it back in my pocket. "Nia wore it all the time. She never took it off."

"No—I mean, yes, I've seen Nia wearing it," he says. "But I've seen it somewhere else as well."

"I'm not following! What does that have to do with it being in my house mixed in with my aunt's things?"

He grabs my hand and leads me toward the building exit. "I have to show you something."

"What is it?" I'm tripping over my feet as he pulls me toward the door. "Tre, what's going on? Just tell me."

He looks back at me as we walk out of the building. The sun is blinding, and I have to shield my eyes from its glare. "I'm not even sure myself," he says. "But I think you may be more connected to Nia than you realize."

CHAPTER 37

TORI

WE LEAVE CAMPUS IN A HURRY. THE MORNING TRAFFIC IS light, and the drive back to Magnolia Springs is smooth. I sit in the passenger seat, my hand clasping the necklace in my jeans pocket. When we arrive back at his uncle's place, Tre parks in the driveway and glances around the exterior of the main house. He's acting strangely, and I am beginning to lose my patience with him. I wish he'd tell me what he knows.

"Are you going to tell me what's going on?" I ask.

He ignores the question and gets out of the car. He waves at me to follow him as he runs into the yard. "Come on."

He passes the side gate and goes straight to the front of the house, where he unlocks the front door. We step inside. The house is quiet, and I'm beginning to have second thoughts about going any further.

"What are we doing back here?" I whisper.

"Follow me."

He walks quickly down the main hallway toward the back of the house, and I follow close behind. We stop in front of the office door I'd been in earlier. He turns on the light and takes my hand, leading me over to the fireplace with the large collection of fraternity photos. He reaches toward the back of the mantelpiece and hands me a photo. I recognize it as the partially hidden photo from earlier—the one of Nia's dad and Tre's uncle from years ago.

The picture is unframed, and its edges are beginning to yellow. Also pictured in the photo is Nia's mom, Mrs. Bryant. She is posing with another woman whose face I don't recognize. I turn my attention back to Mr. Bryant. He is smiling happily in the photo with his arms wrapped tightly around the waist of another young woman—the woman whose side profile I'd seen briefly earlier.

My body goes stiff. My heart feels like it has stopped in my chest. The woman Mr. Bryant is holding in the picture isn't his current wife. Standing in his arms with a proud, beaming smile is the younger version of Aunt Lyn.

I finally look at Tre. "My aunt and Nia's dad?"

He nods and points back to the photo. "But that's not all. Look at that."

I look at where he's pointing. Draped around Aunt Lyn's neck is Nia's necklace—the same necklace that's in my pocket.

"I—I don't understand," I say. "What does this all mean?"

"When I saw you at the vigil with your aunt, I knew she looked familiar," he says. "It wasn't until you told me about the necklace that I realized where I'd seen her before."

"From this picture?"

He points at the photo again. "She's a member of the sorority. Look at her jacket."

I take a closer look. Aunt Lyn is wearing a black jacket with the letters for Kappa Theta Theta embroidered across the front—the same as Mrs. Bryant and the other woman in the photo.

"I never knew she was a member of Kappa Theta Theta," I say. "She's never mentioned it before. She knew Nia had pledged after I told her about the probate. Why didn't she mention that she was a member?"

"Well, she wouldn't be wearing the jacket if she wasn't a member. I know that for sure."

"Do you know who this is?" I ask, pointing at the woman standing next to Mrs. Bryant.

"Yeah, that's Diana's mom," he says. "I've seen her before."

"Where?"

"From some of Diana's family pictures on her Facebook and Instagram."

I turn the picture over in my hand. On the back, someone has written the names of everyone in the photo in neat cursive. *Dwight. Ray. Evie. Cassandra. Patricia.*

"So, Diana's mom must be Patricia," I say.

"And your aunt, her name is Evie?" he asks, pointing at the list of names.

"Our family calls her Lyn. It's short for her real name, Evelyn. I've never heard anyone call her Evie before."

"But that's her, right?"

"Yes, that's definitely her. Evie. Lyn. They're both short for Evelyn. Aunt Lyn *is* Evie."

CHAPTER 38

TORI

I TWIRL THE PHOTO BETWEEN MY FINGERS, MY EYES GLUED on Aunt Lyn and Dwight Bryant. I look at Cassandra Bryant standing at the other end of the photo with Diana's mom. They're smiling with their arms wrapped around each other's shoulders, like best friends.

What happened between them? And what does it have to do with Nia?

Tre is staring at me from across the kitchen table. I place the photo face down on the table and force myself to look away. "What do you think it all means?"

He shrugs. "I don't know."

"It looks like Nia's dad and my aunt were involved at some point. But this is the first I'm hearing about it."

"Yeah, and then there's Nia's necklace," he says. "Why is she wearing it in the picture? Do you think they just happen to have the same one?"

I shake my head. "No, that's not possible."

"Why not?"

"Because the necklace Nia had was one of a kind. I remember asking her about it one day when we first met. She was always wearing it, so I was curious."

"One of a kind?"

"Yes, it was custom-made. It belonged to her late grandmother."

"So why is Evie, or whatever her name is, wearing it?"

I turn the photo back over and look again at the necklace around Aunt Lyn's neck. "That necklace was special to Nia. Her parents passed it down to her when she turned sixteen. She never took it off. And she was wearing it before she went to the rehearsal. I saw it myself when she came by my house."

"Then why was it with your aunt's things?" he asks. "And it looks like there's blood on it."

Nia's necklace is lying in the middle of the kitchen table. There is a dried red stain on the pendant that looks like it could be blood.

"I don't know," I say. "None of this makes sense. It looks like someone may have framed Diana for Nia's murder. What if someone is trying to frame my aunt too?"

"Why would they do that?"

"I don't know. I don't know anything anymore."

"Do you think she would do something like this?" he asks. "You did say you didn't know her very well before moving up here."

"You're right. But I can't see her being involved with Nia's death. What reason would she have to kill Nia?"

Our conversation is interrupted by the sound of the lock turning on the front door. Tre glances down at his cell phone as an alert appears on his screen.

"It's just my Uncle Ray," he says.

"How do you know?"

He holds up his cell phone. "Doorbell app."

"He's home?"

"Yeah, his flight must've just landed."

The front door opens. There is a loud thud as a bag is dropped on the tiled floor in the front hall. "I thought you said he was in Japan?" I whisper.

"He was. When he found out about Nia, he caught a flight back. He still keeps in touch with Mr. Bryant from time to time."

I hear footsteps approaching, and I slide Nia's necklace into my pocket. The photo is still in the middle of the table. I'm about to grab it when a man appears in the kitchen doorway. I yank my hand back.

Tre's uncle pauses in the doorway and looks at me before turning to Tre. "Hey, Tre!" he says. "Didn't expect to see you here."

"Hey, Unc. How was your flight?"

"Eh, long. I'm just glad it's over." He looks at me again and smiles. "And who is this young lady?"

"Oh, um, this is Tori. Tori, this is my Uncle Ray."

He shakes my hand. "It's nice to meet you, Tori."

"Nice to meet you too." I do my best to muster up a smile, but my eyes keep darting to the photo.

Ray shoots Tre a look of approval as he takes off his suit jacket. He drapes it over the dining room chair and spots the photo lying in the middle of the table.

"What are you guys up to?" he asks.

"Nothing much." Tre clears his throat. He's trying his best to appear casual, but I can hear the nervousness in his voice.

"What are you doing with this?" Ray asks, picking up the photo.

"Tori had class with Nia and me. We were just talking, and I was telling her how you and Nia's dad know each other."

Ray's smile melts. "Yeah, me and Dwight go way back to college days. I still can't believe this all happened with his daughter."

"Neither can we."

Ray walks over to the refrigerator and pops the top on a can of beer and takes several sips. "I'm actually about to go freshen up and head over to see Dwight and Cass. I can't imagine what they're going through."

Tre signals me with his eyes and then turns back to his uncle. "I was showing Tori some of your old pictures from college. You and Mr. Bryant have a lot of pictures together."

"Oh yeah," says Ray, undoing his tie. "We were pretty tight."

"I was kind of surprised to see Mr. Bryant with this other woman in this picture. In all your other pictures, he's with his wife."

"That is an old picture from before Dwight and Cassandra."

"Who is she?" Tre asks. "The woman he's with?"

Ray picks up the photo and points to Aunt Lyn. "Who, her? That's Evie."

"Evie?"

"Yeah, she and Dwight dated for a while in college."

"But Mrs. Bryant is in the picture too. They all knew each other?"

Ray smirks and places the photo back on the table. "Yeah, that's a long story. One that I tried to stay out of."

Tre presses him. "Why? What happened?"

"I don't know all of the details. Evie and Dwight dated for years. Then one day, Dwight was with Cassandra."

"And you don't know what happened between them?"

He shrugs. "Dwight never really wanted to talk about what happened, and I didn't push him about it. I try to stay out of other people's business. All I know is it wasn't Evie's idea for things to end, but I don't think she really had a say in the matter. Dwight wanted Cassandra."

"That sounds like it got pretty messy," says Tre.

"It did. I didn't agree with how things went down, but like I said, I stayed out of it. Cass and Evie were friends once, but what happened with Dwight basically put an end to that."

I finally speak up. "What happened to Evie?"

"She dropped out of school shortly after that all happened," he says. "I never saw her again. I always wondered what happened to her. Everything was so private, and Dwight didn't want to discuss it, so I let it go. Everyone kind of forgot about it after a while."

He takes his coat off the chair and slings it over his shoulder. "Well, if y'all will excuse me, I'm past due for a shower after that long flight. I'm going to go upstairs and get out of these clothes. It was nice meeting you, Tori." He grabs his beer and walks out of the kitchen, leaving me and Tre alone again.

"Well, now we know," Tre whispers.

"I don't know," I say. "Some things still aren't adding up. What about Diana?"

"Tori, Diana wasn't there! You saw the video. We need to go to the police."

"And say what? That I found this necklace in my aunt's bag, and she's wearing it in an old photo from over twenty years ago? It doesn't prove anything."

"That's not for us to decide." He steals a look at the doorway to make sure we're still alone before continuing. "Something is wrong about this whole situation."

"But what if we're wrong?"

"If we're wrong, then we're wrong. But how else would she have gotten the necklace unless she was there that night? You said yourself Nia never took it off."

I feel for the necklace through the pocket of my jeans. "I guess you're right."

"Uncle Ray said things ended badly between them. What if this has nothing to do with Nia at all? What if this all has to do with her parents?"

He reaches across the table and places his hand on mine. "All I'm saying is let's tell the police what we know and let them handle it. I think this thing is much bigger than we thought."

CHAPTER 39

CHRIS

My lunch sits untouched on the table. I mash it with my fork until it no longer looks edible.

"Are you going to eat or are you going to continue to play with your food?" Rosalind stares at me disapprovingly from the other side of the booth.

"I'm sorry," I say. "I guess I'm not really hungry. I just have a lot on my mind."

"Well, you have to eat, Chris. I'm a little worried about you."

"I'm fine." I pick up the fork and force myself to take a bite of the cold food.

"You look like you haven't slept in days."

"It's just this case. I feel like we're spinning our wheels."

"You guys just need a little more time," she says. "These things happen."

"We arrested the wrong girl, Ros."

"You don't know that. You said yourself she could still be involved. Maybe she had an accomplice?"

I shake my head. "I doubt it. And the media hasn't made things any better. I don't know if you saw the paper this morning."

She looks down at her food, avoiding my gaze. "Yeah, I saw it. Look, don't let those people get to you. They sensationalize everything."

The local paper had run the story. It was a scathing piece highlighting the failures of the investigation. The article even included several quotes from residents that had been interviewed. Our mistake was now front-page news, and the community was beginning to question our ability to get justice for Nia.

"It's hard to ignore when it's right in your face," I say.

"I know but try to tune it out. Focus on what you can control." She takes another bite of her food. "Do you have any thoughts on what really happened?"

"I wish I knew. We've re-interviewed everyone—the boyfriend, the lover, the sorority sisters. Everyone has an alibi. There's no evidence tying any of them to this, and we don't have anyone new on our radar. This looks bad, Ros. We've already screwed up once, and now we have no other suspects."

My cellphone rings. It's been ringing all day. "It's Cramer. I gotta take this."

"Sure. Go ahead," she says.

When I answer, Cramer is whispering. "Where are you?" he asks.

"At lunch downtown. Why? What's up?"

"A couple of Nia's friends are here at the station. They say they have something."

"Did they say what it is?"

"No, I haven't sat down with them yet. How soon can you get back here?"

I can feel Rosalind watching me, but I don't look at her. "Give me ten minutes."

"Alright, make it fast."

He doesn't wait for my response. The line goes dead in my ear.

"I'm sorry. I gotta run," I say.

She smiles politely, but I can tell she's disappointed that our lunch has been cut short. "It's fine. I get it."

"Something just came up with the case." I place enough cash on the table to cover the meals. "Cramer needs me back at the station ASAP."

"Go take care of work," she says. "We can catch up later."

I head for the door. I take one last look back at her before walking out of the restaurant. Whatever this is—whatever information Nia's friends have, I hope it's worth it.

———

Back at the station, Cramer has already set everyone up in an interrogation room. When I arrive, I recognize Nia's friends as the young students from the day we'd delivered the death notification at the station. They're seated at the far end of the table, their faces tense with worry.

I close the room door and take a seat next to Cramer. "Hey everyone, sorry I'm late."

"It's ok," Cramer says. He looks across the table at the young pair. "We were just getting acquainted. This is Tori James and Tre Thomas."

"We've met," I say. "You all were at the station the day we found Nia's body. What brings you all in today?"

Tori looks nervously at Tre, and he places his hand on her shoulder. "Go ahead. Show them."

She reaches into her pocket and places a crumpled napkin down on the table. She snatches her hand away quickly, putting as much distance between herself and the object as possible. I carefully unfold the napkin. Lying in the middle of the table is Nia's necklace—the same one that was reported missing from the crime scene. There are traces of what looks to be dried blood on the small pendant and caked between several of the chain's links.

"Where did you find this?" I ask.

"I found it this morning." Her voice shakes as she stares at the necklace. "It was in one of my aunt's bags."

"Your aunt? Who is your aunt?"

"Her name is Lyn—I mean Evelyn. Evelyn Shaw."

Cramer turns to me. "You recognize that name?"

"No, I don't. How did you come to find this?"

"I'm living with her right now while I'm in school," she explains. "When I was leaving home today, I saw that she'd left her closet light on.

I went to turn it off, but I knocked over one of her bags. The necklace fell out of the bag."

"Do you know any reason why she would have this?" I ask. "Did she know Nia Bryant?"

"Nia was my best friend. We hung out all the time, and she was always over at my aunt's house visiting me. So yes, she knew her."

"What was the nature of their relationship?"

"I don't know," she says. "Aunt Lyn seemed to like her. She would always tell me to invite her over for dinner. I never got the impression that she didn't like Nia."

"So, you have no idea why she would have this? Or how she came to have it in her possession?"

She shakes her head. "I don't know how she got it."

Tre finally breaks his silence. "There's something else we need to show you."

He slides a medium-sized photo across the table toward us. The photo is several years old and is slightly frayed around the edges. I notice Congressman Bryant. He's smiling happily in the photo next to another man I don't recognize. Mrs. Bryant is in the photo as well, standing alongside Diana's mother, Patricia. I also notice another woman in the photo—a woman standing in the arms of the congressman. I bring the photo close to my face and the woman's face comes into full view.

"I recognize her," I say.

Cramer grabs the photo from my hands. "Who?"

"The woman standing with Congressman Bryant. I recognize her from the vigil."

Cramer looks at me, confused.

"Remember I told you that I thought I saw someone watching the Congressman? A woman who I thought he recognized?"

Cramer's eyes grow wide as he stares at the photo.

"That's her. I only caught a glimpse of her face, but I'm almost sure that's her."

Tori gulps and points a shaky finger at the woman. "That's my Aunt Lyn."

An unsettling feeling comes over me. Nia's parents, Diana's mom, and this Evelyn woman all know each other from years earlier, but what does it have to do with our investigation?

As I stare at the photo, I notice the jackets that the women are wearing. "This woman is Diana's mother, Patricia. Did you all know that?"

"Yes," says Tre, "I've seen her in some of Diana's photos."

"Mrs. Bryant confirmed that she and Patricia are line sisters. They pledged together. Tori, your aunt has on the same jacket. So I'm assuming she's a member of the same sorority, Kappa Theta Theta?"

Tori nods. "I never knew before today, but when I saw the photo, I put it all together. There's so much I don't know about her. First her relationship with Nia's dad, and now the sorority. And apparently, she not only goes by Lyn ... but Evie as well."

"Did you say Evie?" I say, lifting my eyes from the photo.

Tori flips the picture, and I see that someone has written something on the back. I read the names slowly. *Dwight. Ray. Evie. Cassandra. Patricia.*

"So, this Evie ... is your Aunt Lyn?"

"Yes. Aunt Lyn is my dad's sister. The family has always called her Lyn—short for Evelyn. But I think—I think her college friends knew her as Evie."

I glance over at Cramer sitting quietly next to me. "The sorority advisor, Maggie Price, mentioned an Evie at the courthouse yesterday. She said that someone named Evie stopped by the sorority house on the day of the probate."

"Really? You never told me this."

"It was weird. When she mentioned the name, Patricia started acting strangely. I asked who Evie was. Patricia kind of brushed it off, but I could tell there was something bothering her. She seemed almost scared when Ms. Price mentioned the name."

Cramer turns to Tre. "Where did you find this picture?"

"It's my uncle's." He points at the other man in the photo standing next to Congressman Bryant, the one I don't recognize. "My uncle Ray. He pledged Lambda Nu Phi with Nia's dad. I found it in his photo collection. I've seen the photo before, but never thought much about it until Tori told me how she found the necklace. That's when I realized I recognized her aunt from the night of the vigil."

"Tori, do you know anything about your aunt and Congressman Bryant?"

"Not before today," she says. "I had never even met Mr. Bryant until a few days ago when we found out about Nia's death. Aunt Lyn has never mentioned him before."

"Well, it looks like they definitely have history."

"And she's wearing Nia's necklace." Tori points at her aunt's neck in the photo, and I notice the necklace. It's wrapped around Evelyn's neck and appears to be the exact same necklace as Nia Bryant's necklace—the same one that is now sitting on the table in front of us, stained with blood.

"It looks like the same one," I say.

"It is the same one," Tori says matter-of-factly. "Nia told me that necklace was one of a kind. It belonged to her late grandmother. Her dad gave it to her mom when they got married."

"So there's no way it could be a duplicate?"

"It's the same one. I'm sure of it."

"This has to be connected somehow," I say out loud, more to myself than to them. "Tori, what can you tell me about Evelyn?"

"To be honest, I don't really know much about her," she says. "I'm not that close to my dad's side of the family. He died when I was young, and his family lived across the country from us when I was growing up. When it was time for me to go to college, my mom reached out to her because she knew Aunt Lyn lived near MSU."

"And you live with her now?"

"Yes. She offered me a room in her house after my first semester. It made sense to move with her since she's not charging me to stay there."

"Before you moved in, was she living alone?"

"Yes, she got divorced a few years ago. I never met her ex-husband, so I don't know much about him."

"Do you know his name?"

"It was Curtis, I think." She shakes her head. "I'm sorry; you must think I'm horrible for knowing so little."

"No, no," I say. "It's fine. You're being very helpful, believe me."

"And you've never heard her talk negatively about Nia or the Bryants?" asks Cramer.

"No, not about Nia. But ..." Her voice trails off, and she looks over at Tre.

"But?"

"My uncle mentioned something today when we asked him about the photo," Tre says, cutting in.

"Ok, and what was that?"

"My uncle told us that Evelyn and Mr. Bryant dated in college for a few years. But he said Mr. Bryant broke it off with her and started dating his current wife."

"Apparently, Mrs. Bryant and my aunt were friends before this all happened," says Tori.

Cramer turns and looks at me. "And not just friends—sorority sisters. Which means she also knows what goes on in the sorority."

"I got the impression things ended badly between them," Tre continues. "Uncle Ray didn't go into too much detail, but whatever happened, it sounds like it was bad."

I look back at the photo as I try to make sense of it all. This Evelyn Shaw woman had been nowhere on our radar during the investigation, but now she has my attention. Someone else was there that night, someone who knew where the girls would be. Someone who knew their routine, even down to their clothing.

"So what happens next?" asks Tori.

"We're definitely going to have to look into this further," I say.

"I can't believe this is happening," she says. "Things just keep getting worse and worse. If she did this, I don't know what I'm going to do."

"I'm going to ask you both not to mention what you've found to anyone. We need some time to dig into this."

Tori doesn't respond. She stares angrily at the wall behind us.

"Tori, do you have somewhere you can stay?"

"You can stay with me," Tre says to her. "I don't think you should be in the same house with her if she's involved."

She shakes her head. "I can't stay out again. Besides, she will know something is up when she gets home and the necklace is gone. If she did what I think she did, I want to be there. I want her to look me in the eyes and tell me why."

"Tori, as I said, we need you to be discreet about this," I say. "Just give us twenty-four hours to check things out. Stay with Tre tonight, and we will try to have some answers for you tomorrow."

She seems to consider the idea. "We would all feel more comfortable if you didn't go home," I say. "At least until we get to the bottom of this."

She's reluctant but agrees. "Ok."

"May we hang onto the photo?" I ask Tre.

"Yeah, sure," he says. "I don't think my uncle is going to go looking for it tonight after all this time."

"Well, we thank you both for coming in," I say. "I know this wasn't easy, but you've given us some very valuable information. You're both free to go."

They gather their things, and I open the door as they prepare to leave.

"We'll be in touch with you both soon. In the meantime, please try to go about business as usual. If Evelyn is associated in some way, we don't want to tip her off."

Tori and Tre say their goodbyes and walk out of the interview room. I can hear their footsteps receding as they head down the steps toward the exit.

"I didn't see this coming at all," says Cramer.

"Me neither," I say. "The question is, what was Evelyn doing with this necklace? And there looks to be blood on it. Of course, we'll have to have it tested to verify that it's Nia's."

"And we now know this Evelyn has some bad blood with the Bryants."

"You know when we first interviewed the Bryants, we asked them if they could think of anyone who would want to hurt Nia or who would want to hurt them."

"Yeah, and they couldn't think of anyone," he says.

"Exactly, but now we know Congressman Bryant was romantically involved with this woman before Cassandra Bryant."

"Uh huh, for several years at that," he says.

"And to make things even more complicated, this Evelyn woman and Cassandra Bryant are part of the same sorority. Tori says she thinks they were friends at some point. I think we need to find out what happened between the three of them all those years ago. If we can find out what happened, I think we may be one step closer to finding out what really happened to Nia."

"I think you're right," he says. "Evelyn knew Nia through her niece. She was someone who Nia would've trusted. And she was one of the only people outside of the girls that were there that night that might've known the location."

"That's true," I say. "But there's one thing that's not fitting together?"

"What's that?"

"How does Diana play into all of this?"

My eyes land on Patricia in the photo. She is standing with Cassandra Bryant; her arm wrapped around her shoulder.

I tuck the photo in my file folder. "Let's get the parents in here. I think it's time we make these people talk. One way or another, they're going to tell us what we need to know—whether they want to or not."

Chapter 40

Evie

The necklace is gone.

I can feel the panic creeping in, the dread building in the pit of my stomach. I yank open the door to my closet. My eyes dart frantically from left to right. I start ripping through everything—clothes, shoes, purses—I toss it all on the closet floor. I tear through it all in a matter of minutes until nothing is as it was. The once perfectly organized space is now destroyed—a gaping hole stretching out in front of me.

I scramble to my feet and run back into my bedroom. The bag is still sitting on the edge of my bed. I grab it and turn it upside down for what seems like the hundredth time, pumping my arms as I unload its contents onto the bed. Everything falls out—a makeup pallet, pens, scrap pieces of paper—everything except the necklace.

I toss the empty bag to the floor and run out of my bedroom. I am halfway down the hall when I notice Tori's room door partially open. The sound of my heavy breathing fills the empty space. Suddenly, a thought occurs to me.

I go to her room and push the door open wide. Her bed is still made, but a pair of crumpled jeans have been left in the middle of the floor. A jar of hair gel sits open on her dresser next to a brush. She's been home at some point during the day. I begin pulling open drawers and tossing her clothes out onto the floor. I search every inch of the room, even the large walk-in closet, but I find nothing.

The necklace isn't here.

I sit down on the edge of Tori's bed and try to catch my breath. It wasn't supposed to go like this. This wasn't part of the plan. Tori was never supposed to get involved—to find out the truth.

I bring my knees to my chest and rock my body back and forth. Tori won't keep this to herself—I'm sure of that. She and Nia were close, and she'll do anything to find out what happened to her. She has no loyalty to me—nor I to her.

I try calling her. It rings once before going to voicemail. I dial again, but she doesn't answer. She knows what I did—and now she's dodging me.

Run, I think to myself. *Run while you still have time.*

Running would be the smart thing to do. I could pack my bags and withdraw all my money. I could disappear—I've already done it once before. It's the only thing that makes sense, the only way out of this. I should be scrambling right now, throwing everything I can fit into an overnight bag and taking off before the police have a chance to figure out what really happened.

But I don't move from the bed.

My breathing begins to slow as a calmness comes over me.

I'm *not* running anymore.

It's time for the world to know what *really* happened—what those closest to me tried to bury. It's time for them to answer for what they did.

CHAPTER 41

CHRIS

PATRICIA IS THE FIRST TO ARRIVE. SHE ENTERS THE STATION a little before 5 p.m., accompanied by her lawyer and her husband. She still wears the same unfriendly expression from our first meeting, and I brace myself for what is sure to be a difficult interview. When I approach them at the information desk, I overhear her speaking to the on-duty officer in a nasty tone. It isn't long before she refocuses her anger on me.

"What is this all about?" she asks. "What reason do you have to call me down here?"

"Good afternoon," I say. "Thank you for coming in."

She scowls at me. "Detective, what is going on here?"

"If you all would follow me, we just have a few questions that we'd like to clear up. Is that ok?"

Patricia doesn't move. She glances at her lawyer, and he nods his head at her. She turns back to me, her hands on her hips. "Fine. But I want my lawyer and my husband in the room."

I lead them up the stairs to the second floor and show them to an empty interrogation room. Cramer joins us inside and pulls me to the side.

"We were able to make contact with the ex-husband," he whispers to me. "He's agreed to come in and speak with us."

"Oh, thank God."

"He doesn't live too far away. He says it'll take him thirty minutes to an hour, depending on traffic."

"Ok, and what about the Bryants?"

"They should be here soon too. I told Jacobs to let us know when everyone arrives."

"Ok, well, we better get started."

Patricia and the others are watching us impatiently.

"Thank you all for your patience," I say. "This is my partner Detective Albert Cramer. We're leading the Nia Bryant murder case."

Cramer takes a seat next to me. "Nice to meet you all."

"The reason we called you in is because we just need a little help clearing some things up, Mrs. McNamee," I say.

"It's not Mrs. McNamee," Patricia snaps. "It's Mrs. Grimes."

"Oh, my apologies."

"McNamee is my maiden name. I've been married for quite some time now."

"Well, Mrs. Grimes, we wanted to ask you about your relationship with Cassandra Bryant," I say.

"What about it?"

"What is the extent of your relationship? Where'd you meet? Whatever you can tell us to help us to get a better understanding of how you two came to know each other."

Patricia glances at her lawyer again. "It's ok, Pat," he says. "You can answer the question."

She turns back to us and crosses her hands on the table. "Cassandra and I are line sisters. We pledged together when we went to MSU."

"So you met in college?"

"Yes."

"And you remained friends after college?"

"Yes. Well, we kept in touch. I lived overseas for about fifteen years, so we mainly talked on the phone and kept in touch on social media."

"So, would you say that you two are close?"

"We were close in college. We talked on and off over the years after graduating, but I wouldn't say we're best friends."

"I see."

"That tends to happen when you move across the globe," she says. "You aren't always able to maintain those same relationships."

"Yes, we spoke to Mrs. Bryant, and she tells a similar story. Since you both are in the same sorority, we assumed that maybe Diana and Nia knew each other before coming to MSU. But now we know that's not the case."

"She's right; they never met. Diana was born here in the States, but it didn't work out with her father. I met my husband shortly after her first birthday. Once we were married, we all picked up and moved overseas for his work in the military. We didn't come back to the States until Diana's senior year of high school. So the girls never met before coming here."

"Ok," I say. "Well, what about her husband? How is your relationship with Congressman Bryant?"

Patricia frowns. "What does Dwight have to do with this?"

I take the photo from the file folder and slide it across the table in her direction. The color drains from her face.

"Where did you get this?" Her hand shakes as she reaches out to touch the photo.

"We uncovered it today," I say. "Can you confirm that that's you in the photo?"

She nods her head slowly. "Yes, it's me."

"And this woman here?" I ask, pointing at Evelyn Shaw. "Do you know her?"

"What does this have to do with the case?" She looks over at her lawyer, but he appears confused as well.

"Mrs. Grimes, just answer the question," says Cramer. "Do you know this woman?"

Her husband places his hand on her shoulder and finally speaks. "Pat? What is it? What's wrong?"

She looks at him briefly before turning to face us. "Yes, I know her. That's Evie."

"Evie," I say. "Evelyn is her real name, correct?"

"Yes, but we all called her Evie."

"And how do you know Evelyn, or Evie as you call her?"

"She's my other line sister."

"So, you and Evelyn and Cassandra Bryant all pledged together?"

"Yes, that's right."

"Looking at this photo, I can only assume that there was some history between this Evie person and Dwight Bryant. Am I correct in my assumption?"

"Y—yes," she stammers. "Evie and Dwight dated in college."

"Ok. So, what can you tell us about Evelyn Shaw and Dwight Bryant?"

Patricia takes a deep breath and exhales slowly. "I don't even know where to begin with that. It was so long ago, and I still haven't forgiven myself for what we did."

Chapter 42

Chris

"Evie and I used to be best friends." Patricia stares at the faded photo and smiles for the first time. "It's hard to believe that now, but we were inseparable back in college."

"Even closer than you were to Cassandra Bryant?" I ask.

"Cassandra came after, so yes. Evie and I were like sisters. We did everything together. And it was like that for a while."

She points at the small photo lying in the middle of the table. "I even remember when this picture was taken. It was Spring of '98. We had all gone to campus to see the new Lambda Nu Phi spring line. Evie, Cass, and I had just crossed into the sorority a few months before, and we were really excited for the guys, especially because Dwight had pledged."

"How long had Evie and Dwight been dating?" asks Cramer.

"They started dating during our freshman year. So almost three years at this point. They were really in love, or so it seemed. I was genuinely happy for Evie. Dwight seemed perfect for her."

The smile suddenly fades from her face as she reaches to pick up the photo. "But this picture is probably one of the last pictures of them together. Actually, now that I think about it, things were probably already in motion at this point. I just didn't know it at the time."

"What happened between them?" I ask.

"Cassandra happened. When Cass came into the picture, everything went to shit ... and fast."

"Can you tell us about that?"

"Evie and I decided to pledge Kappa Theta Theta the semester before. We were excited, and we knew we wanted to do it together. That's when we met Cass."

"So you didn't know Mrs. Bryant before that time?"

"Not really," she says. "She was a year younger than us. I recall seeing her around campus, but we'd never spoken or anything."

"So you all got selected to be on the pledge line," I say. "How was that?"

"It was rough. But the process brought us all closer. There were eight of us total on the line. By the time we crossed, we were all like sisters. But me, Evie, and Cass were really close."

"So things were good between them initially? Between Evie and Cassandra?"

"Yes, things were good. They really seemed to click, and I kind of got looped in because of my friendship with Evie. After that, the three of us began to hang out all the time." She pauses and puts the photo back on the table. "But it didn't last long."

"What happened?"

"One day, shortly after we crossed, we were at Evie's place hanging out, and Dwight showed up. Cass had never officially been introduced to him before that time."

"So Evelyn introduced them?"

"Yes, she did. It seemed fine. I didn't notice anything at the time, but that quickly changed. A couple of weeks later, I noticed a change in Cass. I couldn't quite put my finger on it, but I knew something was off. She was acting strange and distant. And she wasn't coming around as much. Every time we called her to meet up or hang out, she had an excuse."

"And that was unlike her?"

"It was very unlike her. But I didn't think too much about it. I just figured she was busy or had her own things going on. Plus, I was seeing someone new at the time, so I was kind of wrapped up in my own stuff.

But one day, it all came to the surface. I was on campus late after a study hall at the library one day. I was walking back to my car, and I noticed Cassandra's car parked not too far from mine. It looked like someone was in the backseat, so I walked over to the car, and that's when I caught them."

"What did you see?"

"Dwight and Cassandra. They were having sex … right there in the backseat of her car."

Tears form in her eyes, and her voice begins to quiver as she fights to hold them back. "I was so shocked; I couldn't believe what I was seeing. I started banging on the window."

"What did they say when they saw you?"

"They were just as shocked as I was! Cass was crying and kept saying how sorry she was. Dwight kept begging me not to say anything to Evie."

"And did you?"

She lowers her eyes. "I didn't. Looking back on things, I know I should've; after all, Evie was my best friend. But I decided to stay out of it. I knew it would crush her, and I didn't want to be the cause of that."

"But I take it Evelyn found out?" Cramer asks.

"Not initially," she says. "Things actually seemed to return to normal for a while. Cass was back to her normal self and coming around more. I thought she and Dwight had kept their word—but I was wrong. Everything sort of came to a head the fall of our senior year. Evie ended up getting pregnant."

"By Dwight?"

"Yes. She came to me one day while we were on campus and swore me to secrecy. She told me she was pregnant."

"And what about Dwight? How did he take the news?"

"Well, let's just say he wasn't too thrilled," she says, rolling her eyes. "That surprised Evie because she told me that they had always talked about starting a family."

"But he wasn't happy?"

"Not at all. It caused a big thing between them. He used the excuse that he was young and wasn't ready for a baby. But Evie was over the moon, and she decided to give him time. She thought that he would eventually come around to the idea of being a dad."

She looks at the photo again. "But he didn't. I remember Evie came to me crying a few weeks later because they'd just had a huge fight. Dwight wanted her to terminate the pregnancy. She was heartbroken."

"That had to have been difficult for her," I say.

"It was. But getting an abortion wasn't an option for Evie at that point. She really wanted that baby. And that's when ..." She stops mid-sentence and glances at her lawyer again.

"It's ok, Pat," he says. "Tell them."

"And that's when what?" I ask.

She turns back to us and sighs. "That's when Dwight came to me."

I glance over at Cramer, but he looks almost as confused as me. "He came to you for what?"

"You have to understand—I didn't mean to hurt her. I didn't mean for anything bad to happen."

"What did he come to you for?" I ask again.

"He came to me, and he asked me to convince Evie to get an abortion. He knew how close we were. If it was anyone she would listen to, it was me."

"And what did you do?"

"At first, I flat out told him no! I was so angry at him for even asking me to do such a thing."

"At first?"

"Yeah, at first. But then he started spilling everything, and I knew Evie was fucked. He admitted to me that he and Cass were still seeing each other. He told me that he was in love with her and had been planning for months to find a way to tell Evie. According to him, there was nothing left between them. He wanted out of the relationship."

"But then the pregnancy happened?"

"Right. He didn't see a way out except to convince Evie to get rid of the baby so that he could be with Cass. If Evie had a baby by him, he could kiss his relationship with Cass goodbye. So, he asked for my help."

"And did you?" I ask. "Did you help him?"

"Like I said, at first, I refused. But Dwight came from money—a lot of it. And me, I wasn't so fortunate."

A single tear falls down her cheek. She wipes it away quickly. "I struggled all through college. The only reason I was even able to go to MSU was on an academic scholarship. My mom was a single mom with five other kids at home, and I was the oldest. Money was always tight, and I sometimes had to work two jobs while still attending school in order to support myself and send money home to my family."

"So he offered you money?"

"Yes, and at the time, it seemed like a fortune."

"How much did he offer you?"

"Five grand. He told me it was mine—all cash and no strings attached. He wrote me a check right then and there. I just needed to convince Evie to go through with it."

"So you took the money?"

"I met up with Evie a few days later at campus, and I convinced her to get rid of the baby. I know it sounds bad, but I need you to understand that it wasn't just about the money. I knew what was going on between Cass and Dwight and that he wanted to end the relationship with Evie. I knew she would be a single mother if she had that baby. I couldn't help but think of my own mother and the way I had watched her struggle for so many years. I didn't want that for Evie, so I told her maybe it wasn't a bad idea. Dwight had told her he wasn't ready for a baby. I told her it would probably strain their relationship and run him away."

"And she went for that?"

She looks me square in the eyes. "You don't understand, Detective —Evie *loved* Dwight. She would do anything for him. The last thing she wanted was for him to leave her. So when I said that, I could see something change in her. She wanted the baby, but she couldn't stand to lose Dwight. She practically worshipped him."

"But you knew he already had one foot out the door."

"That's true; I did. I know it sounds awful, but I didn't have the heart to tell her."

"So, did she go forward with the abortion?" Cramer asks.

"I helped her set everything up," she continues. "It was supposed to be a simple procedure—in and out. I went with her to support her, to be there for her. But they wouldn't let me go back. I wish I had insisted because something went wrong."

"Wrong? How?"

"The procedure didn't take long. She stayed with me for a few days while she recovered, but she seemed to be getting worse. Four or five days later, I had to rush her to the hospital. She had a high fever and was in a lot of pain. They ended up admitting her."

"Do you know what was wrong?"

"She had an infection. They suspected improper techniques were used during her abortion. By the time she made it to the hospital, she was already septic. If we had waited another day or two, she probably would've died."

"Wow," I say. "That's awful."

"She was discharged, thankfully, but she became really withdrawn after that. I think she went through some sort of depression. She didn't want to talk to anyone, not even me. But it didn't matter because things fell apart between us shortly after that when everything came out."

"She found out about the deal you'd made with Dwight?"

"Evie was barely out of the hospital when Dwight broke things off," she says. "He didn't even have the fucking decency to wait until she had completely healed. He told her that he didn't want to be with her anymore—that he loved someone else. Cassandra."

"And how did she take that?"

"Not good. A few days after the breakup, I went to her place to check on her. I hadn't heard from her, and she wasn't returning my calls. I found her on the floor in her apartment. She had slit her wrists and was bleeding out. I called 911, and they came and picked her up."

My mouth drops. Her lawyer, who has maintained a stoic expression during the interview thus far, looks shocked.

"She tried to kill herself?" I ask.

"Yes," she says. "She was committed and spent three days in the psych ward at the hospital."

"So, how did she find out about your agreement with Congressman Bryant?"

"I went to pick her up after they let her out of the ward. I still had the check that he had written out to me in the center console of my car.

After everything that happened, I didn't have the heart to cash it. I felt like everything Evie was going through was my fault."

Tears form in her eyes again. "I stopped to get gas after picking her up and went into the station to pay. When I got back in the car, she was holding the check and asked me what it was for."

"So you told her?"

She begins sobbing. Mr. Grimes reaches for the tissue box sitting in the middle of the table and hands it to her. "I couldn't lie to Evie," she cries. "I told her about everything—the money, Dwight and Cass—everything. I thought if I told the truth, we could start over with a clean slate. I loved Evie, and I told her I was only looking out for her."

"I take it that didn't happen?"

She shakes her head. "She was so angry with me. She told me that I didn't care about her—that I was only thinking about myself. She got out of the car and went inside the gas station and called a cab. She wouldn't even let me drive her home."

"So that's how it ended between you two?"

"I never saw Evie again after that," she says, dabbing her eyes. "I found out a couple of days later that she withdrew from the university. I felt horrible that things ended that way between us."

We all sit quietly for several minutes as we try to absorb everything. Patricia continues to sob quietly, and Mr. Grimes wraps his arms around her as he tries to comfort her. "Why are you all asking about this woman now?" he asks. "How does this relate to Diana and what happened to Nia Bryant?"

"Evie is now a person of interest in this case," Cramer says. "We can't disclose too much, but we have reason to believe she may have been involved."

Patricia gasps and sits up in her chair. She suddenly looks terrified. "What? What did she do?"

"As my partner said, we can't go into much detail," I say.

She turns and looks at her husband. Her bottom lip trembles as she speaks. "Ms. Maggie, she—she said something about Evie showing up the day of the probate."

"Pat, please calm—"

She interrupts him and turns to face us. "She did this, didn't she? Evie did this?"

"Mrs. Grimes, we are just trying to piece this all together," I say. "We don't know for sure yet."

She scoots back from the table and jumps to her feet. "Oh, God! I think I'm going to be sick!"

Mr. Grimes reaches out to stop her, but she makes a run for the door. He follows behind her, shouting her name as he tries to keep up. Suddenly, Detective Jacobs appears in the doorway of the interrogation room. "Everything ok?"

"It's fine," I say. "She just needed a break. We're just finishing up."

"Good. Because Evelyn Shaw's ex-husband is here."

CHAPTER 43

CHRIS

Curtis Shaw is pacing nervously back and forth in the next room. He is a tall, lanky man and is dressed in a long-sleeved business shirt with matching slacks. He has undone the knot in his tie and draped it over his broad shoulders.

"Good afternoon, Mr. Shaw."

"Detective Cramer? Are you Detective Cramer?" he asks.

"Um, no, I'm Detective Chris Evans. Detective Cramer is my partner."

"Well, I was contacted by a Detective Cramer. He asked me to come down."

"Yes, that's correct. We have some questions for you about a case that we're working."

"Is Detective Cramer coming? Should we wait for him?"

"He's actually finishing up another interview right now. Please, why don't you have a seat."

He doesn't make a move to sit down right away and glances uncomfortably at the door.

"If he finishes before we're done here, I'll have him join us," I say. "Please sit, Mr. Shaw. Is there anything I can get for you before we start?"

He shakes his head and finally takes a seat in an empty chair. "I'm fine. What is this about? He mentioned something about my ex-wife."

I take a seat in the chair across from him. "Yes, sir. That's correct. Detective Cramer and I have been working the murder case of Nia Bryant."

"The college student that went missing?"

"You're familiar with the case?"

"How can I not be? It's been all over the news."

"Well, we've come across some evidence that seems to tie your ex-wife to the case, and we would like to clear up some things based on information we've gathered thus far."

He looks down at the table and whispers to himself. "Dammit, Lyn! What did you do?"

"Excuse me?"

His eyes meet mine. "I knew something like this would happen. She just couldn't let it go."

"What? What couldn't she let go?"

"Dwight Bryant. She had this hatred for him. Actually, hatred is a nice way of putting it—she detested the man."

"So you're aware of their history?"

"I know enough. Lyn didn't like to talk about it too much, but I found out over the years the whole story."

"How long were you married to Evelyn?"

"We were married a little over ten years. We divorced a few years ago."

"If I may ask, what led to your divorce?"

"There just wasn't anything there anymore. The last few years were rough, and we weren't equipped to handle it."

"Can you tell me what happened?"

He leans back in his chair. "Things started to go bad when we tried to start a family. It just wasn't happening for us."

"So you had problems conceiving?"

"Yeah. It didn't bother me as much. I was happy at the time as long as I was with her. But Evelyn always wanted children."

"That type of thing can really put a strain on a marriage."

"Yes, it did. We tried for years and saw countless specialists. Evelyn was consumed by it, and every day she became more and more obsessed. We grew apart. We started arguing more, and our finances took a hit because we spent thousands on fertility treatments. I was working double, sometimes triple overtime, to try and keep our heads above water. But she was never satisfied. Nothing could replace her want for a child, and it eventually became too much. I began to feel like all she cared about was a baby. I wanted more out of life—and I wanted more in a wife than what she was giving me. After ten years, I couldn't take it anymore, and I told her I wanted a divorce."

"How did she take that?"

"Well, I think she had been expecting it for a while. She didn't put up a fight. It was actually very amicable."

"Really? You don't hear that too often."

"Surprisingly, yes. We agreed on the terms. It went relatively smoothly ... not like some of those nasty divorces you hear horror stories about."

"Well, you're a lucky guy in that sense."

"I guess you can say that," he says. "It was hard emotionally on me. I loved Evelyn—and in a way, I'll always love her. But I always felt like I was paying for what he had done to her."

"For what Congressman Bryant had done?"

"Yes. In the beginning, she told me a little about what happened. She told me about Dwight Bryant and how he had left her for his current wife when they were in college. She told me they used to be friends. The breakup devastated her, so much so that she had even tried to hurt herself. But it wasn't until years later that I finally found out the whole truth. When we started trying for a baby, Evelyn was diagnosed with Asherman's Syndrome."

"Asherman's Syndrome? What is that?"

"I don't really know too much about it, but from what I know, there's usually some scarring in the uterus. In severe cases, it can cause infertility."

"So I'm assuming she had a severe case?"

"Very severe. Her doctor said it was one of the worst that he had ever seen. It can happen from a few things. In Lyn's case, he thinks it happened as a result of an abortion she had in college."

I think back to the interview with Patricia Grimes and her mention of an abortion she'd convinced Evelyn to have at Dwight Bryant's request. Mr. Shaw's story is beginning to tie everything together.

"Lyn was devastated," he says. "And that's when she told me she had gotten pregnant by Dwight in college. She told me he didn't want the baby and bribed one of her friends to convince her to terminate."

"So you think she blamed him?"

"Oh, I don't think—I know she blamed him," he says. "She changed so much after the diagnosis, and things started going downhill with us. She was never the same."

"Since things ended amicably between you two, do you still keep in contact with Evelyn?"

He shakes his head. "No, I remarried. My new wife, Veronica, and I just welcomed our first baby."

"Oh! Well, congratulations! Boy or girl?"

"Thank you!" he says, smiling proudly. "It's a girl. She just turned eight weeks this past Sunday."

"Well, that's some good news. And I know with a newborn things can be hectic, so I won't hold you much longer. I'm sure you need to be getting home. I just have one more question, if that's ok?"

"Sure, what is it?"

"Did Evelyn ever show any erratic behavior during or after your marriage? Anything that ever made you think she could be capable of harming someone?"

"No, not while we were married," he says. "But something did happen a couple of months ago right after my daughter was born."

"Can you tell me about that?"

"It was the day after my wife had given birth, and we were still in the hospital. We got a delivery to the room. It was from Evelyn."

"A delivery?"

"Yes, some flowers and a balloon. Nothing major. There was a small card that came with it, and it said congratulations from Evelyn."

"That's odd. And you hadn't had any contact with her?"

He shakes his head. "We haven't spoken in years. I don't even know how she knew about the pregnancy—better yet, how she even knew where to send the flowers. How did she even know about the birth?"

"That's interesting. Maybe she follows you guys on social media, and you didn't know."

"Yeah, that's the only thing I could think of. Maybe she had a fake account. My wife posted a birth announcement on her account after the birth, so it's possible. Anyway, it completely freaked Veronica out. She had the nurse throw out the arrangement. She made me change the locks at our house. I even had the alarm company come out to reset our alarm code."

"Well, I can understand her concern. That had to have been frightening."

"Oh yeah, I'll admit it was creepy. And Veronica was coping with being a new mom. I just wanted to do what I could to help her feel comfortable coming home with the baby."

"Has anything happened since then?"

"No, nothing. I pretty much put it out of my mind—that was until I got the call today to come in and talk to you guys."

"Well, I'm glad you took the call seriously and took the time to drive all the way over here. I know you don't live in the area."

"It's fine," he says. "I just hope Evelyn is ok. Even after everything, I still care about her. She's a good woman, Detective. She just has some demons she's dealing with."

"Well, what you've disclosed today helps answer some questions for us."

"Can you tell me what's going on?" he asks. "What is she accused of?"

"I'm sorry, I can't say just yet. We are still investigating."

"But I thought an arrest was made? Why are you guys looking at Lyn?"

"That's true; we had a suspect. But some new information has come up that we are looking into. That's all I can tell you right now."

He lets out a frustrated sigh. "Fine, ok."

"Well, I won't hold you any longer," I say. "Thank you again for coming down."

He stands and shakes my hand. "Anytime. I hope it all works out."

When we step out of the room, Mr. Shaw pauses outside of the doorway. He stares at something at the other end of the hall, and I look to see what he's looking at. The Bryants have just arrived and are being led down the hall by another detective. They disappear into one of the interrogation rooms.

"That's him," he says. "That's Dwight Bryant."

I place my hand on his back and lead him toward the stairs. "Come on, let's go."

We walk down the stairs to the station entrance, and I hand him my business card. "It was nice meeting you, Mr. Shaw. If you think of anything else that may be useful, don't hesitate to give me a call."

"Have a good night, Detective." He slides the card into his jacket pocket and walks out of the station. I watch him until he is safely in his car.

Back upstairs, Cramer is standing in the hall waiting for me. "I just spoke to Jacobs," he says. "They reviewed some of the surveillance footage again from the businesses surrounding Nia Bryant's apartment from that night."

"And did they see anything new?"

"Footage from the gas station across the street shows a car matching the description of Evelyn Shaw's vehicle parked in the gas station parking lot on the night of the murder."

"Were we able to get a visual of her near the vehicle?"

"Unfortunately, no. The way the vehicle was parked provided us with a view of the trunk area. Her license plate was in full view, which was how they were able to match it up. But there was a blind spot on the driver's side, so they were unable to make an ID on her."

"Well, I think that should at least be enough for a warrant," I say. "Her car was in the vicinity of Nia's apartment. There was a lot of blood in Nia's car. If she was the one who stabbed her, there is probably some blood transfer in her vehicle as well."

"We also found out how she might've exited the apartment complex. There's a side pedestrian gate that many of the residents use. It's next to the bus stop on the main road. My guess is she ditched Nia's car and exited the complex through that gate and went across the street to where she'd parked her vehicle."

"But how would she have gotten to Groveland Park if her car was parked at the gas station?"

"That's something we're still trying to figure out."

"And were there any cameras near the pedestrian gate?"

"Nope. She would've had a clear path to the gas station without being seen. And at that time of night, there's very little traffic in that area."

"She knew just where to go. It almost seems like she knew the place."

"Exactly what I was thinking," he says. "So, did you get a chance to talk to the ex-husband?"

"I just finished up with him. But how'd it go with Patricia Grimes?"

"The woman was hysterical. It took fifteen minutes just to get her to calm down. I sent them home and told them we'll call if anything else comes up."

"Well, now we just have to talk to the Bryants."

"Wait, aren't you going to tell me what happened with the ex-husband?"

"Yeah, let's get out of the hall."

We move into the employee's lounge. I spend the next few minutes recounting for him my conversation with Mr. Shaw. He listens carefully and waits until I'm done before speaking. "So that's it, huh? That was the trigger?"

"I think it was a culmination of things," I say. "Her niece and Nia were friends. Seeing Nia on a regular basis was probably a constant reminder of Dwight Bryant."

"And then her ex-husband remarries and finally has a child of his own."

"Exactly! She had to watch again as another man that she once loved moved on with another woman. Everyone was living the life that she felt that she deserved ... everyone except her."

"That's enough to make any person snap," he says.

"I think Evelyn finally got her revenge for what she believes was done to her. I think she killed Nia to get back at Mr. and Mrs. Bryant in some sick way by taking away their only child. And I think she framed Diana to get back at her former best friend. In her eyes, Patricia Grimes is just as responsible for the loss of her unborn child as Dwight Bryant. She was the one who talked her into going through with it."

Cramer seems to be considering my theory. "Patricia betrayed her ... and all for money," he says. "If Diana was convicted of murdering Nia, it would've sent her away for life. That's enough to devastate any mother. Patricia would've lost her daughter as well ... not to death, but to the system."

"You know the saying," I say. "An eye for an eye ..."

He shrugs. "Or, in her case, a child for a child."

CHAPTER 44

CHRIS

THE BRYANTS STARE BLANKLY AT US FROM ACROSS THE interview table. The news we've just broken to them has come as a shock, and minutes pass before they finally speak.

"Evie?" says Mrs. Bryant. "You found evidence linking Evie to Nia's murder?"

"Yes," I say. "Evelyn Shaw."

"Well, what evidence did you find?" asks Congressman Bryant.

I place the evidence bag that contains Nia's necklace on the table. "This was found in her home."

"It's—it's my necklace," says Mrs. Bryant.

"We were told that you passed it down to Nia. Is that correct?"

"It belonged to my mother," says Congressman Bryant. "She died when I was in high school. That was the last thing she gave me before her passing. I gave it to Cassandra on our wedding day, and it was passed down to Nia on her sixteenth birthday."

"I see."

"And you're sure Evie had it?" he asks.

"It was recovered by someone who lives at her residence. It was found amongst her things. We're still working on verifying everything, but the necklace was never found at the crime scene, even though Nia was wearing it before she died. And that information was never released to the public."

"We've already spoken to several people about Ms. Shaw," says Cramer. "Including Patricia Grimes."

The congressman's eyes shift. He looks uncomfortable.

"I—I don't understand," says Mrs. Bryant. "We haven't seen Evie in over twenty years. And you're saying she just popped up out of the blue and murdered our daughter?"

"We don't have all of the answers just yet, but that's what we're thinking," I say.

"But the knife was found on Diana. I'm sorry, but none of this makes sense."

"Actually, I think it makes perfect sense when you put all the pieces together." I turn my attention back to the congressman. "Wouldn't you say so, Congressman Bryant?"

"I'm not sure what you mean?" he says.

"You don't remember seeing Evie the other day at the vigil?"

"I told you I didn't see anyone."

"I know you saw her," I say. "Because I saw her."

Mrs. Bryant's mouth drops. She stares at her husband.

"I saw you two watching each other. But when I asked you about it, you denied seeing someone in the crowd."

"There were a lot of people there that night," he says. "It was dark. It could've been anyone."

I lean forward and look him square in the eyes. "Congressman Bryant, don't lie to me."

"I told you what I saw!"

"Congressman Bryant, we're talking about your daughter here! Do you understand that your daughter is dead? And we're telling you that this woman may be involved. You can help us."

"I'm aware of that, Detective! Don't you think I know that Nia is dead? You don't think I know that she's never coming back?"

"So you're telling me that you didn't see Evelyn Shaw at the vigil?"

"I'm saying that I can't be sure that it was her."

"Ok, fine. Let's try another angle." I take the photo from my file folder and slide it across the table. "This is you with Evelyn Shaw, is it not, Congressman Bryant?"

He looks down at the photo, and his face drops. "Where did you get this?"

"Answer the question. Is that you in the photo?"

"Yes, that's me."

I slide the photo to Mrs. Bryant. "And is that you, Mrs. Bryant?"

She nods. "Yes—yes, that's me. But I don't understand what this has to do—"

"Let me explain. You see, we spoke with Patricia Grimes after uncovering this photo and finding out about the necklace in Ms. Shaw's possession. We had some questions about Evelyn's connection to Nia—only to find out that she's actually connected to you."

"Congressman Bryant, you dated Evelyn Shaw," says Cramer. "Back in college, is that right? She's wearing your mother's necklace in the photo."

He shrugs. "Yeah, so?"

"But things got a little complicated," he says. "You see, we learned that you and Evelyn Shaw dated for several years—that is until you dumped her for her sorority sister."

Mrs. Bryant looks down at her lap and shrinks in her chair.

"You all crept around behind Evelyn's back for months, according to Mrs. Grimes. Isn't that right, Mrs. Bryant?"

She raises her head. She's crying now. "I—I never meant to hurt Evie. I know it was wrong, but Dwight and I were in love."

"What is going on here?" asks Congressman Bryant angrily. "We came here to find out what updates you have on Nia, and here we are in the hot seat!"

"So, you broke things off with her?" asks Cramer.

Congressman Bryant throws his hands up in the air. "Yes—yes, I broke up with my girlfriend. Is that a crime?"

"And the necklace? What's the story with that?"

"I gave her the necklace a few years into our relationship. We were serious, and I thought she was the one. When my mom gave me that necklace, I said that only the woman that I married would wear it."

"So you were planning to marry Ms. Shaw?"

"Look, I was young," he says. "I was a stupid kid. I hadn't proposed or anything, but at that time, I didn't see myself with anyone else. I thought I had it all figured out. But things changed when I met Cass."

"So, you broke up with her? And I'm assuming you took the necklace back?"

"It was my mother's!" he yells. "What was I supposed to do—let my ex keep the family heirloom? Yes, Detective, I took it back."

"How did she take that? I'm sure she was aware of how significant that necklace was to you?"

"She was upset, of course. But I didn't want to keep sneaking around. I had to end it with her so that we could both move on."

"But that's not all you did," I say.

He tenses up. Mrs. Bryant looks over at him and frowns. "What is he talking about, Dwight?"

"Oh, so your wife doesn't know. You never told her?"

"Told me what?" Mrs. Bryant looks from me to her husband.

"You never told your wife about the pregnancy?"

"Pregnancy?" she gasps. "What pregnancy?"

"According to Mrs. Grimes, Evelyn Shaw got pregnant her senior year of college—by your husband."

Congressman Bryant shifts in his seat.

"What?" says Mrs. Bryant. "Evie was pregnant? I never knew!"

"I don't think Ms. Shaw had much time to announce the news," I say. "The pregnancy was terminated early on, isn't that right, Congressman?"

He doesn't respond. His eyes are fixed on the photo on the table.

"What? I don't understand," she says.

"Your husband didn't want the baby," I reveal. "But Evelyn did. She confided in Mrs. Grimes about the pregnancy. According to her, Evelyn was excited to be a mom."

"Yes, but the father wasn't," says Cramer. "He tried to convince her to get rid of the baby, but she didn't budge. He didn't want Evelyn anymore—he wanted to be with you. So, he went to the one person that she trusted—the one person she would listen to. Patricia."

Mrs. Bryant lets out a loud gasp. Her hand goes up to her mouth.

"He offered Mrs. Grimes money to talk to Evelyn—to convince her to get rid of the baby. Luckily for him, his plan worked. Evelyn terminated the pregnancy."

Mrs. Bryant stares at her husband in disbelief. He maintains his silence; his eyes fixed on Cramer and me.

"But things didn't go as planned," I say. "There was a complication, and Evelyn ended up being hospitalized."

She turns back to us. "I remember Evelyn being in the hospital at some point. I never knew why. She was very tight-lipped about it!"

"It was a complication from her abortion. She recovered and was released—only to be dumped not too long after."

"Good God!" whispers Mrs. Bryant. "I never knew she was pregnant."

"That's the whole truth, isn't it, Congressman? But it doesn't just end there."

Now it's his turn to look confused. "What are you talking about?"

"You see, we did a little research on Evelyn Shaw. We even spoke to her ex-husband. That complication she had—it did some major damage."

"What do you mean?" he asks. "What kind of damage?"

"The kind that prevents you from ever bearing children."

His eyes grow wide. "What?"

"Evelyn Shaw, she was never able to have children after that," says Cramer.

"We think this may have something to do with why she targeted you both—as well as Patricia Grimes," I say. "As you can imagine, she wasn't too happy to find out that the advice she'd been given by her best friend was actually at your request."

"So, this was all some sort of revenge?" asks Mrs. Bryant.

"You all went on with life and had families of your own. Evelyn Shaw never got that chance."

"So, you think that she was getting back at us in some way?" he asks. "She blames us for what happened to her?"

"We think when she crossed paths with Nia that it triggered something in her. She wanted to make you all hurt the same way she's been hurting all these years—by taking away your children."

"This is ridiculous!" he says. "You don't know that that's true. Have you even spoken to Evie?"

Mrs. Bryant turns angrily to her husband. "It makes perfect sense to me!"

"What? Cassandra, you can't believe—"

"This is all your fault!"

"My fault! Don't put this all on me! You weren't completely innocent yourself, you know?"

"Don't you dare try to flip this, Dwight! You were the one conspiring behind everyone's back."

The Congressman takes a deep breath as he tries to compose himself. "Cass, you don't understand—"

"You lied to me!"

"I never lied to you! I just didn't tell you everything that went on. I was trying to protect you!"

"Oh fuck off!" she screams. "You were trying to protect yourself, Dwight! It's always been about you!"

He scoots back from the table, knocking over his chair. "Forget this! I don't have to sit here and listen to this!"

Mrs. Bryant jumps to her feet and lunges at him. "I hate you!" she screams. "You killed our daughter!"

She begins pummeling his back with her fists. Me and Cramer move around the table to separate them. I grab the congressman by his arm and pull him toward the door. Cramer holds on to Mrs. Bryant as she tries to wriggle herself free.

"Get your hands off me!" He yanks his arm away from me and storms out of the room. Mrs. Bryant frees herself and screams after him as he disappears down the hall.

"You killed her, Dwight! You killed my baby!"

CHAPTER 45

TORI

JUST GIVE US TWENTY-FOUR HOURS.

I can't get the detective's words out of my head. I sneak a quick look at the clock again. Only a few hours have passed since we were at the police station, but it feels like an eternity.

"Tori, are you alright?" Tre asks.

"Huh?"

"Are you alright? You've barely touched your food." He points to the container of Chinese take-out that has gone cold on my lap.

"I'm not really hungry." I place the lid on the container and move it to the coffee table. "I just keep thinking about everything."

"Like what?"

"I don't know. Little things are beginning to stand out to me, like how Aunt Lyn used to always ask about Nia. It came off as concern, but now I know that she was probably keeping tabs on her. It never occurred to me before now. She was always listening ... always watching. And then ..."

"What? What is it?"

"The night before the probate—I remember she went out."

"Did she say where?"

"No, and I didn't ask. But I remember hearing her come in late after I had already gone to bed. She killed Nia."

He takes my hand in his. "We don't know that for sure. Let's see what the police find."

"I know she did it. It's the only thing that makes sense. She used me. All this time, she was using me to get close to Nia. She built trust with Nia only to turn around and kill her. She's sick." I can feel myself getting angry.

"Maybe she did," he says. "It's nothing you could've done. Some people are just evil."

"I was the one who brought Nia around her! If I hadn't, maybe she would still be alive."

"Do you hear yourself?" he says. "You're blaming yourself for something that was completely out of your control. You didn't know what she was planning ... no one did. You can't blame yourself."

"I just feel hurt—betrayed. She's supposed to be my family."

He wraps his arm around my shoulders and kisses me softly on the forehead. It's the first time he's ever shown any type of affection toward me. "None of this is your fault, Tori. You were a good friend to Nia. She wouldn't want you to blame yourself over this."

He lifts my chin, turns my head toward his, and kisses me gently on the lips. I don't pull away.

He finally releases my lips and smiles. "I've been trying to find the right time to do that."

I can feel myself blushing, and I look at the floor.

"Do you feel better now?"

I take a deep breath, and my body relaxes. "A little."

"Good," he says. "Try and finish your food. I'm going to jump in the shower. I'll be right back."

He goes into the back bedroom. I sit in silence, listening to the distant sound of the shower as I fight the urge to call Detective Evans. Even though hardly any time has passed, I'm anxious to find out if he's found anything connecting Aunt Lyn to Nia. I take a quick glance back at the bedroom door to make sure Tre hasn't come back out before I make the call.

"Hello. This is Detective Evans."

"Hi, Detective Evans; this is Tori James."

"Yes, Miss James. What can I do for you?"

"I'm sorry to call so soon, and I know you told me to wait, but I was just wondering if you've found anything on my aunt?"

He doesn't answer right away, and I take the phone away from my ear to make sure the call hasn't disconnected. "Hello! Are you there?"

"I'm here."

"Have you found anything?"

"We've spoken to some people, including her ex-husband. We're still tying up some loose ends."

There's another male voice in the background. I overhear the man mentioning Aunt Lyn's name and an arrest warrant. My heart feels like it has stopped in my chest.

"Miss James, are you still there?"

I'm suddenly at a loss for words. "I—I'm here. Um, listen, I gotta go."

"Is everything ok?"

"Yes, everything's fine," I say. "Thank you for the update."

I hang up before he has a chance to respond. My hands are shaking as I stare down at my phone. Tre is still in the shower. I can still hear the sound of running water coming from the other room. I grab my keys and slip quietly out of the front door before he can realize that I'm gone.

———

The drive home is a blur. I speed toward the house, my hands gripping the steering wheel so hard that my fingertips numb. My heart is beating so fast that I have to take deep breaths to keep myself from hyperventilating. Flashbacks of Aunt Lyn and Nia continue to plague my thoughts, fueling my rage. Everything is so clear now, and I want answers.

I take a sharp left into the neighborhood and floor the gas. I am going way over the speed limit, but I don't let up on my speed. My cell phone has been vibrating loudly in my purse for the past fifteen minutes, but I continue to ignore it. I know it's Tre. He has probably realized what I'm about to do and is calling to make one last attempt to stop me. The truth is, I don't know what's about to happen. Confronting Aunt Lyn was the one thing I was told not to do—but I feel like she's given me no choice. I want her to face me—to tell me why.

I pull my car into the driveway, barely missing the trash can that is still sitting out on the curb from Monday. The house looks completely dark from the outside, and I hesitate for just a moment.

What are you doing?

I don't even stop to consider a response as I step out of the car. An unseen force pushes me forward, overriding my attempt to reason with myself. I pause when I reach the porch. The street is quiet except for the distant barking of a dog. The doorknob turns easily, and I let myself inside without using my key.

The house is completely dark except for the glow of a small night light plugged into the wall. It takes a few seconds for my eyes to adjust to the darkness. I move quietly toward the kitchen. It's deathly quiet except for the sound of my footsteps.

For a moment, I think that she's gone—skipping town before the police can make a move on her. I round the corner to the kitchen. Our eyes lock in the dark, and I freeze. She's seated at the kitchen counter, a half-empty glass of wine clutched between her fingers.

A chill runs up my spine as she brings the glass up to her lips and smiles.

"Hello, Tori."

You can turn back now, I think to myself. *It's not too late.* The thought briefly crosses my mind, but I stand firm. She owes me an explanation—to tell me why this all happened.

I don't return her smile. "Hello, Evie."

CHAPTER 46

CHRIS

"WE GOT IT!" CRAMER BURSTS INTO THE SQUAD ROOM, waving a piece of paper around in the air.

"Is that the arrest warrant?" I ask.

"Yep! The judge just signed off on it. We can go pick her up now."

I grab my badge. "Round everyone up. I'll let the Lieutenant know."

Lieutenant Stokes' office is through a small door that is connected to the squad room. He looks up when he hears me enter.

"We got it, sir. We got the warrant."

"The judge signed off?"

"Yes. Cramer just informed me. We can bring her in."

He lets out a sigh of relief. "Finally, some good news."

"We're gathering everyone now to go execute the warrant."

He slants his eyes at me. "You know, Congressman Bryant isn't too happy with how that interview went today."

"I'm sure he isn't," I say. "I wasn't trying to ruffle his feathers, sir. We just needed the truth, and he was being elusive about his relationship with this woman."

He holds up a stack of papers. "Yeah, I know. I just read your report update. What the hell went on in there?"

"Let's just say Mrs. Bryant uncovered things today about her husband that she never knew. She wasn't thrilled—I'll say that much."

"I'll deal with him," he says. "You just worry about getting the Shaw woman in here. Bringing up the man's old skeletons is only going to pay off if we're right about her involvement in this."

"Yes, sir. We'll keep you updated."

I turn to leave when he calls my name. "Hey, Evans."

"Yeah?"

He nods his head at me in approval. "Good work."

"Thank you, Lieutenant."

Cramer and Jacobs are waiting for me outside of the office. "Are we good?" Cramer asks.

I grab my cell phone from my desk and place my gun in the holster. "We're good. Let's go."

We are halfway down the hall when I get a call. The male voice on the other end of the line is frantic.

"Detective Evans! It's me Tre Thomas! I was in earlier today with Tori."

"Yes, yes I remember. Is something wrong?"

"I didn't know who else to call. It's Tori."

I stop walking. "What's wrong?"

"She was acting strange earlier," he says. "She was blaming herself for what happened to Nia and for bringing her around Evelyn."

"Tre did something happen?"

"We were at my place, and I left her alone while I went to shower. When I got out, she was gone."

I think back to my earlier phone conversation with Tori. When we were talking, Cramer had mentioned the arrest warrant. Tori had ended our conversation abruptly. Now I'm wondering if she somehow overheard.

"I've been calling her, but she's not answering my calls," he says. "I'm worried she might do something like try and confront Evelyn."

Cramer and Jacobs have noticed that I'm no longer behind them and are walking back toward me.

"Tre, where are you now?"

"I'm headed out to look for her."

"Tre, stay where you are! We're on our way to Evelyn's now."

"What's going on?" Cramer asks once I'm off the phone.

"That was Tre Thomas. We gotta get to Evelyn's now. Her niece may be headed there. If we don't hurry, we may have another dead girl on our hands."

CHAPTER 47

TORI

"Sit down." Aunt Lyn points to an empty barstool at the counter and pats the cushion.

"No, thank you," I say. "I'm fine where I am."

She shrugs and takes a sip of her wine. "Suit yourself."

I take a few steps toward her. My heart pounds in my ears. "It was you, wasn't it?"

"You're going to have to be more specific."

"You know what I'm talking about. You did it, didn't you? You killed Nia."

She lowers the wine glass. "You're right; I did."

"Why? How could you do that to her? She was my best friend."

"Tori, some things are just more complicated than you realize."

"Is it because of her father? You couldn't have him, and you wanted a way to hurt him?"

She shoots me an angry look. "You don't know what you're talking about."

"Don't tell me what I know! I know all about you and Dwight Bryant. I saw a picture of you two together. He left you, didn't he? He left you for her." I can feel my rage boiling over, spilling out of my pores like lava.

"Tori ..."

"You were jealous!" My words are like knives, cutting deep. "You never got over how he dumped you for her! You did all this—and for what? To still be bitter and lonely!"

She's up in a flash, lunging toward me before I even have the chance to react. Her body collides with mine as she pins me up against the wall. I fumble with my cell phone. She grabs it from my hand in one quick motion, throwing it across the room, where it hits the wall and shatters into pieces.

Her hand is now on my neck ... squeezing ... *crushing*. I gasp for air, but my breaths are trapped under the force of her hand. Her eyes are soulless ... *merciless*. I should've run while I had the chance. I should've thought about what I was walking into.

But it's too late.

She killed my best friend ... and now she's killing me ...

CHAPTER 48

CHRIS

The whir of the helicopter is deafening. It drowns out my thoughts until I can barely hear myself think. I stand at the edge of the barricade. It's been over an hour since I received the phone call from Tre. The street outside of Evelyn Shaw's home has gone from a quiet residential neighborhood to something that looks like a warzone.

A growing crowd of people congregate on the street, taking up the sidewalks and spilling out into the road. Several officers are positioned around the barricade and have been charged with the task of keeping the crowd at bay. The sounds of the sirens and the helicopter hovering overhead have lulled people out of their homes, many of them dressed in bathrobes and pajamas.

Lieutenant Stokes comes barreling toward me; his pudgy face flushed red. "What the hell is going on, Evans?"

"Evelyn Shaw—she won't come out," I say. "Her niece is held up inside with her. That's her car parked in the driveway."

He throws his hands in the air. "Jesus Christ! This is the last thing we needed!"

I look toward the house. The SWAT team sergeant ducks underneath the barricade and walks up to us, his thumbs hooked in the loops of his bulletproof vest.

"We got eyes on them," he says. "They've moved into this front bedroom." He points to a small window at the front of the house that faces the street. "My guys have the place surrounded. I have a guy positioned on the side of the house where the other window into the room is located. From there, he has a clean shot."

"Don't shoot yet," I say. "Let's try to talk her down."

"Evans, this woman is unpredictable," says Stokes. "If we have a shot, we need to—"

"No! Please let me ... let me just try and talk to her."

"We've tried that," says the SWAT sergeant. "She's refusing to speak to anyone, and we don't know what kind of state the hostage is in. If she's injured, we need to get to her now."

I plead with Lieutenant Stokes. "Lieutenant, please! Give me a chance to try. I think I know how to get in her head. Just give me five minutes with her before you give the order."

Stokes is apprehensive. "Evans ..."

"Five minutes, sir. That's all I'm asking for."

He sighs. "Alright, Evans, five minutes! That's it!"

"Thank you, Lieutenant! Thank you!"

The SWAT sergeant shakes his head and walks away. "Your call. We'll stand by."

The next ten minutes are hectic as I'm fitted with a vest and an earpiece. The SWAT lead gives me quick instructions on what to do once inside while Lieutenant Stokes watches nervously from his post. I tuck my gun into the back of my waistband.

Rosalind stands near the front of the crowd behind the police barricade. Our eyes meet. She looks worried, her eyes darting from me to the house. I jog over to her.

"What are you doing?" she asks. "You're not going in there, are you?"

"She's got a hostage in there."

She tries to reason with me. "Chris, this is dangerous."

"I know. But I have to try."

"We both know why you're doing this. You don't have to prove anything to anyone."

"I know I don't have to, but I don't want anybody else to die—not on my watch, at least."

"Evans!" Lieutenant Stokes yells my name. "Evans! Let's go!"

"I'll be fine," I say. "I promise."

She smiles, but I can see the sadness in her eyes. "Don't make promises you can't keep."

I force myself to walk away. I don't look back as I walk through the barricade surrounding the house. The sound of the helicopter hovering overhead seems to grow louder the closer I get to the house. At the front door, I am relieved to find that the knob turns easily. I take one last look back before stepping inside.

CHAPTER 49

TORI

THE POLICE ARE OUTSIDE. I CAN HEAR THEM.

I should feel safe knowing that they are just outside these walls—but I don't. Instead, I'm more terrified than I've ever been. Aunt Lyn has moved me into my bedroom and is pacing up and down the floor. A black gun is gripped firmly in her hands. I don't know how long I've been here or how long she plans to keep me here. The clock on my nightstand is turned away from me. The shattered pieces of my phone still lay on the floor in the kitchen. I can't call for help even if I want to. She blocks the only way out of the room.

I watch her closely as she walks back and forth. She is unusually calm for a woman whose house is surrounded by the police. Her face is relaxed—almost peaceful.

She walks to the window and moves the curtain to the side. I slowly bring my hands to my throat. The skin on my neck is sore. My throat is raw from the attack. I don't speak, fearful of sending her into another rage.

There is a flicker of movement near the bedroom door. I look out of the corner of my eye, taking care not to appear too obvious. Detective Evans appears in the doorway. He takes several steps inside the room.

Aunt Lyn whips her head around and raises the gun, pointing it straight at my head.

"Easy now, Evelyn," he says, raising his hands slowly in the air.

She comes to stand next to me and presses the cold muzzle of the gun against my scalp. "Don't make me do it."

"It's ok, Tori," he says, seeing the panicked look on my face. "Just calm down. Everything is going to be fine."

She cocks the hammer back on the gun. "Are you sure about that?"

He turns to her, his hands still raised up in the air. "Yes, I'm sure. Because this isn't you, Evelyn. You don't want to hurt anyone else."

She lets out a short laugh. It makes me shudder. "What makes you think you know anything about me?"

"I won't pretend to know everything," he says. "But I know enough."

"You need to leave. Now!"

"Evelyn, you know I can't do that. Please just put the gun down."

She pushes the gun further into my scalp, and I begin to plead with her through tears. "Please! Please don't!"

"You don't think I'll shoot her?" she asks. "Trust me; I won't hesitate. Family or not."

Her voice is strangely calm, and Detective Evans raises his hands higher in the air as he takes a step back. "Ok, you have my attention. Just help me understand how we got here."

"Since you claim to know so much, why don't you tell me how we got here?"

"Evelyn, please—"

"Go on!" she yells. "Tell me everything you know since you *think* you know so much!"

He takes a deep breath and takes a step forward. "I know you had a horrible thing done to you by people you trusted. I know that you wanted them to feel the hurt that you've felt all these years."

I watch her out of the corner of my eye. Her face is blank, emotionless.

"This had nothing to do with Nia Bryant or Diana McNamee, did it?" he asks. "This started long before them."

"You don't know what you're—"

"I know what he did," he says. "I know about your baby."

She flinches, and the gun nudges my scalp.

"I know what happened between you and Dwight Bryant. And I know about Patricia's involvement. I also spoke to your ex-husband. He told me all about your medical troubles."

She finally speaks. "People don't care about the consequences of their actions anymore. They don't think of how their decisions can impact everyone around them. They got to have everything while I was left with nothing."

"I know—"

"No," she says, shaking her head. "Don't pretend to know what I've been through because you don't. I lost everything ... my marriage, my career, my chance at being a mother. All the things I wanted for myself, I never got to have. Do you know what it was like getting the news from the doctor that I would never have children? Do you know how that made me feel after so many years of trying? All that money gone down the drain for all of those treatments ... all that time wasted?"

"No, I don't know how that feels. I can't imagine." He appears sympathetic, but I can't tell if it's genuine or a ploy to get her to let her guard down.

"I was the first in my family to go to college," she says. "Do you know I was even considering med school? I had my whole life planned, only to have it taken from me. When everything happened, I couldn't cope. I lost it all."

"So you went after the ones who you feel wronged you?"

"Things have a funny way of working out," she says. "I didn't even have to look for Nia; I knew who she was as soon as I saw her. She looked just like him. After all those years, there she was. Dwight's daughter was standing in my house, and I wanted him to pay."

"And what about Diana? Was she your way of getting back at Patricia?"

"I overheard Nia and Tori talking about her one day. When I heard the last name, McNamee, I knew she had to be related to Pat."

"So, you set out to find her?"

"A quick internet search was all it took," she says. "These kids, they have their entire lives posted on social media. Their families, their homes

—they record everything. It didn't take much for me to put everything together. They practically handed me what I needed."

Her words cause me to cringe. She had been watching them all this time. Even worse, she used my friendship with Nia to get the information she needed. She was plotting for months right under my nose. I had never known.

"So you planned all of this?" he asks.

"I watched and I waited," she says. "I saw everything. And I learned so much about them, especially Nia. I saw past the good girl façade. She was conniving and deceitful, just like her mother. What she was doing to Diana was the same thing Cass had done to me. It was history repeating itself."

She turns and looks down at me before turning back to Detective Evans. "Don't you see—I did the world a favor! People like Nia Bryant destroy lives. She needed to be stopped!"

"So you stabbed Nia that night out at Groveland Park?"

"I knew where they would be. Nia came by the day before the probate. I stood right outside this room. I overheard everything about what had gone down between her and Diana. Diana was angry, and I knew everyone would look at her first."

"So you planted the knife on Diana to throw attention on her? Maggie Price said you came by the day of the probate. Is that when you did it?"

She smirks and tightens her grip on the gun. "Well, I guess you do have me all figured out, Detective."

"Not quite," he says. "Tell me, why the car? Why drive Nia's car back to her apartment?"

"Leaving it at the park would've been too easy. The park would've been searched from top to bottom, and her body would've been found immediately. Driving it to her apartment was risky, but I needed her parents to have hope that she would be found alive."

"So, this was all about control?"

"They had hope because I gave them hope," she says. "I controlled what happened. As long as she was missing, there was always hope that she would be found."

"But you knew she was never coming back. And when her body was discovered, you got to see that hope snatched away from them."

She smiles for the first time. "Hope is a strong emotion, Detective. It'll have you wishing for something that you know will never happen. I know all too well what that feels like."

"And what about the necklace?" he asks.

"What about it?"

"Why take it?"

"Why wouldn't I take it? Dwight gave it to me first. That was supposed to be my necklace. But then he took it back, and he gave it to her. He is so used to treating people any kind of way. He uses people to get what he wants. I wanted to take away everything that ever meant something to him."

"Even his dead mother's heirloom?"

She rolls her eyes. "He took everything from me. I don't give a damn about his mother."

"So, I guess you got exactly what you wanted."

She shakes her head. "What I want—I'll never have. I can't get my life back. I'll never have a family of my own. So no, Detective, I didn't win."

"It didn't have to be this way," he says. "Those kids were innocent. They didn't deserve to pay for their parent's sins."

"There are always casualties in war, Detective." There is no remorse in her voice—no emotion.

He points toward the window facing the street. "Evelyn, the police are gathered outside. The house is surrounded. How do you really think this is going to end?"

"I'm perfectly aware of how this all ends."

"What can we do to make this end peacefully—where no one else gets hurt?"

She inches the gun further against my head. "I don't think that's possible, but I've told you everything that you need to know."

He takes another step toward us. "We can work something out. No one else has to die. Please, let Tori go."

"You know I can't do that, Detective."

My heart pounds harder in my chest as I feel the muzzle of the gun pressing deeper into my scalp.

"Evelyn, please, put the gun down," he pleads. "Let her go."

She doesn't seem to hear him. The gun stays pressed to my head. "I've lived in a prison my entire life. There's not a box you can put me in that can be worse than what I've lived through."

"Evelyn—"

She suddenly looks down at me, cowering on the floor, and smiles. "I'm sorry, Tori."

"Evelyn, no!" he screams.

Aunt Lyn lifts the gun from my head and aims it directly at him. I barely have a moment to react when the ear-splitting echo of a shot rings through the air. Blood splatters everywhere. It covers my face and hands. A bullet has been fired from outside, striking Aunt Lyn in the head. Her body crumples to the ground. She's motionless, blood pouring from the single gunshot wound. It pools on the floor around her body.

Detective Evans runs over and kneels next to me, his eyes searching my face. "Tori, are you ok?"

He searches my body for injuries, but I'm unharmed. He asks me again if I'm ok, but I can't speak. I reach out to touch her, but he pulls my hand back.

"I'm sorry, Tori. She's gone."

Chapter 50

Chris

The blood pressure cuff tightens around my arm for the second time. It restricts my circulation and causes my fingertips to numb. I watch impatiently as it slowly deflates, and little numbers flash on the monitor. The EMT jots down my blood pressure reading and carefully removes the cuff.

"I told you I'm fine. This isn't necessary."

"Oh, for God's sake, just let them check you out, Evans," says Lieutenant Stokes. He watches from outside of the ambulance. I open my mouth to respond but decide against it. I can tell from the look on his face that it's a losing battle. I sit back against the wall of the ambulance and rest my head on the vehicle's aluminum interior.

The EMT continues her exam as I watch the activity in front of Evelyn Shaw's house. Two male technicians have just emerged from the house and are hauling out a black body bag.

It's finally over.

I should be grateful that we now know the real person behind Nia Bryant's death, but I know that there isn't much closure to be had for the people involved.

"Ok, you're all set," says the EMT. "Everything looks good. Just try and get some rest, Detective."

"I'll certainly try."

Lieutenant Stokes rushes over to me once I'm out of the ambulance. He places his hand on my shoulder. "Are you sure you're ok?" He looks me up and down like a parent inspecting their child for injuries after they've fallen from a bike. "That was a lot to witness in there."

"I'm fine, Lieutenant."

"Well, nevertheless, I think you should take a few days. After all of this, you could use some time off."

Cramer comes walking down the front porch steps of the house. He gives me a quick hug. "You good, kid?"

"EMTs gave me the all-clear, so I guess so."

Stokes motions toward the house, which is now roped off with yellow crime scene tape. "How's it going in there?"

"It's gonna be a while," Cramer says. "There's still a lot to sift through."

"What've you found out so far?" I ask.

"Well, we've already uncovered a TracFone. When we searched it, there was only one outgoing call, and that was to a rideshare company on the night of the murder."

"A rideshare company?"

"Yes. A call was made a few hours before Nia was murdered. We contacted the company, and they were able to pull their records from that night. The request made was for a ride to Groveland Park."

"Let me guess. The pickup location was from the gas station across the street from Nia's apartment complex?"

"Yep, you guessed it. From what it looks like, she drove her car to the gas station and parked it there. Then she took the rideshare to the park. And then, after the murder, she drove Nia's car back to her residence. From there, she was able to jump in her car and drive home without anyone knowing she was ever there. She was never a suspect, so we never thought to look for her vehicle on any traffic cams."

"Jesus Christ!" says Stokes. "She may have gotten away with it if that necklace had never been found."

"We've also started looking through her computer," says Cramer. "We uncovered fake social media profiles and saved articles on Nia and her parents. It looks like she's been watching them for years. Her niece and Nia becoming friends was a stroke of luck that worked out in her favor."

"So this was all planned out over years?" asks Stokes.

"We are still trying to piece everything together, but I think so," says Cramer. "This house was purchased a few months before Nia started college at MSU. It looks like she knew Nia was coming here and moved close by. I think she always knew she would kill her; she just needed the perfect opportunity."

Lieutenant Stokes shakes his head.

"Her confession from the body camera you were wearing was the nail in the coffin," says Cramer. "We have everything we need to close the case."

I stare at the crowd of people. The Bryants have arrived. They stand on opposite sides of the crowd. Congressman Bryant glances at his wife, but she doesn't look at him. Diana, Patricia, and Byron are standing a few feet away. They watch closely as the black body bag is wheeled past them. Drew stands off to the side, away from the group.

Rosalind is standing near the medical examiner's van. I excuse myself from Cramer and Lieutenant Stokes and make my way over to her.

"Thank God you're ok." She takes me into her arms. I don't care that people are watching; I let her hug me.

"I told you I would be."

"So, I guess everything worked out?"

I look back at the Bryants on the other side of the barricade. "I'm not so sure about that. A lot of lives were destroyed over this."

"How's the girl?"

Tori is being examined by an EMT in a nearby ambulance. She's wrapped in a heavy blanket, and the EMT shines a small light in her eyes. Tre is standing guard next to her, his arm draped around her shoulder. She has a blank look on her face, and I can still see the shock in her eyes.

"She's got a long road ahead of her," I say. "But I think she's going to be ok."

"Poor kid," says Rosalind. "She's gonna need therapy after this.

Held hostage and then had to witness her aunt executed right in front of her eyes."

"Our guys may have pulled the trigger, but what happened in there was all Evelyn's doing."

She turns to look at me. "You think she wanted to die?"

"She spilled her guts out, Ros. She gave a full confession. She raised that gun at me knowing that there was someone ready to take her out. I don't think she had any plans on leaving alive."

CHAPTER 51

TORI

Six weeks later

A LARGE, MOSS-COVERED ARCH MARKS THE ENTRANCE TO the cemetery. It's a wrought iron fixture suspended high above the ground, with vines that interloop around its base and travel up to the keystone. Large flowers sprout from the ground around it, and I watch as it passes overhead. I hug the bouquet of flowers close to my chest as the car bumps along the winding road. I can feel myself growing nervous as we near the burial site. Even though it's been almost seven weeks since Nia's death, I've only recently gotten up the nerve to visit her grave.

Tre pulls the car over onto the side of the road and slows to a stop. I look to my right at the small, fenced plot. Toward the back of the plot is a newly erected tombstone that's surrounded by various assortments of flowers.

"She's over there," he says.

I don't move. The bouquet is heavy in my arms.

"Do you want me to come with you?"

I shake my head. "No, I need to do this. I've put it off long enough. Besides, my therapist says this is all a part of the healing process."

He turns off the car and sits back in his seat. "How's that going?"

"It's ok, I guess. It gives me a distraction for an hour three times a week."

"Well, I'm glad you decided to go. What you witnessed is something no one should ever have to go through."

"Well, I didn't really have a choice. When my mom moved up after everything happened, that was one of the first things she made me do."

"She's just worried about you."

"I know she's just trying to help," I say. "Even though she didn't witness what happened firsthand, the whole situation has been traumatizing for her too. The first time I'm out on my own without her, and something like this happens."

He places his hand on mine and gives it a small squeeze. "Well, I'm just glad she agreed to let you go out today."

I smile. "Well, that's because she likes you."

"You sure you don't want me to come?" he asks, giving my hand another squeeze.

"No, I have to do this on my own."

The hot afternoon sun beats down on my head as I make my way toward the gravesite. I stop when I'm a few feet away and look back at the car. Tre is watching me from the driver's seat and waves me forward. I take a few more steps but stop again when I realize that I'm no longer alone.

A woman has entered the plot from a side gate and is walking toward me. I use my hand to shield my eyes from the afternoon sun. It isn't until she's a few yards away that I realize that it's Diana.

She looks up, and our eyes meet. "Oh, hey."

"Hey, Diana." My heart is pounding, and I suddenly have the urge to run back toward the car.

"I'm sorry, I didn't know anyone was—"

"Oh no, it's ok." I place the bouquet of flowers on Nia's grave. "I was just leaving."

"Oh, you don't have to leave on account of me," she says. "I won't be long. I just wanted to pay my respects before I get out of this place for good."

"You're leaving?" I ask. "Like not coming back?"

She nods. "Yeah, I decided to finish out my senior year at a college closer to home."

"Oh. I didn't know."

"Yeah. Even though my name has been cleared, things just haven't been the same. I'm just looking for a new start."

"I understand."

She turns to look at Nia's grave. "But I couldn't leave without ..." Her voice trembles. "I just want her to know that I forgive her and that I never meant for any of this to happen."

"It's not your fault," I say.

"If I could do things differently, I would never have asked her to stay behind that night at the park. I keep thinking that maybe she would still be alive."

I take a step toward her and place my hand on her shoulder. "There's nothing you could've done. This isn't anyone's fault but the person who decided to take her life."

She smiles at me for the first time. "You know, I never got a chance to thank you."

"Thank me?"

"Yeah," she says. "I never got a chance to say thank you for what you did. If it weren't for you, I could still be tied up in all that legal mess. Because of you, the truth finally came out. And I know that couldn't have been easy ... you know, with Evelyn being your aunt and all."

"Well, I'm just glad it all worked out. But ... you're welcome."

She smiles again and turns her attention back to the tombstone. Tre has gotten out of the car and is slowly making his way over to us. Suddenly, I'm no longer in a rush to leave. For the first time in weeks, I feel like I'm going to be ok. A feeling of peace comes over me as I stand over my best friend's grave—shoulder to shoulder with the most unlikely companion.

Epilogue

Before

THE COLD METAL OF THE STETHOSCOPE SENT SHOCKWAVES through her body.

"Take a deep breath in," said the nurse. The woman took a deep inhale and then exhaled slowly. The chest piece moved to her back as the nurse took a listen to her lungs. She did as she was told, counting to five with each breath. The nurse draped the stethoscope around her shoulders and typed something on the little portable computer next to the bed.

The recovery room was bitterly cold, colder than the first room that she'd been in earlier that morning. Goosebumps covered her arms. She brought the thin blanket that covered her body up to her chest to warm herself.

The nurse checked the clear IV bag next to the bed. "How are you feeling, Evelyn? Any pain?" The kind nurse from earlier was gone and had been replaced by this woman. She was younger, her voice upbeat. She moved with the quickness of someone who knew her job well.

The woman grimaced as she tried to reposition herself. "A little sore, but I'm ok."

"Well, the good news is your procedure went well. If everything looks good when the doctor comes to check on you, you'll be discharged home."

The woman didn't respond. Something across the room had caught her attention. She fixed her eyes on the small TV mounted on the opposite wall. A red banner blinked across the bottom of the screen. Her entire body stiffened as she read the caption: *Candidate Dwight Bryant wins Congressional seat.*

She knew the face on the screen, the man waving to the crowd. He was just as she remembered him—the walnut-brown skin, the captivating smile, the enigmatic eyes. It was almost as if time had stopped. Suddenly, she was no longer cold. The frigidness of the room seemed to melt away as a surge of heat came over her.

His wife and teenage daughter stood next to him, their faces proud as they waved to the crowd. He had forgotten her after all this time and had moved on with his life. He was on to bigger and better things, a promising future.

Anger billowed up inside of her, a seething rage that couldn't be controlled. He didn't just get to forget what he had done. He didn't deserve to move forward. All was not forgiven—and it never would be.

One thing was for sure—she would see him again.

About the Author

Sharhonda Exantus is a practicing pharmacist with a love for whodunits and cozy mysteries. She is a native of Miami, Florida, and received her Doctor of Pharmacy from Florida Agricultural and Mechanical University. In her spare time, she enjoys writing and binge-reading mystery and crime novels, particularly psychological thrillers. *Sins of the Lines* is her debut novel. Sharhonda currently resides in Florida with her husband and three children. To learn more, visit her website at www.sharhondaex antus.com.